D1650576

Possession

The Fallen One roamed the city all night, after they finally let her out of that maze of pain where they claimed they needed to fix her. They kept prodding her new body for fractured places, sliding her into machines to photograph her skeleton, drawing her blood to test it for poisons. She wanted to claw and kick herself free, but she'd waited too long for this body to risk letting them keep it.

What a body! What a windfall of muscle and bone! And the skin – she can't stop touching her new skin, the silk hills and smooth valleys, the lightly furred notch between her thighs. Hair the same colour as the hair she once had, the red of alchemy, its heavy ends brushing the small of her supple new back. With this body, she'll take hearts and souls the way she's longed to for so many years.

Possession

Mathilde Madden

Madelynne Ellis

Anne Tourney

BLACK LACE

Black Lace books contain sexual fantasies.
In real life, always practise safe sex.

First published in 2008 by
Black Lace
Thames Wharf Studios
Rainville Rd
London W6 9HA

Copyright © Mathilde Madden, Madelynne Ellis, Anne Tourney 2008

The right of Mathilde Madden, Madelynne Ellis and Anne Tourney to
be identified as the Authors of the Work has been asserted in
accordance with the Copyright, Designs and Patents Act 1988.

A catalogue record for this book is available from the British Library.

www.black-lace-books.com

Typeset by SetSystems Ltd, Saffron Walden, Essex

Printed and bound in Great Britain by CPI Bookmarque,
Croydon, CR0 4TD

The paper used in this book is a natural, recyclable product made
from wood grown in sustainable forests. The manufacturing process
conforms to the regulations of the country of origin.

ISBN 978 0 352 34164 8

*All characters in this publication are fictitious and any resemblance
to real persons, living or dead, is purely coincidental.*

This book is sold subject to the condition that it shall not, by way of
trade or otherwise, be lent, resold, hired out or otherwise circulated
without the publisher's prior written consent in any form of binding
or cover other than that in which it is published and without a similar
condition including this condition being imposed on the subsequent
purchaser.

The Silver Chains

Mathilde Madden

1

Misty was strutting along the queue of patrons outside Wonderland. She was toying with them and camping it up using this black and white cane she had found the day before in a junk shop. She liked the cane. It didn't really go with the rest of her outfit. Except that it was all monochrome too.

She was wearing this Gothic Lolita look. She thought she looked damn fine. Alfie had said he liked it, but also that the weird Victoriana stuff slightly disturbed him. He had gone as far to say that it was almost as disturbing as that time she had gone to a fancy dress party as *The Ring* complete with her hair gelled into wet-looking rat tails and a TV casing to crawl out of.

Misty smiled to herself as she thought how odd it was that a man as big and powerful as Alfie would admit to being 'disturbed' by a tiny Asian girl in a silly costume. And that memory was especially delicious because when that conversation took place her beautiful big man had himself been dressed as a sexually ambiguous pirate with lashings of eye liner and a frilly shirt open to the navel.

Misty always felt sort of gooey inside when she thought about Alfie. He was meant to be meeting her inside the club. She hoped he liked it. She knew he thought some of her friends were kind of wild. But this has been his idea. Really. He had tried almost everything else.

Reaching the front of the queue Misty was about to nod to the bouncers and swan inside like she did most nights she came to Wonderland, but instead she found herself eavesdropping on an argument. A man in a pair of jeans and a blue shirt – an outfit that was decidedly non-dress-code – was trying to talk his way inside.

Misty sniggered as the man made some rather valid arguments about some of the style failings of the rubber, leather and PVC-clad patrons that the bouncers were letting in while denying him entry. The man had a point. He was very, very beautiful, even in his dress-code-flouting outfit.

He was also Alfie. Her Alfie. He should have been inside the club by now.

Rolling her over-made-up eyes, Misty swanned over on four-inch heels.

'Hey Biff, hey Billy,' she said to the doormen. She didn't know their actual names. That didn't matter. Everyone knew her.

The larger of the doormen, the one with a bright orange crew cut, said, 'Hi Misty. Be with you in a sec.' And he turned back to Alfie, clearly about to say something a little more threatening to get rid of him.

'Just a minute, Biff,' Misty said.

The doorman turned around. Maybe he actually *was* called Biff. 'Yeah?'

Behind Biff, Alfie was grinning at Misty.

'He's with me.'

2

Caroline Ray was too old for nightclubs. In truth, she had been too old for nightclubs at the age of twenty-one. She lacked the gene that gave a person the ability to tolerate the pound-pound-pound of dance music. She liked to be able to linger over a drink. To sit down. To talk.

But she had been single for three months and Wonderland seemed like a good place to find the type of man she was looking for. A strong man who liked an even stronger woman.

But Wonderland was so hot and loud and intimidating. Everyone was dressed in the most outlandish leather, rubber and PVC outfits. And the way they sneered at her made it clear that she – in her simple black leather trousers and black T-shirt which was just enough to get her in the door – was the one they considered outlandish.

Caroline felt strangely alone in the throng. She hadn't been out on the pull for ages. Hadn't needed to come to a place like this. She was hoping to see a familiar face, but everything was different from how she remembered it. It all felt hopelessly cliqued and unwelcoming.

Why had she thought this would be a better bet than the internet?

She was just about to head for the basement, when her eye was caught by a woman sitting in a corner of a booth, playing cards on her own. She looked incredible. This place was full of very wildly dressed people, but this woman was astonishing. Caroline was here looking for a man. A kinky dirty-minded man. She hadn't expected to have her head turned by a woman. But she couldn't stop looking at this one.

She was Asian – maybe Japanese, although Caroline couldn't be sure – and wore her glossy jet black hair piled up on her head in a heap of tumbling curls and ringlets. Her make-up was a mask of white, her lips blood-red, her eyes outlined in black. She wore a dress – Caroline could only see the top of it, the table hid the rest – that looked vaguely Victorian. A frilly bib part, with puffy mutton-chop sleeves ending in long buttoned cuffs. Caroline found herself staring at the girl. For too long. Because she raised her head and grinned.

Caroline smiled back and the woman beckoned her with a jerk of her head. Caroline wasn't sure. Embarrassed to be caught looking. This was her first time at a place like Wonderland. She wasn't quite certain what the woman's invitation might be about. She half shook her head, only a vague tiny movement.

The woman in the booth made a sort of chastising face, raising her eyebrows and cocking her head. Then she picked up a couple of playing cards and waved them. Caroline found herself nodding. Relieved. The woman was offering a game of cards not a full-on heavy duty S&M sex session.

'Mercy,' said the woman holding out a hand for Caroline to shake as she slipped into the booth.

Caroline took her. 'Er, *merci*? *Je ne comprehend pas Francaise?*' She stuttered. Unsure even about how to say that she didn't speak French in French.

The woman laughed. 'No. I'm not French. I wasn't speaking French. I was saying Mercy was my name. Although it isn't really, it's Misty. Sorry. That happens all the time. I do it on purpose, really.'

'OK, so, Misty?'

Misty nodded. 'Misty Sun.'

'Oh. Right. Misty? What like Mistress Misty, kind of

thing?' Caroline said as she sat down opposite Misty in the booth.

Misty made a face. 'Nah. Not really. Well maybe. It's not my real name. And a lot of the kinky guys love it. But, actually, my real name is Mindy. I just think Misty is better.'

'Better?'

'Than Mindy. But I do like Mercy. Hmm . . .'

'Well, yeah, for sure. I'm Caroline, by the way.'

It was about then in the conversation that Caroline realised that this booth, tucked away in the corner of the huge cavernous vastness of Wonderland, seemed weirdly sheltered from the ear-bleedingly loud thump of the music playing in the rest of the club. It was like an oasis of calm – Misty's little oasis.

'So, what you doing here, Caroline? It's your first time, right?'

'No, no. I've been here before. Just not for a while. I split with my boyfriend and, well, I thought this might be a good place to meet someone new. I don't know what I was thinking. I should've just used the net.'

Misty nodded. 'Ha. So, what are you looking for? Apart from a game of rummy with a Japanese Gothic Lolita. A big burly master? A big burly slave boy? Are you the binder or the bindee?'

'The binder. Um.' Caroline looked at the table, slightly shy of her desires.

Misty tapped her round-tipped black and white finger-nails on the tabletop. 'There's nothing to be embarrassed about. And you know, a friend of mine is here tonight and he's really keen to find a woman who's down with hurting him while having sex. That's why I brought him. It's kind of a new thing for him.'

'Yeah. Well that might be interesting. Right now I'm just after someone who could keep it casual. I don't really want a full-blown live-in slave or anything. Just some kinky fun. See where I am, you know.'

'Sure. That's cool. Actually, he doesn't do relationships or anything, right now. He can't really. Um, personal stuff. But I think you and him might get on. He'll be in the basement. Experimenting.'

Caroline smiled. 'I was heading down there anyway.'

3

Out of the little bubble of calm that was Misty's booth, Caroline found herself back in the sensory overload of the thumping music and flashing lights that defined Wonderland. Misty was holding her hand dragging her through crowds that were getting thicker and thicker. Over the dance floor. Through gyrating hips and flailing limbs. It was like hiking through a dense forest of PVC and corsets and men with leather waistcoats and goatee beards.

Then Misty tugged her through a familiar door that was all wood and iron like a dungeon from the days of yore, and into a cooler, quieter, far kinkier place. Stone steps led down towards noise of whips, yelps and all kinds of moans. Caroline felt the hair on the back of her neck stand up. In the medley of sounds she picked out the crack of a whip and a deep masculine moan of twisted pleasure that followed it. Her blood started to beat harder between her legs.

At the bottom of the stairs Misty led her through Wonderland's basement.

Oh, it was wonderful. Men were crawling on the floor dressed in leather collars and not a lot else. She saw one particularly exquisite specimen crouching in a tiny cage, all dark eyes and desperately bulging underwear. Caroline's breathing was getting ragged as she weaved her way through St Andrew's crosses and stocks. She had to step over a cute blonde girl who was tied up on the floor, hogtied so tightly that her head almost arced right round to touch her toes.

But Caroline registered her for little more than the

seconds it took not to tread on her, because it was then that she saw him.

His big muscled arms were braced against one of the basement's stone walls. He wasn't bound. He was just standing in position. His big bare back making an excellent target for a spry short-haired woman wielding a single tail whip. The woman was something of an expert, cutting the thin tail of leather through the air, making shapes and sounds, making it seem like the whip was alive. And over and over it was landing on the man's back, eliciting a combination of vivid marks and muffled grunts that had turned the inside of Caroline's mouth to dust.

She hadn't even seen his face.

While Caroline was frozen to the spot Misty let go of her hand and moved through the crowd towards the man. Somehow she got the attention of the woman with the whip, who handed it over to Misty with a sly smile.

Misty raised the whip and cut it through the air, her strange Victorian pinafore dress billowing. Caroline noticed for the first time that Misty was in character right down to her toes, even wearing little black button-through boots and black tights. But she didn't notice that for long. When Misty sent the whip flying through the air it seemed to land harder and far more viciously than before. A fact born out by the way the man's arms seemed to buckle a little at the elbow and he collapsed into the wall slightly.

'Goddamnit, Misty,' he said, in a voice that was low enough to carry even with his face up against the wall.

Misty stilled the whip as he turned around. 'You're meant to say, "Red".'

He looked angrily at her, then cracked a lopsided smile. Misty ran into his arms, jumping up and linking her ankles around his big back.

Caroline's main thought, the one accompanying a weird stab of jealousy was, god, he's a really big guy.

A moment later Misty dragged Mr Big over to where Caroline was standing. 'Here you go.' she grinned. 'Alfie Friday, at your service.' And she winked dramatically, turning to Alfie. 'How about you take her home and show her a good time?'

'Misty, I don't need you to . . .'

'I thought you said . . .'

'Shush. She *can* hear you.' Alfie and Misty turned around and Alfie grinned sheepishly. 'Look, sorry. It's just . . .'

Caroline held up her palms. 'No, no, it's OK. I mean, you're not obliged to.'

Caroline's voice sort of dried up as Alfie fixed her with his eyes. She noticed they were a very unusual colour. A sort of deep gold. 'Maybe we should have a quick drink though, the three of us,' Alfie said.

'OK,' said Caroline.

'Cool,' said Misty and, as Caroline looked over at her, she noticed that her eyes were the exact same colour. How odd. Caroline would have assumed they were related, brother and sister even, if they weren't so clearly from different sides of the world.

'It's Alfred, really,' Alfie said, setting the drinks down on the table in Misty's secluded booth, 'but everyone calls me Alfie.'

'OK Alfie,' Caroline raised her glass. She took a quick drink and then smiled at Misty, who smiled right back; clearly the conversation was down to her. She looked back at Alfie. 'So, er, this is your thing, then? You're really into kinky stuff?'

'Well,' Alfie leant back in his seat, 'let's just say I'm experimenting with a few things right now. Different things. Different kinds of sex.'

'Oh right, OK.'

Misty looked around. 'Where's Leon?'

Alfie said, 'I don't know. He was marking me downstairs.'

'I thought you said you didn't need to be marked if you were here. I thought you said pain kept you stable.'

'That's just a theory,' Alfie said. 'I asked Leon to be there in case I was wrong.'

'God, I thought you were sure. You should be more careful. You're flipping to non-sex triggers more and more. If you flipped somewhere like this it could be bad.'

'I am being careful,' Alfie said. 'There's enough warning to get the sedative and get hidden.'

'Not if you don't know where Leon is.'

'I'm with you now.'

'Yes but I haven't got any...' Misty just shook her head, exasperated.

Just as Caroline was wondering whether it would be rude to ask what they were talking about, she noticed another man coming up behind them. He was tall, but not as tall as Alfie. A little older. He had long dirty-blond hair and was dressed in tight fitting denims – jeans and a waistcoat – and nothing else. He looked like a refuge from an 1980s metal band. Or a roadie.

'Shit, sorry,' he said in a broad Birmingham accent as he approached the table. 'I was watching you, sire, honestly. I just got talking to this girl, and – oh fuck, hello, sweetheart.' He turned a bright, white smile on Caroline.

'Hi,' Caroline said, holding out a hand. She could have sworn she heard Alfie growl as Leon took it and shook.

Leon gave her a blatant once-over, letting his eyes drift salaciously over her legs. 'Nice trousers. Not every chick can carry off leather.'

Alfie growled again. More distinctly. There was no mistaking it.

'Anyway,' said Leon, 'are you taking over now?'

He was looking at Misty, who shrugged and nodded.

'Great. 'Cause I really want to finish that conversation I was having with that chick down . . .'

'Fine,' Alfie snapped. 'Go.'

And Leon reached into his pocket, pulled out a syringe, and threw it onto the table.

It bounced once and then rolled. Caroline's mouth dropped open and she felt herself cowering away from it.

Misty reached out and whisked it away.

'Look, er,' said Caroline, 'if this is some kind of, I don't know . . . um, maybe this isn't my thing.'

'It's not like that,' said Alfie. 'It's not what you think. I'm diabetic, that's all. I can get unwell really fast sometimes. I need someone to keep and eye on me. In fact . . .' He leant across the table and fished the syringe out of Misty's hand, then shifted, holding it out to Caroline. 'You should take it, if I'm going home with you.'

'If you're going home with . . . ?'

Alfie stared deeply into her eyes. 'You don't want to?'

Caroline swallowed. Alfie had the strangest expression on his face. Looking at him she felt a little confused. Mesmerised, even. 'I don't know. I don't even know what you like. What you want.'

Alfie held her eyes. 'I don't want to come,' Alfie said. 'Don't let me come. It isn't good for me.'

'Oh,' said Caroline. 'You like that, do you? Denial kink?'

'I wouldn't say I *like* it, exactly.' Alfie grinned then. 'But I can go home with you and give you a great fucking night. And, I won't even get an orgasm myself at the end of it. Does that appeal at all?'

Caroline felt her pussy thump at this petulant declaration. But she shook her head. She'd never met a kinky man quite like this before. 'I don't know.'

Alfie shrugged. 'Want to find out?'

4

In the large kitchen of Caroline's flat in Tooting, Alfie bent down a little and Caroline – perched on the table – kissed him.

She could feel Alfie letting her kiss him. Just letting his head go back and opening his mouth under hers. He bent his knees a little more and she bore down on him all the harder then, feeling a desperate need to possess him totally.

Alfie said something, but it was lost in the meld of their mouths. Caroline pulled away. 'What?'

'Hurt me,' he said, low, like a confession. 'Pull my hair, bite me, anything. I need it.'

Caroline didn't need telling twice. She tangled a fist in his dark hair and twisted. Alfie moaned. Caroline pressed her thigh between his legs and felt his cock there. It was hard. She twisted his hair more. He moaned again. His cock got even harder. Alfie was rolling his head back on his shoulders. 'OK,' he said, 'but I need more.'

Caroline twisted harder again. 'What?' she whispered, almost unable to hear herself over the thumping of her heart and the roar of blood in her ears.

'Yeah. I need you to hit me or something, though. You saw what I was having done to me at the club. You know I can take a lot more than this. Need a lot more than this.'

'Hit you where?'

'Hit my face, slap my face. Hard as you can.'

Caroline stopped and took her hand out of his hair. 'Are you sure? You said you were new to this. I don't want to hurt you.'

Alfie grinned. 'Yeah, you do.'

'But I don't know your limits or anything. I mean, I know your safe word is red but...'

Alfie sort of smiled. 'No limits. No need. Look, really, trust me, unless you have silver bullets you are not going to be doing me any lasting damage anytime soon. Now, hit me. Hit the damn wolf in me.'

The wolf in...? But Caroline pulled her arm back and slapped Alfie's face hard. His head jerked. His mouth fell open a little. He was so easily, instantly aroused by it. He was so sexy. And Caroline didn't even think. She slapped him again.

Then she kissed him some more. Harder this time. Wilder. She bit his lips hard and then his tongue. Her hands were in his hair again, but this time even she was feeling it wasn't enough. She could feel his need coming off him in waves. He was burning with it. Fuck, but he was hot. Hot in every way.

Caroline pulled back from the kiss and looked at Alfie. His lips were swollen from kissing and biting. There wasn't a single mark on his face where she had slapped him though. She wished there was. 'I want to see you kneeling. See you on your knees.' It turned her on so much she could barely choke the words out.

Alfie fixed Caroline's eyes with his and lowered his body slowly. First onto one knee, then both. Then he watched her, waiting for the next order.

Caroline ran her teeth over her bottom lip. 'Fuck, you look so hot like that,' she said softly. 'I wish you were tied up, but I don't want to stop and get any stuff.'

'You don't need to tie me up. How about I link my little fingers behind my back?'

'Yeah. Oh, yeah. Do it.'

Alfie put his hands behind his back. His chest expanded a little. The muscles at the tops of his arms went taut.

Caroline sighed. He looked like a hero. A brave man

offering himself to her, offering himself up to be sacrificed to whatever her twisted desires demanded of him. She felt she could look at him – look into his golden eyes forever.

But forever, it turned out, didn't last so very long.

Caroline bent at the waist, leaning right down from her perch on the table and kissed Alfie on the lips again. It was delicious having his face so much lower down than hers. Her hands found his big smooth chest. She closed her fingers over his nipples, twisting and pulling. Each time he gasped into her mouth and she felt very sure his cock was getting harder and harder.

'Fuck,' said Alfie when Caroline took her mouth away from his. 'I really want to come.'

'You can't though, can you?'

'No.' Alfie sighed. 'You've still got the insulin, though, right?'

Caroline frowned. 'Er, yes.'

Alfie smiled. 'I just want you to use me, then. Let me find a pleasure in pleasuring you.'

Caroline found the idea that Alfie would be denied any kind of sexual release unnervingly sexy. She squirmed on the table.

Alfie said. 'If I could come though, I'd like to come on your shoes. Can I kiss them?'

Caroline looked down at her shoes. They were black shiny Mary Janes. Cute, but nothing special. 'You like them?' she said, breathy suddenly, with the need for his mouth to be plastered back over hers. 'I was going to change into something more in keeping. I have some boots upstairs.'

'No. They're great. You want to see me licking them?' He swallowed. 'I will. If you tell me to. I'm in the right place to obey any orders you might give me.'

Caroline looked down at him. He looked so amazing, there, on his knees. His arms were still linked behind his back and he was looking up at her with those big golden eyes. There was something animal-like about him. All that power, like a coiled spring, offered to her. So beautifully controlled. A noble beast, submitting himself to her, but still wild, untamed.

'I want to see your tongue working on my shoes,' she said, her voice husky and cracking. Suddenly she was feeling close to orgasm. It seemed strange as – in some ways – they had only just begun.

Alfie kept his hands behind his back as he moved his head forwards and began to run his tongue over the toe of one of her pumps. Her feet were off the floor. Almost at the perfect height. He only had to duck down a little. Caroline squirmed. The way his long pink tongue glided over the leather of her shoe just made her think about that same talented tongue working between her legs.

She let him lick them some more. Then she said, 'I like the way you use your tongue, Alfie. How about you use it to make me come?'

Without taking his mouth off her shoes Alfie turned his head a little and smiled at her. Then, with his hands still in position behind his back, he let his tongue glide all the way up one of her leather-clad legs, stroking softly through the hide.

By the time he reached the top Caroline had unfastened her buttons and was shucking the trousers down her legs. Her underwear followed and, as she slid forwards, Alfie pushed his nose and mouth into position. Caroline's legs turned to liquid as soon as she felt his soft damp-velvet tongue caressing her clit.

He stroked her over and over with his tongue and then pushed back, down, deeper, and thrust the length of it inside her. Caroline's hands gripped the table edge. She looked down at those powerful shoulders. Those big arms. His neat waist and arse still snugly covered in tight jeans. She thought about the hard column of his frustrated cock. The sweet urgent needy taste of his mouth. That strange smell of cut grass and coppery blood that he seems to exude. In some ways he barely seemed human at all. Some fantastical creature.

He drew his tongue back over her clit once more and it nearly tipped her into orgasm. One more time and she was there. Screaming. Her hands leaving the table and finding his scalp again. Twisting in his hair. Hurting him and holding his mouth on her. Almost levitating with the power of it.

When she opened her eyes he was still on the floor in a kneeling crouch, hunched over her shoes and pooled jeans.

He looked up at her. 'Thank you. God, I wish I could come too. You could make me beg for it.'

Caroline laughed lightly. She pushed her foot forwards and grazed it up the distinct bulge in his jeans. 'You want to come, huh?' she teased. Tracing the bulge of his erection once or twice more.

'Yeah. God.'

With a couple of kicks, Caroline slipped off her trousers and underwear that were tangled around her ankles. 'You want to beg for it?' she said as she did it.

'Mmm-hmm.'

'Well go on then.'

And he was on his knees, with his hands behind his back, begging to come. 'Oh god. Please. I need to. I'm so turned on. Please, tell me I can.'

Caroline looked at him. Kept looking at him. She couldn't take her eyes away. 'I'd like to see you touch yourself. Take yourself to the edge.'

Alfie nodded.

'Mmm. Take off the rest of your clothes first.'

Lifting himself a little way from the floor Alfie shed his open shirt and his jeans. Naked he looked even more like a beautiful animal. He got down on his haunches. Poised to pounce. Big powerful thighs spread wide. Hard cock. Jutting. Shining and wet.

'Touch it,' Caroline said.

Alfie snaked a hand between his legs and made a fist around his cock. He pumped it twice, quickly. Gasping as he did. Wanting and needy.

'Do it slowly,' Caroline said. 'I want to watch.'

Alfie moaned a little. Clearly not wanting to slow down, but he did it. He stroked himself more gently, still crouching at her feet, until his head was tipped right back and he was incoherent with desire.

And then his eyes snapped open. 'Fuck!' he said. 'Where's the sedative?'

'The what?'

'The sedative? Uh, the syringe. The insulin?'

'You need . . . what?'

Alfie's face was hard as stone. 'Inject me. Right now.'

Caroline reached for the syringe, but she wasn't wearing her trousers.

She slid off the table and dropped onto the floor next to Alfie. He'd let go of his cock and was frozen. Crouched on the floor looking terrified.

Caroline scrambled in the pocket of her crumpled trousers. Nothing. She turned them around and tried the other pocket, exhaling with relief as her fingers touched the cool glass.

She straddled Alfie's body. As he lifted his face to look at her she saw it looked weird, swollen. She didn't pause to think. She shoved the hypo into his neck.

He bucked under her a couple of times and then stilled. Unconscious. Oh fuck. Too much.

Caroline turned, looking for Alfie's jeans. Didn't diabetics carry glucose sweets in case they had too much insulin?

But there was nothing in Alfie's pockets. And when she turned back, there was no Alfie. Just a gigantic unconscious wolf.

* * *

Caroline didn't really remember going to bed, but she woke up with a muzzy head and fuzzy teeth.

She pulled on a T-shirt and sweatpants and stumbled into the hall. She stared at the kitchen door. Not sure what she would find behind it. She'd closed it the night before and jammed a chair under the handle, after staring in disbelief at Alfie's sedated form which had transformed into the body of a huge sleeping wolf.

She knocked on the door. 'Uh, Alfie?'

'It's OK,' said Alfie's voice from behind the door. 'I'm OK.'

Caroline opened the kitchen door to find Alfie sitting at her kitchen table, he smiled, sheepish. 'I can, uh, I can explain. Sort of.'

Caroline turned to make some tea. 'You don't have to.' The sight of Alfie sitting there was making her feel light headed. He looked like he might be naked, but he probably had his underpants on under the table. *He did have a pair of underpants with him, didn't he?*

'It wasn't a fit. I mean, if you've convinced yourself I just had some kind of fit, I didn't. I . . .'

'You're a werewolf.' Caroline said, turning away from the boiling kettle.

'Yes.'

'You're a werewolf who has got too old and whose body is becoming unstable. You change when you come, don't you? So you thought you'd be OK with me. A kinky woman who gets off on you not having an orgasm. Except it didn't work, did it? Because even without a climax the excitement was still enough to make you change.'

'Uh . . . ? So you're – what? – some kind of werewolf expert.'

Caroline couldn't help looking at the red marks across his back from the whipping he got at the club. 'No. Not really. My sister Cate is a witch.'

'Oh? I didn't know witches had . . .'

'Sisters?'

'Well, yeah. Families.'

'Well, they do. Of course they do.' The kettle boiled and Caroline poured the water into the pot. Then she turned and set it on the table, fetching cups and some milk from the fridge. 'So you know. I know. In fact, she told me about you.'

'About me.'

'Yes. She told me I'd meet you. An unstable werewolf. A man who became a wolf and not just at full moon. And, believe it or not, she said I needed to set you on your path.'

'Oh?'

Caroline poured tea sloppily into both cups, 'So I was thinking last night, after you, *you know*, what I could do. Why I might be meant to set you on your path. I don't know much about werewolves. Or anything paranormal. But I do know about bondage. So I kind of wondered if that might help.' Caroline picked up her cup and sipped her tea.

Alfie drank his own tea and then said, 'I don't see how.'

'Well, I mean, what if you had bondage sex? Why not just get tied up. Then you'd be safe if you changed.'

'I've thought of that. And it wouldn't work. You didn't see how I change if I'm not sedated. Rope won't hold me. Even chains. The heat that comes out when my body breaks and reforms . . .'

Caroline said, 'Well I guess you're right. What about The Silver Chains?'

Alfie reached out and poured some more tea into his cup, adding the milk as he spoke, 'God, I'm so fucking thirsty.' He took a huge gulp. 'Wow, this is good tea. Silver would burn me. But I don't see how that would . . .'

'No, no, The Silver Chains. They're a werewolf legend.'

'Well what are they?'

'They're meant to control shapeshifters. Maybe they stop the change somehow. There are a lot of stories about them. And, I don't know, they just seem to be something that might help. I can't believe you've never heard of them.'

'I was bitten by a lone wolf. I've pretty much had to work stuff out for myself. There's no one who can tell me about these Silver Chains. Even if they're real. Even if they would help.'

Caroline said, 'There's me. I can tell you.'

'You? How come you know about them?'

'Because I like chains. I guess Cate knew what she was doing when she mentioned them to me.'

Alfie set his cup down and looked at her. 'God, I hate witches. Why do they always have to be so weird about everything?'

'Honestly, I don't think they think it's weird. But look, I know it sounds a bit out there, by our standards, but Cate said I would set you on your path. She said it was the path to your one true love, actually.'

'My one true love. Well now I know you're talking bollocks.'

'Why? Don't tell me, you don't believe in love. Typical werewolf.'

Alfie laughed, bitter, pithy and sarcastic. 'Oh I believe in love. I just don't think it believes in me.'

Caroline poured some more tea. It looked very dark brown as it came out of the spout. Strong. Normally it would be too strong for her, but this morning she felt like she needed it. The extra strength. Somehow she wanted this conversation to go on forever. She felt trippy, shivery, achy; it all seemed too real, too immediate. The werewolf Cate had told her she would meet one day was sitting right here.

She watched him drinking his tea. Everything about him seemed to be calculated to be ridiculously sexy and yet, at the same time, it was thoughtlessly casual: the way he blew over the surface of the liquid; the way his lips formed a tiny pout when he did that; the long lashes that grazed his cheekbones when he blinked; the way he looked at her, didn't speak, then looked away with a half-smile. Caroline was finding the silence that had taken hold of the room a little bit uncomfortable, but, somehow, she couldn't bear to break it.

Alfie drained the last of the tea from his cup. 'OK, tell me about these chains then.'

'Come upstairs,' said Caroline. 'I have a lot of stuff to show you. I think I know where they are. I warn you – it's going to be a bit of a trek.'

And after he'd gone with two fat wallets of documents detailing the last known locations of The Silver Chains, Caroline felt sure that she wasn't the first woman whose life Alfie Friday had walked into and then walked right out of.

5

'I can't believe we're doing this.' Misty was standing at the luggage carousel in Rio airport and she had never spoken a truer word. 'I mean, fuck it, Alfie. Brazil. We're in Brazil.'

'Yep,' said Alfie, heaving the second of Misty's enormous suitcases onto a trolley. 'We're not going to be able to take all this stuff with us, by the way. You'll have to find some kind of storage facility.'

'What?' Misty looked like she didn't understand him. She looked around again. 'I can't believe we've done this. I just can't.'

Alfie hadn't really explained. Had come home from the night he'd spent with that strange woman from Wonderland and declared that she had told him to go and find The Silver Chains. On the plane, while Leon was sleeping, Misty had tried to get him to tell her more. Tell her why the chains were going to help him – they'd already explored containment options and only something that held his body without constraining it, like a cage, could do the job of holding him while he changed. But all he would tell her was that The Silver Chains were different.

Behind Alfie, Leon grabbed his own bag and flung it onto the trolley clumsily. Alfie had to jump out of the way. 'Damnit, Leon, watch out.'

'Sorry, sire.'

Alfie turned to Misty. 'I don't have any choice. That thing with your kinky friends didn't work out. I need to find a way to have sex. I've got to, Misty. And this is the only lead I've got. There's a werewolf pack in Brazil that can help me. I know they can.'

Behind him Leon heaved the last of the bags onto the trolley. 'Yeah, yeah, sire, we know. Kinky Caroline told you they had The Silver Chains.'

'Yeah. Right. Now come on.' And Alfie turned, leaving Misty to trot after him and Leon to bring the rickety trolley.

In hot and noisy Rio, Misty was amazed at how Alfie seemed to know just what to do. They'd taken a train and then picked up a ride in the back of a truck deep into nowhere.

In the rainforest everything was hot and damp. Sultry. It was gloriously lush and so uncomfortable.

Misty lay back against her holdall in the back of the truck – the only luggage Alfie had let her bring from Rio. She was wearing just a brightly printed sarong. Alfie had hardly left her any interesting clothes. She felt practically naked.

Across from her Leon looked like he was asleep, his body juddering as the truck shook over the unsurfaced road. He looked so sexy. Leon was always the most animal looking of the three of them. His long blond hair the only soft thing about him. He was topless – only wearing his jeans – and when he growled and rolled over a second later, she could see the long stretch of his muscled back.

Alfie was wearing jeans too. And a white vest. The two of them looked like aging teen pop stars. He was reading a paper from the document wallet he hadn't stopped leafing through since he got home from his night with Caroline. Alfie never really took any notice of werewolf history. Werewolf lore. Leon had told Misty things about lycans that Alfie never had. But since this trip had been proposed Alfie had been reading up on the kind of stuff he usually sneered at.

As she was staring at him, he looked up and smiled a lazy hazy-heat smile. His big body was sweat-shiny.

Wetness glistened on his forehead and upper lip. Misty knew every inch of it – but they hadn't slept together for nearly a year. She knew she could never have him again.

'Everything OK?' she said.

'Yeah, yeah. I think we might need to get out and walk soon.' He pulled a compass out of his pocket. 'The bearings for the Carci Gate are different in different documents, but I think we can get to the general area.'

Misty nodded and at the same time Alfie reached out and banged on the back of the truck's cab. The engine rumbled lower and lower as they pulled over and came to a stop.

A skinny Hispanic woman slipped out of the cab and said something to Alfie in rapid Portuguese. Alfie said something snappy back.

Alfie had gone into a bar the night before to arrange this lift. Misty was sure – had been certain when she saw their driver was female – that Alfie had used his sex appeal to get what he wanted. But, of course, he wouldn't have been able to sleep with her. Perhaps she was snippy about that.

Alfie had always been a charmer. A man who knew how sexy he was and knew how to use it – the way he moved his body, the way he pitched his voice – but once the flipping had started it had been like watching someone trying to get used to having a limb missing. He'd seduce and charm women (and a not inconsiderable number of men) wherever he went and then he couldn't take them to bed. There had been so many tears. So many fights. One charming female doctor had even offered to 'prescribe something'. And Alfie, lost and confused, had become more withdrawn, more sullen, more deep-down angry.

Whatever Alfie had dragged them around the world for, and he hadn't really given a proper explanation, Misty just hoped it worked.

* * *

'She said we ought to be careful.' Alfie said casually, as they trekked through the undergrowth. 'Lot of dangerous stuff out here.'

'Yeah, right,' said Leon. ''Course that was what she was shouting about. Anyway, what's for us to worry about? Unless any of the snakes have silver fangs.'

Alfie gave Leon a look. 'Still no harm being careful. We're a long way from home, Leon.'

'We're werewolves, sire. Practically unkillable. Did you forget that? Did you think Misty and me were hanging out with you because you're such great company these days. Newsflash – we're your pack. You're our alpha. We're bound to you by ancient ties. Worse for us.'

'Leon,' said Misty, 'leave it.'

'Leave what?' Leon stopped and pouted at Misty, his hands on his hips.

'Leon, move, I can't get past.'

Leon didn't move. He just cocked his head at Misty. 'I said, "Leave what?" All I was saying was how daddy's acting more and more grumpy these days. Must be that sore *head* of his.'

Misty swallowed.

Alfie, who was a few yards ahead, leading the way, whirled around. He launched himself at Leon – lightning fast, exploding from a standing start – grabbing him by the scruff of his neck and barrelling him up against a tree. 'She said,' Alfie snarled, his face right in Leon's, 'Leave. It.'

'Huh. Touchy today, sire? I suppose it's been a while since you've been able to lock yourself up in your cage and have a wank. That being all you can do without turning into the big bad wolf. *Hard*, is it?'

Alfie stared at Leon. Misty was watching the muscle twitch in Alfie's jaw. He wasn't saying anything but Misty knew from Leon's face what Alfie was doing. Pulling alpha. Staring Leon down with the power he had as pack alpha and Leon's sire. Alfie had never had to discipline Misty this way – but she still didn't envy Leon right now.

'All I am asking,' Alfie said eventually, speaking through his teeth, 'is that you respect your surroundings. We're a long way from home in a place that could be hostile. You don't know what there is out here in the rainforest. You think we can be sure that nothing here is dangerous to lycans? You think anyone's done tests on that?'

Leon was several shades paler than he had been a moment ago, but he still inhaled and said, 'We're were-wolves. It isn't like that. Silver. Mercury. That's it.'

'There's no scientific basis . . .'

'Don't start that, sire, we're werewolves. Science has left the building.'

Alfie growled deep in his throat. The dark sound made Misty shudder. The last shreds of pink life drained from Leon's face.

'OK,' Leon muttered, weakly, 'OK. I'll be careful.'

If she hadn't been distracted Misty might have scented something, but she was staring at Alfie and Leon so intently. The way they were looking at each other. It was weird but it was just so sexy. The heat. The humidity. The sweat. Alfie's shoulders – the way the taut muscles rolled in his tight vest. Leon's bare back up against the alien looking tree. Misty felt her clit swell softly. Heat and humidity inside her and out.

It was pure sex. For a moment or two at least. Then her lust drained out of her body and she felt nothing except the point and sting of a silver blade at the base of her skull. Around the perimeter of the little clearing where they were standing the points of several cross-bows appeared out of the undergrowth.

A cool female voice said, 'Oh how perfect. Fresh blood."

6

It was hard to believe they couldn't break out of the small round wooden hut they were locked in – it seemed so flimsy – but Misty had watched Leon as he tried every crack and slit in the walls, every join, every square inch. Cursing and muttering as nothing yielded.

He turned to Misty. 'Wolves escape. You ever heard that line? A place like this shouldn't be able to hold us.'

Misty just shrugged.

Alfie was slumped in a corner. They'd been locked in the hut a few hours without food or much water.

Werewolve's bodies ran at higher speed than human ones. They needed to eat and drink (and sleep and fuck) a lot more than humans. But these bodily needs always seemed to hit Alfie hardest of all. Misty had got used to seeing Alfie looking glazed and grouchy if they were stuck somewhere without access to anything fleshy and high protein. She knew all it took to get him back to his funny bouncy self was a cooked chicken and a couple of pints of milk.

'Damn it!' Leon kicked at the section of wall he'd been trying to pry apart from it's neighbour and Alfie looked up.

'Sit the fuck down, Leon.'

Leon turned and looked down at Alfie with his hands on his tightly denim-clad hips. Misty shifted. Time for round two. 'Let me get this straight, sire. You drag us across the planet to find some magical bondage gear for you to have a kinky fuck with, but you're too busy making sure we don't forget what a big tough daddy-wolf you are and you drop the ball and get us caught by some kind of, what? Jungle werewolves? Because they are wolves, right? These guys?'

'I didn't know they even had wolves in the rainforest,' said Misty.

'There's only one werewolf pack in the whole of the Southern Hemisphere,' said Alfie. 'No one really knows why. But these wolves guard the Carci Gate. There the ones we were looking for.'

'What is the Carci Gate?' said Misty. She'd heard Alfie mention it several times – but he'd never really explained what it was.

Leon turned to her. 'Oh, it really is a lovely story. Trust daddy to choose this bit of werewolf lore to latch onto. The Carci Gate. How werewolves help humans. How we save the stinking world. It's the favoured myth of those who like to think that werewolves should all roll over and be good little doggies. Keep humans safe – safe from us and safe from monsters. It's the bloody Uncle Tom Werewolf. The weredog. You know, man's best friend.'

Misty shook her head. 'What? I don't understand.'

Leon sighed. 'He really never taught you anything, did he? There's this magical gate, somewhere on earth ...'

'Here,' said Alfie, 'it's here.'

'They do say it's in South America. Anyway this gate – think of it as a portal to some kind of evil dimension, if you like. So this portal opens at full moon and unmentionably horrible creatures come through it. From this other dimension, or other planet, or whatever, fuck knows really. But anyway they do and the only creatures that can kill them are lycans. Lycans in wolf form. So every full moon when the gate opens the wolfies troop off and kill anything that gets through. Woo-hoo! Lycans help humans. Protect them from the yuks.'

'Is that true?' said Misty to Alfie.

'Yes. It's true. And the pack that guard the Carci Gate have The Silver Chain. Or were the last known custodians. That's why we're here.'

'The chains that can hold any shapeshifter?' said Misty. She'd heard of those.

'And they'll hold me,' Alfie said.

'But what?' said Misty. 'They're just going to give it to you. Aren't they sacred werewolf treasures, or something.'

Alfie held her gaze. 'I'll just have to persuade them, won't I? There's something else notable about this pack. Almost unheard of. They have a female alpha.'

Leon made a hooting noise. 'Great,' he said. 'No really, that's fantastic. You're going to shag queen bitch and she'll just give you her sacred treasure. Is that how it works for pretty boys like you? Except it doesn't really seem to be going according to plan so far, does it?' Leon kicked at the hut wall again.

'Stop that. This is part of my plan. I expected to be captured by them. By the Carci Gate guardians.' Alfie said it slowly. 'It was the only way. You don't find them. They find you. They have lycan detectors set for fifty miles around the gate.'

'Why?' said Misty.

'Because they have a code. Any lycan who gets this near to the gate either joins them in their fight against the evil that comes through that thing every full moon, or dies.'

Misty gasped. 'Alfie!'

'Oh my god, sire,' said Leon. He turned to Misty. 'He's joined us all up to the foreign legion just so he can get a shag. You didn't mean to take the chains at all, did you? You meant for us to stay here.'

7

An hour later, none of them had any energy left to argue.

The door opened so suddenly that Misty jumped backwards. Then felt her stomach flip over when she saw the food. Fruit and meat. Perfect. She got shakily to her feet, half watching Leon and Alfie doing the same from the opposite corners where they had deliberately positioned themselves.

The three of them approached the two burly men holding out the loaded trays. Leon and Alfie both snatched up handfuls of food. And Misty wasn't far behind.

About half of the food was gone when another figure appeared in the doorway, a woman with long dark hair in a slick plait down her back. Her body was taut, wrought from activity, especially her bare arms which were patterned with long distinct muscles. The golden skin on her bluntish face was lined in a way that suggested she smiled a lot. But she wasn't smiling right now.

She was standing so erect and upright. Regal. Misty was certain she was the female alpha that Alfie had mentioned.

The woman said, 'Would you come with me please, Alfie?'

Alfie stared at the remaining food for a second. Misty saw his nostrils flare a little. Then he nodded, turned and followed the woman out of the cell.

Following the woman out of the hut, Alfie walked through a busy encampment. He, Misty and Leon had arrived blindfolded. This was his first glimpse of the place.

Werewolves were renowned for making homes in all kinds of odd places. What were usually called 'pack houses' were as likely to be old warehouses, caves or forgotten basements as actual houses. Werewolves were often squatters. Lacking the money to pay proper rent. (There was also a long tradition of werewolves taking over the homes of people they had killed – if the victim was lonely and isolated enough. But Alfie didn't hold with that sort of thing. Leon probably did.)

Alfie had seen the insides of all sorts of weird and wonderful places, turned into werewolf pack houses, but he had never seen anything quite like this bizarre and eclectic camp. Huts, like the one they were locked up in, and much older looking stone buildings – the largest of which seemed to be some kind of temple – cluttered around an open space. A square with a raised wooden platform containing nothing but a wooden post. So far, so place out of time, but dotted around the buildings – filling almost every scrap of space – were vans, trucks, cars, tents, all kinds of makeshift and permanent dwellings. It looked like a refugee camp. But Alfie knew what this was. This was a conflict zone. This was the trenches. The front. This pack guarded the Carci Gate.

The woman led him down a small path between a mobile home and a large static caravan. Through a small empty space and into the trees beyond. After a few yards she stopped below a rope, which hung down from overhead.

'Climb it,' she said.

Alfie looked up. The rope disappeared into the canopy – he couldn't see where it went. 'Look,' he said, turning to the woman, 'what is this all about?'

'Climb it.'

Alfie shrugged, took the rope and began to climb.

Alfie was strong, but his body was big and heavy. His

arms were sore, muscles screaming, as he hauled himself higher and higher into the trees.

And then, just as Alfie began to wonder what would happen if he just let his deadened arms let go of the rope, it took him up through a trap door, a hole in a wooden floor above his head. He climbed up and on through it and found himself in a large room.

When he was high enough up the rope – which continued up to the room's roof – he put his feet down on the wooden floor. Then he let go of the rope and looked around.

The room he was in was beautiful. A huge airy entirely wooden space up in the trees. A loose gauzy white fabric hung at the huge windows cut out of the four walls, revealing views of the distant blue and purple tipped hazy mountains over the tops of the trees. The sticky oppressive heat was lessened up here. The only sounds were of bird calls and the curtains billowing in the wind. Scented candles burned in carved stone holders, filling the airy space with the scents of musk and sandalwood and jasmine.

In the middle of the room was a huge bed. A four-poster made of wood so dark it seemed almost black and hung with the same wispy fabric that draped the windows.

The place swam with seduction, romance, sex.

Alfie knew exactly why he had been brought here. And he already had his vest off when the woman emerged through the hole in floor.

She smiled.

She was dressed for utility in a tight brown vest and khaki parachute pants. Her feet were bare and she had a single leather thong around her neck with a lozenge shaped wooden bead resting just above the dint in her collar bone. Looking at her now, she seemed so overtly lycan. It wasn't always so easy to tell, but some were-wolves moved in a lightly sinuous, slightly animal way.

Leon certainly did. And she had that stance too. Also shared with Leon. Shoulders right back. A certain pride.

Alfie didn't know if he looked blatantly lycan to other werewolves. But he'd always assumed not. Alfie was a big man – tall and wide. And like a lot of big men he walked the path of the gentle giant. Trying to make his body small. Holding back. Always trying not to seem intimidating unless he really needed to.

Alfie looked at the woman. He didn't speak. He began to weigh up his options. Did he want to escape? Wolves escape. Should he be making a plan? Maybe Leon was right – he couldn't just join them up to this unknown warrior pack for the sake of him getting his hands on The Silver Chains. He didn't even know for sure what the chains did. Maybe he should try and escape – easier to escape from this love nest than the hut. And once he was free he could go back for Misty and Leon. They could rethink in the jungle now they knew the location of the camp

An escape plan. If the woman wanted sex it was too easy. If she had sex with him he'd flip when he came. Not much killed werewolves. Like Leon had said, silver and mercury accompanied by a wound that would be fatal in humans. A drop from a height – even one as high as this wouldn't kill him. He was sure she knew this too. Sure she was keeping a close eye on him to make sure he didn't try it. But if he flipped – if he was a wolf – well, she'd want him out of there as quickly as possible.

All he needed to do, to escape her, was orgasm.

And orgasms seemed to be her plan too.

Alfie had never thought about his flipping like this before. As something actually useful. The fact he had access to his wolf whenever he wanted him. That could be a blessing as well as a curse.

She had both hands behind her back as she approached him. She was loosening her plait. As she got nearer it fell away from its fastening and she shook her head so the shiny crinkled-up dark hair twisted free and fell all around her shoulders.

She was handsome, not beautiful, practical and a little worn away by time and trouble. But so elegant. She was incredibly sexy. Alfie made a low involuntary noise in his throat and she laughed. Just a light momentary noise that said she appreciated his obvious arousal, even in the midst of her own.

'I don't often do this,' she said, reaching out and putting her hand on his bicep. 'I'm the alpha here. I can take whatever I want. Whatever pleasure I want. But I usually look to my pack. I rarely bring prisoners up here.'

'Oh, well that's OK then,' said Alfie. 'So long as you don't make a habit of it.' And he lowered his head so he could kiss her.

Suddenly she was demanding and it was alpha and alpha. A power struggle.

Alfie knew that the woman kissing him – the woman whose name he still didn't know – was a more powerful *alpha* than he was. She had a large and complex pack under her control. But Alfie had been bitten by an Ancient Beast. In the werewolf hierarchy – in the line – Alfie was probably a more powerful *werewolf* than her. It was complicated. Not to mention the whole basic part where he was her prisoner.

Which made the power twist around between them. Unresolved, delicious. She pushed him backwards, holding the kiss and guided him to the bed. He went down into a sitting position, steadied with an arm, then right onto his back with his feet still on the floor.

She climbed on top of him and pulled off her T-shirt. She didn't have a bra on. Her tits were neat. Tight and pointed. Her body reminded Alfie of Iris's – an old girlfriend. The woman's skin was far darker than Iris's had been, but her physique, her body shape was so similar.

Her nipples were already hard and so dark they looked almost black like the wood of the beautiful bed. Alfie gasped at the sight of her and he saw the woman swallow hard in response.

'What do you, what do you want me to do?' Alfie whispered.

The woman was running her hands over his prone chest. Her hands were rough. Well worked. She was a warrior. She saved the world every month. Fought the Carci. Suddenly Alfie felt overwhelmed by her – by what she was, what she must have done in her life. 'What, you mean like what do I command you to do, because you're my prisoner?'

'Mmm, yeah.'

The woman rested her hands with a thumb over each of Alfie's nipples and caressed then, teasing him with the rough nap of each pad. 'OK, butch. Listen. I want you to fuck me. Nice and long. Nice and hard. Very hard. I can tell from those biceps that you're capable of just what I need. A good hard fuck. And I don't want you to come until I say you can. I want to see those big hard arms start to shake as you hold your body over me.' She was panting lightly as she finished her sentence. Then she leant down and kissed him deeply, pinching both his nipples at the same time.

Something in the mass of sensation – the pain, the pleasure, the overwhelming everything of her bare skin hitting his – meant that Alfie felt nothing so much as all the blood in his body rush to his cock. Suddenly he was stone-hard, not thinking straight.

He shivered into her kiss. He was going to get to orgasm. To come inside her. He could allow himself. He had to, to escape. He'd come here for sex. And whether he found The Silver Chains or not, he was going to get some at least. A taste.

But a single taste. Could that make it worse? Like

Tantalus in Hades, tortured by the water that he couldn't reach to drink. His thirst was far worse after Persephone had stopped and helped him get one scoop to his lips.

No. Surely. Nothing, nothing could make his frustration worse. Sex. Really. Not like what he'd had with Caroline. Real sex. Fucking. And, god, it had been so long.

The woman knelt up over him and started to unfasten her parachute pants. Alfie made another noise in his throat as he reached out and knocked her hands away.

It wasn't really intentional, but as he tried to get them undone he ripped the delicate material. The sound of the tearing excited him. He'd done this once with Iris. Asked her to wear old clothes just so he could indulge a fantasy of ripping them away. *Iris*. Again. Even before he'd lost control of his body he couldn't lie with another woman without thinking of Iris. Even with Misty – whom he'd felt he might be able to fall in love with – he'd found himself thrusting into her thinking of his ex-girlfriend who now hated him for what he was. A werewolf. Hated him for being the same as the thing that had killed her brother.

But right now, visions of Iris aside, Alfie didn't – couldn't – think. He growled, ripped the nameless woman's clothing away and flipped her onto her back. He paused for one suspended moment, over her, using one of his arms for balance, the other twisting and fumbling at his jeans. He got them off, kicking and twisting, as fast as he could – his underwear going with them. Then he lowered himself onto the woman's taut smooth body and kissed her.

She was soft beneath him. Small. Eager and willing. She pushed her fingers up into his hair and pulled him close.

'Pull,' he muttered into her bottom lip. 'Pull my hair.'

She did. Hard. She jerked his head back, away from the soft safety of her mouth. The sudden heat in his cock echoed the pain in his scalp. He looked down into her eyes. She flickered her lips into a little pout, inviting his kiss. But she didn't release her grip on his hair. He pulled against her fist as he strained to meet her lips and she teased him by pouting again and then wetting them with her tongue.

'Please,' he whispered as she teased him with the promise of her lips.

'Please what?'

'Please let me kiss you. Please.'

Laughing she finally gave into him and let him get near enough to kiss her. She tasted so much sweeter for those few moments wanting and waiting. He kissed her harder – she still held his hair firmly. God it was good.

When he broke the kiss, pulling back panting, she said, 'Fuck me now, werewolf. Alpha. Wolf and man. Fuck me.'

And he did. He didn't need telling twice. He reached down and guided his cock inside her. And he was already thrusting hard, watching her roll and moan beneath him before he remembered just why this was so hot. He hadn't done this for a year. He hadn't had sex for a year. The pain while she had pulled his hair had kept him grounded for a while, but now he was just fucking her, gliding on liquid pleasure. His cock was opening up inside her like a flower. She was tight, wet, around him. Fitting him perfectly. She – her pussy – was everything his own fist wasn't.

And the wolf was coming. He could feel it. Hot breath on the back of his neck. It couldn't be real. His imagination. But it felt so real. He looked down at the woman underneath him. So pretty. Like Iris. He'd kill her if he changed now. She wouldn't stand a chance. Even though she was a werewolf herself she'd stay human. Her human could still be killed by his wolf. He knew it. Silver, mercury and him.

'I ... I can't.' He stopped moving and tried to pull back. Her legs were locked behind his back. She tightened them. 'No please, you have to let me go.'

'I told you to fuck me,' she said, her voice soft and low. Even with the weight of her demand.

'No,' Alfie said, 'no. You don't understand.'

She grabbed at his shoulder and tried to draw him to her. 'Fuck me.'

'No!' Alfie ripped free of her, forcing his way through her locked ankles, and slid back off the bed.

She sat up and looked wildly at him. 'Don't even think of the window. I have men on the ground ...'

'I'm not going to try and escape.'

'Then come back here and fuck me. You're my prisoner, remember, you're meant to be pleasuring me.'

'I can't.' Alfie suddenly felt so weak and small. A big man with a big firm erection so hard against his belly. 'I might ... I'll change. Sex makes me change.'

The woman looked at him for a long moment. 'Sex makes you ... ? You're unstable? Close to the skin?'

'Yes. Yeah.'

'You're him.'

'I ... I'm what? Who?'

'We asked ... I don't believe it. We asked the gods to send us an unstable wolf. There didn't seem to be any other way. I never thought they'd answer us. They never normally do ... oh, I'd better ...' She reached behind her and pulled a cord that hung down next to the bed. Somewhere in the distance Alfie heard a bell ring. Then the rope that hung down to the ground began to shake. Someone was climbing up. Several people.

'Why? Why do you need an unstable wolf,' Alfie said, wondering about the window, the people the woman had claimed were 'on the ground'.

She saw him looking. 'No. We need you for the sacrifice.'

'Sacrifice!' Alfie didn't know what or where he was

suddenly. His adrenaline spiked. The wolf was still with him. He could change any second. He turned away from her ready to leap – to throw himself through the window – but she was too quick. He heard her move, grab something, a blow pipe. He dived. As his feet left the floor he felt something hit him in the left arm. A sharp sensation.

He was falling and he looked down and saw a tranquilliser dart in his arm.

He lost consciousness before he hit the ground.

8

It wasn't so hot. Evening now. It was still damp. Alfie's arms hurt. He knew before he opened his eyes why. He was chained. His wrists and his ankles pulled wide. He was standing. Barely balanced. The metal cuffs around his limbs keeping him upright. He was also still naked.

Then, when he did open his eyes, he found he was chained between two thick trees. Stretched like a trophy. Had the alpha really said 'sacrifice'. He looked around him. The forest was darkening. Not quiet or still. But there was no sign of anything that he should particularly welcome or fear.

All he could hear was his own breathing – slightly laboured from the unkind stretch in his arms.

Until finally, someone, something, was coming. Rustles and snaps. Almost certainly footsteps. Coming casually and not sneaking. The sounds were behind him. He tried to look around but his body was pulled relentlessly taut in the chains. He had nowhere to turn. No place to run.

His body felt covered in cold sweat – his senses so sharp it was like he was made of shards of broken glass.

All he could do was twist hopelessly in his bondage. And wait.

Misty watched Leon get more and more frantic when Alfie didn't come back.

'It's going to be getting dark soon,' he said, looking out of the hut's tiny barred window.

'That doesn't matter. She took him for sex. You could tell from how she looked at him.'

'But he can't *have* sex. What do you think she'll do when she finds that out?'

Misty swallowed. 'I don't know.'

'We have to help him. Whatever it takes.'

'Have you got a plan?'

Leon nodded. 'Yeah, but I don't know if you'll like it.'

'If it helps Alfie I like it.'

'I was kind of banking on you saying that.'

Leon told her what he thought they should do. Misty listened without comment. His idea scared her and sort of turned her on too.

She nodded. 'I should take my clothes off.'

'You think that'll work better?'

'Oh yeah. I know how their filthy minds work.' Misty grinned as Leon looked worried. She stood up and raised her hands behind her neck to untie the knot of the sarong. It fell away from her tits and then slid down her body. She stepped out of it, completely naked.

Leon's eyes ran over her body. His jeans were very tight and the bulge at the crotch appeared instantly. 'You sure you're OK with this?' he said as he walked towards her.

Misty nodded.

Leon grabbed her bare waist and drew her to him. Sliding both hands back around to cup her arse as he drew her into a kiss. His hard scratchy denim-covered erection burrowed into her soft stomach.

Misty pulled back from the kiss. 'We ought to wait.'

'Oh babe, we can kiss a bit, can't we? They won't be long. Besides, I need to be ready.'

'You are ready. More than. I can feel it.'

Then Misty froze as she heard sounds outside the door of the hut. They fell quickly into position. Leon dashing to lean up against the wall of the hut, where he was in full view of the door. And Misty kneeling naked in front of him. She wrenched open his jeans and slipped his firm cock into her mouth. Sucking it to even greater hardness.

Above her Leon stroked her hair and tipped his head back, feigning point-of-orgasm bliss. They both pretended to barely notice the shouts of jealous outrage as the door was flung open by their two werewolf guards.

Hands were on Misty quickly from behind. She was dragged off Leon by one burly lycan, lifted right up off the floor by a thick arm around her waist. The other one punched Leon in the face. So hard he slumped sideways. Misty's heart flipped over. She struggled in the man's iron grip – his forearm was like an iron bar across her bare stomach – kicking her suspended legs. 'My boyfriend, my boyfriend, you've hurt him!'

'Serves him right for not sharing the love,' said the wolf who had hit Leon, turning to Misty.

That's right boys, both look at the naked chick.

Misty was panting hard. The wolf holding her must be able to feel it. She tried to calm herself. 'Yeah,' she said, trying to sound sassy. 'You jealous? Don't you get much of that yourself? Never enough women to go round in lycan packs are there? Have you tried sucking each other?'

The werewolf in front of Misty was a big guy like his partner. Not exactly tall, but his big chest was barrel shaped. He had bright blond hair, a heavy, weathered tan and a nasty over-white smile. He wore a checked work-shirt rolled up over his thick forearms. Misty glanced at his crotch. Her mouth went dry at the size of the bulge there. This was a man who knew he had something special in his shorts. 'Suck each other?' he sneered. 'Oh, funny girl. You've got a smart mouth. No wonder your boyfriend likes to keep you quiet with his dick.' He glanced over at Leon who was lying on the ground, eyes closed, not moving. He turned back to Misty. 'And for your information, missy, I get what I want.' Big-dick must have given some kind of signal to his partner because Misty was dropped then, onto the floor.

She landed on her hands and knees in front of Big-dick. 'And what do you want?' she said.

'Oh you must know, cutie. You're in the right position for it. Get it out; I know you can't wait.'

As Misty reached for Big-dick's jeans, the wolf behind her grabbed hold of her arms and pulled them behind her back. He was crouching behind her, his face was by her ear. 'Come on sweetheart, let's see that tongue work.'

Misty leant forwards and started to undo the wolf's flies with her mouth. Something she had no trouble doing and had done a million times before.

Misty got Big-dick's big dick out and took it into her mouth, letting it work it's way down her throat until her nose was almost flush with the werewolf's musk-scented pubic hair. 'Well, goddamn,' he growled, as she took it all, 'you are a clever girl.'

She let his dick slip most of the way out then took it down her throat again. Big-dick seemed to liquefy. The one holding her arms let go of her and she reached around to steady Big-dick, reaching up and grasping his arse through his jeans as she relaxed and let him work back and forth in her throat.

She started thinking of Alfie. His big body over her. The way he used to be. The days back before he bit her and made her terrified of him. The crazy mixed-up joy of their sleeping together. She'd been in love with him. She still was. He wasn't in love with her. Couldn't be. Misty had always known Alfie was in love with someone else.

The cock in her mouth wasn't what was bringing tears to her eyes. She sucked Big-dick hard and let him use her, tangle his big fists in her hair. Let both these men – two big wolves – blot Alfie out of her mind forever. Behind her the other man had dropped into a crouch. He stroked her tits, tweaking at each nipple with spit-moistened fingers. He reached up and touched her mouth, running his fingers around where her lips were stretched around Big-dick. He nuzzled her neck. Bit. Let his stubble graze the crook of her shoulder.

She could tell from the way he was moving and the small groans he made that he was masturbating as he watched. After a few more moments playing with her tight-stretched mouth he moved his big rough fingers and slipped them inside her pussy.

Oh, that was good. Perfect.

She was so wet. From them. From Leon. From thinking about Alfie. She sucked Big-dick harder, took him deeper, made him moan. And that moan, made the guy behind her pump himself faster and make a soft pleasure noise in response. She felt thick hot jets of the other man's come shoot up her back. She let her mouth fall away from Big-dick and let her head roll back so that when he came – super quick – he shot over her face. And then she twisted against the other man's hard fingers inside her and came too.

She knew Leon was long gone.

9

'Who's there?' Alfie said for the third time. But there was no answer and the footsteps kept coming.

Then there was a hand over his mouth and the scent of him was unmistakable.

Leon.

'So, got yourself in a bit of a predicament here, haven't you, sire?'

Alfie mumbled something into Leon's hot sticky palm. The scent of him was overwhelming. His bare chest against Alfie's slick flesh. Alfie could feel Leon's jeans against his arse. He felt strangely ashamed of his nakedness. He didn't usually feel this way about his body – he knew he was beautiful – but now he could clearly feel that Leon was dressed below the waist, and something about that disparity made him burn with arousal and shame.

Leon reached around and pinched one of Alfie's nipples. Hard. Then he let his hand slide away from Alfie's mouth as he said, 'So, you want me to let you go?'

'Yes. Of course I do.'

'What I mean is,' said Leon, sliding his hand down Alfie's side and then slapping his bare backside hard, 'are you involved in some more kinky sex? Are you sure you wouldn't rather I left? Hmm, let me check.'

'Fuck, Leon.'

Leon had run his hand over Alfie's right hip and was taking hold of his flaccid cock. 'You're not going to fuck anyone with this big softy, daddy.'

'Leon!' Alfie turned his head and looked Leon dead in the eye. He meant to pull alpha. To order Leon to let him go. And he really did mean to do that. Right up to the point where he pressed his hot sweat-sticky lips against Leon's similarly sheened ones.

There was one single hot, hard moment where Alfie and Leon kissed each other like they meant it. Alfie's cock began to stir in Leon's hand. And then Leon pulled both his head and his hand away fast. 'God, sire.' Alfie couldn't tell if Leon was aroused or chastising – the breathy words just caught in his throat. Thick and snarling.

And Alfie said, 'Just unchain me, pup.' He turned away. Not looking at Leon. Ashamed. Already making an unspoken agreement with Leon never to mention this again.

Alfie's demand to be released wasn't an alpha command, but Leon obeyed anyway. 'Misty's fine, since you didn't ask,' he said as he walked around one of the trees Alfie was chained to and reached for the manacle that held his left wrist. 'She provided a distraction so I could get away. You know the distraction I mean. The one where she can turn her throat into a velvet tunnel. Although, I guess, you haven't felt that for a while.'

'You left her sucking off the guards!'

'Well yeah.'

'Oh damn it, Leon. And how do you think they'll treat her when they find you sneaked out while she was doing that. Get these damn chains off me. Now!'

Leon fiddled with the cuff for some minutes. 'This is strange,' he said. 'These chains are silver, but they don't burn me. There must be some kind of spell on them.'

'They're real silver?'

'Yes. Well, no, they're silver-plated steel.'

'How can you tell that?'

'I'm good with metals. It's a lycan thing. Although not all lycans have it. You clearly don't. But I've been able to identify metals since I took your bite. And I'm not at all surprised you never noticed that about me.'

Alfie growled. 'Just get it off.'

'Uh, actually, I don't think I can, sire, these mothers are locked up tight. Not shifting without the keys.'

'Well get the chains off the trees then.'

Leon didn't reply, but took two steps to the tree where the chain that held Alfie's wrist was anchored. He wrestled with the chain for a few moments. 'It won't budge, sire.'

'What? No. It's got to.'

'It's padlocked around this tree trunk. Heavy duty fucking chain.'

Alfie sighed. 'OK, well, you're going to have to sneak back into the camp. Get the keys, or something to cut the chain.'

'Or cut the tree down.'

'Yeah. If that's the best you can do. And get Misty out of there too. Don't come back without her . . .'

Alfie's voice trailed off as he saw how Leon was looking at him. Fearful. And then Alfie heard it too. Sounds. Something was coming.

The sounds of whatever it was approaching were horrific. Disturbing and terrifying. A rustle of leaves and a wet thumping, like something was being dragged. Over that silver bells. High, light laughter or singing. And under it all a low droning moan. It was the most monstrous sound Alfie had ever heard.

'Get out of here, Leon.'

'Sire. What the fuck is that?'

'It's for me. Whatever it is. It's what they put me here for.'

'I can't just leave you here. With *that* coming.'

'You can. This has nothing to do with you. Go get Misty.'

'Sire, I . . . she said to get *you* . . .' The noise was getting louder. It seemed to be coming from every direction at once. Like the rainforest was shaking with it.

'Now,' said Alfie, his voice resonating with alpha-tones. 'Get out of here now.'

Leon didn't need telling twice. He couldn't disobey. He took off and vanished into the green.

10

Alfie was alone. Alone, naked, helpless and a long way from home. He listened to the sounds around him. And he waited.

The moaning and rustling and dragging and laughing got louder, but all he could really hear was his own breathing. He could feel his muscles start to twitch and spasm under the tautness of the chains as his adrenaline spiked.

And he began to realise why he had been put here. What was going to happen.

He felt his control leaving him as the creatures emerged from the trees. Three of them. Old and sexless. With long grey hair and peeling skin. A deadness about them. The one in the middle was slightly taller than the others and seemed to be lame – one limb, twisted and elongated, dragging across the rainforest carpet as it moved towards him. The other two were similar and, though seemingly unharmed, moved no faster.

Alfie felt a new surge of fear and panic rush through him. The wolf! The wolf!

His body was changing slightly ahead of his mind, which was rare but sometimes happened in extreme situations. He felt his body twist and change and the chains – for one slip of a moment – twisted and changed with him. He was surprised. That wasn't meant to happen. How could the wolf fight if he was chained.

And then the chains melted away like mist.

And so did Alfie's rational mind.

11

He knew he was back in her bed. He could remember something of what had happened. Sometimes the wolf-memories worked like that. He had killed the creatures easily. They hadn't moved fast.

His big jaws had torn their heads away.

The taller one he had taken last. He knew what they were: Carci. The monstrous creatures that came through the gate at full moon.

As he had killed the tallest one it had said, 'This is not your destiny, wolfman. You should not be here.' Its voice was like a hiss of air escaping.

But his memories were disturbed by a body behind him in the bed spooning him. He rolled over and opened his eyes.

The she-alpha was behind him, crooning, 'Oh you were magnificent, my darling. Only a werewolf in his wolf body can kill Carci. We did not think we could keep the triplets contained until our next moon. But you, you were perfect. What a glorious power you have. Close to the skin.' She touched his face. 'How honoured I am to see it. So rare.'

'Huh,' said Alfie gruffly. 'It's not so great. Really.'

'Because you can't have sex.'

'Well, yeah.'

'But now you've seen The Silver Chains.'

Alfie looked at her. 'Look, er ... actually, I still don't know your name.'

'Hera.'

'Hera. OK, Hera, look, I came here for the chains. I won't lie. Someone told me they might work for me.

Hold me while I came so I could have sex. But they didn't do that. When I changed they let me go.'

'Yes. They did.' Hera was smiling. 'But they don't have to let you go. The chains are magical. If you want them to hold you we can make it so they'll hold you.'

Alfie felt a surge of something inside himself. 'Really?' His whole body was thrumming then. It was instant. He was full of desire. Fire. Sex. Sex finally so close he could taste it. And then there was a second where he thought a little more clearly. 'Misty? Oh god, is Misty OK?'

'Misty. She's fine. She and Leon are down in the camp. We caught him last night, trying to break her out of the prison hut. Somewhat clumsily. We've put them in a nice cabin. The door isn't locked. They're fine.'

Alfie nodded. 'Sorry. I don't understand. I thought we were prisoners.'

Hera rolled her eyes. 'Oh, well, no. Not really. It's complicated. It's true we do capture any wolves that come too close. But we don't force them to join us. They do. They stay of their own free will. This place is special for wolves. Yes, every full moon we fight and kill the Carci that come through the gate, but that's just once a month. We're mostly a good place. We're away from humans, lots of land. Complex pack dynamics that are very satisfying for wolves. It's werewolf paradise. Even The Silver Crown doesn't regulate out here. You should stay. All three of you. I think you'll be happy here. And you, in particular, could be very useful for those times when Carci like the triplets slip through at full moon.'

'You want us to stay? We're our own pack. I'm an alpha.'

'I know. You'd have to give up that status. I'm alpha here. But I think you would find a lot of benefits to staying here. And you don't really have any choice.' Hera ducked forwards and licked his ear. Then pulled herself up and climbed on top of Alfie's body, straddling him.

'The Carci carry a virus. That's why we have to keep them contained. It doesn't affect werewolves, of course, but it's fatal in humans. If a Carci got to a populated area...'

'My cub, Leon, you know what he'd say to that? He'd say why should we care? We're not humans?'

'Yes, we are, Alfie. Only the most foolish wolves, wolves who hate the man they were – the man they are – say that. I know you don't think like that. But that's why you can't leave. The virus won't hurt you, but you're infected with it now. You can't ever be with humans. You're contaminated.'

She leant up over him and pulled down the chains. One cuff already attached to each of the bed posts. She smiled at Alfie as she lifted his right wrist and began to fix it down. 'It's very easy to adjust the spell on them. Just a little elementary magical skill really.' And in the time it took her to say that, she had both Alfie's wrists secure. Utterly secure.

'So they'll change with me? They won't come off?' Alfie said. He was so overwhelmed. Need. Desire. Pure and brutal. He was still thrumming with it.

'Not a chance, my beautiful wolf. I will be quite safe no matter how hard you fight. And I even have a spelled muzzle that will twist when you do too. Those fangs won't be coming out tonight. No matter how much I make you scream for me.'

In response to the realisation that he was going to have sex, Alfie had groaned so loud and so long that it was only muffled when Hera suddenly stuffed a thick pad of leather into his mouth and started tightening straps round his head.

The leather felt strangely soft and satisfying in his mouth. He bit at it and it tasted hot and salty and fleshlike. Hera, on top of him, leant down, kiss-close.

'The only problem is you don't get to kiss me,' she

said, her mouth floating above his sealed and stoppered lips.

Alfie moaned as she flicked out her tongue and nudged at the edges of the muzzle. Somehow the frustration of it was more erotic than a real kiss. He moaned and strained.

'One thing about this situation,' said Hera, drawing her head back from the tease, 'is that when you come it's all over. You come. You change. No more fun for me, you see. We need to make you wait a long, long time. I need to be sure that I'm fully satisfied before you are.' She reached back and drew her hand along the length of Alfie's aching, waiting cock. 'We need to make this poor thing wait.'

Alfie moaned yet again and Hera dipped her head and ran her tongue over the leather that sealed Alfie's mouth. Over and over.

Alfie rolled and bucked his hips, but he knew she was going to make him wait a long, long time.

Her fingernails grazed his chest, raised angry red lines, little tiny beads of his blood. She pinched her own nipples to hardness with fingertips slicked with his own desperate wetness, his helpless needy precome.

She licked his nose and pulled his hair and then, from somewhere, produced a beautiful blue glass dildo. She glanced down at Alfie's straining erection. 'This looks pretty close to your size,' she said as she held it on the base of his belly, jutting right above his real cock.

He gasped and thrust his pelvis making his real cock twitch next to the replacement.

'In some ways,' Hera said, 'the glass is better. Cooler in this heat.'

And she slid herself up and mounted the blue dildo, holding it firm against his abdomen with one hand. Alfie felt her moving on it. His erection was tight up against the groove of her arse. As she moved it teased him, but it wasn't enough to make him come. He was already desperate. He could feel the wolf close but not quite able to break through. He rolled and fought his bonds.

Hera came. Quick and sudden she screamed and pushed her free hand into his hair, falling forwards and ending up thrashing against him with her tits covering his face. He screamed into the gag, wanting nothing more than to be able to flick his tongue over her nipples.

And then she lifted her head, smiled, kissed his hot cheek, dropped the dildo on the floor and slid herself back onto his cock.

An hour of teasing, a year without feeling a woman around his cock, Alfie thought he would die of pleasure. His cock was in fire. Every nerve screamed with heat and need.

This was going to be no great performance of stamina, just a quick bucking fuck. His hips moved, slammed up into her. Over and over and over and down, into the wolf.

12

So they stayed.

Alfie was chained to Hera's bed every night. He fought the Carci every full moon. There was one other time when some of the creatures broke through and Alfie had to change when it wasn't full moon.

Alfie felt like he might have a place in the world at last. He didn't need the sedatives so much. Hera had her priests mix herbs that made him feel more stable in his body than he had done for over a year.

He started taking an interest in the herbalism of the wolf pack. A long-lost interest in medicine reawakening. He'd been studying to be a doctor when he was bitten. He'd abandoned his studies then along with his life.

Even Leon seemed less snippy – delighted to be part of a proper pack. Of course, he and Alfie never mentioned the kiss they'd shared. Alfie was pretty sure Leon wanted to pretend that had never happened. Which was completely fine by him.

Very, very occasionally Alfie thought of the night his wolf had killed the triplets and how, as he had torn into that last one, it had told him that his destiny lay elsewhere.

Misty's heart was so broken it felt as if it were ground to dust.

Leon and Alfie had taken to living with the rainforest pack so easily. Leon loved the complex dynamics of a large wolf pack. The sparring. The jostling for status.

Women do far less well as wolves. It was a known fact. And this pack, despite having a female alpha, didn't treat female wolves much better than the rest of the werewolf world. There was only one female to six or seven males. And most of the jostling for position was about getting a fuck. Rarely did a day go by without some strutting brute turning up to tell Misty of his latest feat of bravery that he thought should earn him a place in her bed.

The only women who seemed to avoid being used as trophies were the priests who lived and worked in the huge stone temple in the centre of the camp. But they were no better off, only getting to have sex at all as part of sacred rites to protect the Carci Gate and stop it widening.

So Misty would sigh, let another wolf take her, and let her eyes drift up to the trees, where the man she loved was in bed with the alpha.

Deep in her heart Misty knew she could have almost anything she wanted of Alfie. Could ask him for anything. Sex, even an exclusive relationship wasn't unimaginable. She knew Alfie felt like he owed her for what he had done. Knew she could name her price. Never wanted to.

She couldn't ever have his heart.

Leon banged in through the door of the cabin. He had several cuts and bruises on his face and upper body. He'd been fighting again.

He slouched over to the bed mat and crashed onto it.

'Good day?' Misty asked him.

'Yeah, yeah, not bad. Want to fuck?'

Misty shrugged.

She walked over to the bed mat. Leon lifted his hips and shucked down his jeans as she approached. She scooted her sarong out of the way and slipped onto his cock.

The slick never-ending heat. The lack of all Misty's favourite things. Crazy music and nightclubs and all her clothes. Damn, she missed her clothes. Leon's cock was thick and firm and felt delicious inside her. But this wasn't her place. She couldn't be this kind of wolf. She was a city girl. This wilderness was all wrong.

She looked down at Leon, his face a close-eyed distant mask of concentration. He wasn't even in the room with her. She said, 'I want to go home.'

'Home? We are home.'

'Home to London.'

Leon opened his eyes. 'Cities are no good for wolves. You heard the saying "Wolves Escape"? I've figured out what that means. It means they make it here. This is where we belong.'

Misty felt her body go stiff and tense. She stood up, pulling herself off Leon's cock and walked out of the cabin, ignoring his cry of outrage.

13

Leon had an itch to scratch. Most of the females would be taken now. There was a clearing in the woods where male wolves often went to pleasure each other. But Leon didn't want that tonight. Other men just didn't do it for him. Most other men.

He wandered around the camp and found himself in front of the temple.

The temple was a stone building. One of the oldest looking in the camp. It looked as if it might have pre-dated the wolves settling here. Maybe the camp had grown up around it. Leon didn't know how long the Carci Gate had been open – how long this fight had been going on.

He slipped inside the open door.

The shady inner chamber of the temple was cool and majestically eerie. It was empty this time of the evening. The main rites were at sunrise.

The only other person was a young female werewolf wearing the robes all the priests wore and dusting down the altar.

'Hi,' said Leon.

The priest turned. 'Oh hello, sorry, I'm just closing up.'

Leon licked his lips. 'So tell me,' he drawled. 'How come you priest girls don't get to have sex like the rest of the females around here?'

The priest looked a little bit startled by this. 'What? Of course we do. There are various special rites, ceremonies where we . . .'

'Oh yes. Well I know all that. But I meant, how come you don't have sex for fun?'

'Sex for fun?'

Leon was very close to the priest now. Her hair was hidden under a white cloth that matched her robes. Her face was pure and clear – she spent all her time in the temple so her skin wasn't sun darkened like everyone else's. Leon felt his heart skip. She was so beautiful. In this exotic place her milky whiteness was the most exotic thing he'd seen yet.

He moved his head and kissed her.

She pulled away, 'No, no I can't. I must keep my energies for the sacred rites. The Carci Gate . . .'

'The Carci Gate is fine, baby. I take care of it.'

He kissed her twice then, long and wet, and she was instantly, wantonly open under him. Yielding. Her protests gone into his damp, coaxing mouth.

There were three or four moments where she seemed to change her mind. Pulling away from him and pleading that she couldn't do this, didn't want to. But Leon could hear her need, see the flush to her pale skin now he had stripped away her robes. And every time she protested he slipped a hand down between her legs and stroked her pussy, coasted into her on the wetness there, and then brought it to her lips. Showing her she wanted this more than she knew.

And then he was fucking her, her white body spread over the altar he had found her cleaning.

He was pistoning in and out of her, his jeans pooled around his ankles, when he felt the sudden sting of a silver blade at the back of his neck. Still inside the priest, he slowly turned his head.

Behind him stood five wolves. Big ones. He recognised one of them as his main jailer when he had first been brought here.

The jailor held out a hank of rope. 'Get your dick out of her,' he said. 'Then kneel and put your hands behind your back.'

14

Alfie was naked. At least Misty was pretty sure he was naked. He was lying in Hera's bed. One of his ankles protruded from the tangle of sheets and was still cuffed to the bedpost. When Misty had questioned this Alfie had said Hera had made a mistake that morning. But when Misty had asked where the keys were and offered to let him free he'd smiled a secretive sort of smile and said no.

'I want to leave,' Misty said, pacing the floor in front of the bed.

'Leave? You can't leave. You carry the virus.'

'I hate it here. I don't have to go anywhere where there are humans.'

'There are humans everywhere except, I don't know. The Arctic?'

'Aren't there meant to be vampires in the Arctic?'

'I have no idea, but, why do you even want to leave? This is a werewolf paradise.'

'Is it? What, so, every werewolf wants the same thing? All female werewolves get to do here is look pretty and get fucked by whoever is top dog at that moment. I never see you. I never have any fun. I've been wearing this thing –' she plucked at her gaudy sarong '– for months.'

'Oh. You mean you don't like ... oh. I never knew. Sorry.' Alfie's face was concerned suddenly. 'I thought you were happy.'

'Why? 'Cause you're happy? It's not like you ever come down and ask me how I feel.'

'No, I know. I've been distracted. Hera's your alpha now. Not me.'

Misty shook her head. 'You're my sire, Alfie.'

Alfie looked sad. Misty knew he was realising he'd neglected her, remembering his debt to her. He'd bitten her. 'I'm sorry. Look, I'll talk to Hera. They need me here to fight the Carci. You know that. I can change outside the moon. But maybe there are other things we can do to make you happy.'

'To make who happy?' said a voice – so familiar. Alpha. Misty looked and saw two strong elegant hands on the rope. Hera pulled herself up into the room.

When Misty looked at Alfie, she saw the tiniest ounce of fear in his eyes. 'Nothing,' Alfie said, snappy-sharp. 'Really, nothing.'

'You should go now,' Hera said to Misty. And Misty knew there was no possibility of argument, of negotiation. She exchanged glances with Alfie and walked over to the rope.

As she started to descend she heard Hera say, 'I'm sorry, darling, some last minute business. Boring punitive stuff. But I'm here now. Let's get you chained down properly for me.'

Misty knew that Alfie was trying not to moan too loudly in response in case she was still in earshot.

Alfie let Hera chain him down, the moves now so familiar. The metal bands drew tight around each of his limbs. The chains contracted to hold him firm – stretch him just a little more than would have been blissful. Every night she fucked him like this and he woke up every morning with a dull ache under both his arms and in his groin.

His cock was sore all the time. Just a kind of heat. He felt used. Helpless to stop himself being used for sex. And he gloried in it. It had been so long.

Sex with Hera was rough. Good rough. She was never soft. Or kind, or gentle. She always made him beg to come. Beg for his release. Called him dirty, filthy, unstable, wrong. Reminded him why he was chained down, why he wasn't in control, didn't deserve to be in control. Reminded him why it had to be her. Why he could never be with anyone else.

As she spread herself over his body and kissed him, she said, 'I can't believe that stupid cub of yours could be so stupid. Wasting time I could have used taking pleasure from your body.'

'What, Misty? She left as soon as you said. She didn't mean . . .'

'Oh no, not the female. Your male. Leon. He raped one of my priests.' Hera shook her head and stroked Alfie's chin.

Alfie pulled his face from her touch. 'Leon wouldn't – What? What are you going to do?'

Hera shrugged. 'I told them to execute him as soon as it was dark.'

'What? No! You can't do that. He's my cub.'

'Alfie, I just told you. He forced himself on one of my priests. I can't have that. I told you. We are beyond the jurisdiction of The Silver Crown out here. We make our own laws. Touching a priest without her invitation means death.'

'Your guards forced Misty to . . .'

'Misty is not a priest. And those were complex circumstances.'

'*This* is complex.'

'No it isn't, Alfie.' And Hera picked up the muzzle and forced the leather pad into his mouth.

He was helpless. Shouting into the leather. She didn't fuck him. She pinched his nipples to tight angry peaks, while he thrashed and fought the bonds beneath her. If he had ever wondered if it would be possible – really – to escape the chains in his human form, he was now convinced it was hopeless.

Hera knelt up over him and slapped his face several times. She was very turned on. Right now Alfie only cared about one thing, that she did not make him change. That he did not become the wolf. He needed his sanity. But he was so angry. He felt like he was fighting to stay inside his own body.

Hera held up her blue glass dildo. 'So, so perfect in this heat,' she whispered as she lifted her pelvis and slid the substitute for Alfie's cock inside herself.

She moaned and looked down at him and said, 'I can't change the rules for you, Alfie. I have over a hundred wolves to think of.' She rolled her hips and Alfie could see her thumb working her clit as the blue glass sliding in and out of her glistened and tinkled in the light from the dying sun.

When she came, head back, small taut breasts in firm peaks, it was almost dark outside.

The drums had started.

15

Misty had been crying. She hadn't climbed down to the ground. She couldn't face the camp. She had thought if she stayed up here in the tree she could fool herself that she might really be somewhere else.

It was magical up in the sky. She could see why Hera lived up here. Why Alfie barely came down except for full moon. He was her toy. Addicted. Drunk on sex. On being able to have sex.

But she wasn't crying now. She was holding her body taut. Hiding in the approaching dark. She'd heard everything. Down in the camp, Leon was going to be executed. Misty was prescient enough to know that her only hope was to get Alfie. And she held her breath as Hera climbed down the rope right past where Misty was crouched.

Once Hera was far enough down the rope, Misty climbed carefully up into her bedroom.

She got onto the bed and managed to get the muzzle off Alfie.

'Oh god,' Alfie said. 'Were you outside? Did you hear?'

Misty nodded. Getting off the bed and looking for the keys to the chains.

'They're here,' Alfie said, tipping his head back to indicate a small leather bag hanging down above his head, right in the middle of the headboard.

Misty took it and started to free Alfie. 'I don't know how . . .' she said. 'There are a hundred lycans down there. I don't know how we can save him.'

'We use the wolf,' Alfie said and his face was pale as he sat up.

'No,' said Misty. But even as she said that, feeling her

particular fear of Alfie's wolf rising inside her, she knew it was the only way.

Alfie got off the bed and looked around. He found a dart of the sedative Hera used to calm him and the blow pipe. He gave it to Misty. 'Here. You take these. If anything happens . . . or, preferably, before it does.'

Misty nodded. Solemn. She made for the rope.

Alfie said, 'Wait, one more thing.' And Misty looked and saw he was taking the chains from the bed.

'OK,' Alfie whispered when they were on the ground, 'I'll change. It'll be chaos. You get Leon. You and Leon need to run. Sedate me before you go. If you can. Leon's the priority.'

'Sedate you? You mean leave you?'

'You can't take me with you in wolf form, can you?' Alfie already had his hands on his jeans ready to fist his cock.

'Alfie, no.'

'It's the only way, Misty. You agreed.'

Misty stared, horror-struck, as Alfie stroked himself. His fear and rage were so strong inside him that he could feel the wolf straight away. He leant up against a tree and let the wolf come to him.

Leon closed his eyes. He was tied to the stake on the wooden platform. Around him a fire was already lit but only smouldering. The smoke was in his eyes. The fire wouldn't kill him – he'd seen the crossbow they'd use after they'd enjoyed watching him suffer.

He was roped, quite comprehensively, to a stake at his back. It was hard to see an escape route. 'Wolves Escape' he repeated to himself like a mantra. Trying not to remember that the last time he had said those words aloud it had been to Misty and if he'd just taken her advice about this place, things might have been so different.

The crowd around him had their backs to the trees, so he saw the wolf first. A magnificent grey and brown and silver animal, hurling itself out of the fringe of trees. It had to be him.

Alfie. Oh, Alfie.

Leon felt his heart soar. Oh, if he had to die right now, to die in those jaws.

The crowd scattered and then he saw Misty. Misty who ran right into the fire. It was only popping and smouldering. Not really alight yet, but she still ran right through it and leapt up onto the wooden base of the stake where Leon was bound. She started to work the ropes, one eye clearly on the wolf.

'What's the plan, Mist?'

'Get you loose during this bedlam, then run. Alfie says to try and sedate him before we go.'

'We can't carry him,' Leon said, feeling the ropes start to fall away from his wrists.

'He said to leave him.'

'We can't *leave* him.' Leon had his wrist free now and pulled away. He was barely aware of everything going on around them, the lycans fleeing as Alfie snarled and growled.

Leon looked at Misty. She seemed to know what he was thinking. 'No, Leon.'

But Leon was already off the platform, leaping through the fire and running towards Alfie who was snarling at a couple of young male lycans. 'Hey! Here!' Leon shouted. 'Hey, daddy, come get me.'

Alfie looked up at him.

Oh god, you stupid creature. You must know me. Come for me.

Leon turned away from Alfie and began to run. Elated and mortified when he felt the wolf turn and chase him. Could he outrun Alfie's wolf?

He'd never tried.

16

Alfie was lying on the grass under some trees. It was hot and sticky as ever. The air was full of the constant noise of insects and birds. He rolled over and opened his eyes.

'Leon,' Misty called, 'he's awake.'

Leon! Misty! All three of them. Together and safe. Alfie, excited, sat up too quickly.

'Steady,' Misty said, reaching out for him. 'Are you OK?'

'Yes. Fine. Mostly. Did we get away? Is Leon OK?'

'He's fine. He's got a few burns and so have I.'

Leon appeared behind Misty. Alfie didn't see any burns. What he did see was blood. Dried blood swirling down and around Leon's arm from a bite on his right bicep. Alfie met Leon's eyes. 'I bit you?'

'Well, yeah,' said Leon, looking at his wound. 'But it doesn't matter, does it? You already turned me once. You can't do it twice over.'

Alfie shook his head. 'No. I guess.' He looked at Misty. 'Did you get the chains?'

Misty nodded towards a bag lying on the ground. 'Yeah. I didn't want you having to go back.'

'I wouldn't have gone . . .' But Alfie trailed off, Leon and Misty were both looking serious.

'Alfie,' Misty said, 'what are we going to do?'

'I don't know,' Alfie said. 'If we stay within their perimeter they'll find us. They have detectors. But if we go outside it . . .'

'We'll infect humans,' Misty said, slumping down against a tree.

Alfie couldn't believe it. Wolves escape. And yet,

where could they go? Was there somewhere deeper in the rainforest? Away from humans and the pack. He was about to say something about that when he saw the sun glint on something in the trees. And he seemed to know instantly that it was a crossbow bolt. And that the person holding the crossbow was Hera.

They'd found them already.

She stepped into the clearing.

Before she could say anything Alfie raised both his hands above his head. 'Take me. Let them go. You don't need them. I'll make sure they stay away from humans.'

'No,' said Hera. 'No, they don't need to.'

'Yes they do. The virus.'

Hera shook her head. 'Werewolves can't carry an infectious form of the Carei virus. You won't spread it if you run. It's just lie, a way of, you know . . .'

Alfie nodded slowly, seeing the trick instantly. 'Of keeping werewolves with you, fighting.' Alfie sighed, shaking his head. 'Oh good god. You people are . . .'

'We do what we have to do, Alfie. What we need to do. We need the wolves to stay. If that virus got out . . .' She tailed off, shaking her head and then looked at him.

Alfie met her sad brown eyes. Solemnly he said, 'I know. And I'll come back with you. I'll come quietly.'

'Unhappily,' said Hera.

'What?'

Hera looked at the ground, then back up. 'Splitting up a pack. That's always bad news. Do you think I want you back just to watch you pine for your cubs in my bed?'

'You were going to have Leon killed.'

'I know,' Hera looked down. 'I thought I had more of a hold over you. I was wrong. The chains. The sex. That was all you wanted from me.' And she dropped the crossbow into the ground. Her eyes were glassy. 'I never found him, you know. My life mate. And now I'm an alpha I thought maybe . . . I thought you . . .'

Alfie walked over to Hera and put his arms lightly

around her. 'Hera, I'm sorry. I thought you just wanted me for fun. And you know I don't even believe in . . .'

Hera pulled herself together and looked up at Alfie. 'I can't take just you. You'd never forgive me if I took you from your cubs. And he –' She pointed at Leon '– can't ever come back to us. So there's no choice. You have to go. But, god, take me with you.'

'Take you!' Alfie stared at her. 'I can't take you. You're an alpha. You can't be part of my pack.'

'You were part of mine.'

'Hera, no. It's impossible.'

'You have to fight the Carci,' Leon said, suddenly. 'The virus could still reach humans if one of them got to a populated area, right?'

Hera nodded.

'You said so then,' Leon continued. 'You do what has to be done. Well, what you have to do is go back. You're the best there is. Everyone says so. Without Alfie you need to make sure none of them slip through again. You're the strongest fighter of them all and no one does strategy like you. They can't lose Alfie and you. It would be a disaster.'

Hera looked at Leon, 'Really?'

Leon nodded vigorously, 'Oh yeah.'

Hera looked like she might cry again. Alfie couldn't believe it. She had always seemed so cold. So gleeful to use him. 'But I can't, I can't leave him.'

'And you won't. You never will. But you've got a job to do. That's your destiny. And it isn't his.'

Hera nodded. 'I guess, the gate . . . it is important work.' She looked at Alfie. 'I'll see you again?'

'Of course you will,' said Alfie.

17

Three Years Later

They didn't like jeans in the bar here, not even for hotel guests. Only Alfie's biggest, dirtiest smile at the slightly effete waiter had got him ushered to a table with the polite and slightly suggestive request that Alfie please not get up and to simply ask the waiter if there were anything – anything *at all* – that he wanted.

He wasn't sure if he'd recognise Hera; it had been nearly three years. A lot had happened since Brazil. But when he saw her, gliding across the open marble space of the cool bar, he knew she wasn't the kind of person you ever forgot. With her sleek dark hair and her flattish, blunt features, she was the most striking woman in this room full of beautiful people.

When the eager young waiter showed her over, he looked at Alfie a little sourly. Alfie placated him with a subtle wink.

'What are you doing this far from home?' Alfie said as he looked back at her, pulling a hypo of sedative out of his pocket and handing it to her. 'Don't you need to stay near the gate?'

Hera shook her head. 'No. I'm an old wolf now, Alfie. My time is almost done. I need to give control to a new alpha. I have a wonderful lycan in mind. I've trained him. He's going to kill me next full moon and ascend.'

Alfie half-choked. He knew this was the correct lycan way of doing things, but Hera made it sound so cool. 'You've groomed a cub to kill you.'

'Yes. I like to be civilised about these things. I don't

want to end up, well.' She looked Alfie up and down. 'End up like you – not in control of my body.'

Alfie didn't respond.

'But I had to see you first. I've got a message for you,' she said bluntly. 'Our priests said it was urgent that I come and find you.'

'What's the message?'

'You have to go back to her. To the woman you love. She has The Silver Collar. The only thing that can save you.'

'The woman I love?' Alfie didn't even think before he said it. 'But she's in Oxford. And I don't even know what this collar is.'

'Alfie, The Silver Collar could be the only thing that can save you. It can hold your form. It's one of the strongest werewolf magical objects. I know your condition is much worse now. Three years ago you wouldn't have had to give me a sedative to hold as soon as I sat down. Your body is breaking apart. Usually wolves whose cubs don't kill them in the correct way age and weaken quickly, but not you, you're still strong. Your wolf is strong, not the man. The wolf will take you over completely. You'll become pure animal. Never mind being able to live a normal life again, this could be your only hope against losing your rational mind all together.'

'Yeah. I get that. But I can't go back to Oxford. I promised.'

'Well break a promise, Alfie. It wouldn't be the first time.'

'Yeah. Except after I promised her I'd never come back, she promised me that if I did she'd kill me. And she knows how to kill werewolves. When I was bitten, her twin brother was killed. When she found out what had happened, what I was as a result of the bite, she read up. Read everything she could about werewolves. She was a smart girl. She found out all about how I could call my sire, the werewolf that bit me, using a summoning ritual.

She wanted me to do that. Call him, so she could kill him. Avenge her brother's death.'

'Woah,' Hera was shaking her head. 'OK, OK, I killed my sire. I had to so I could become alpha. And it was the hardest thing I ever had to do. But my sire wasn't an Ancient Beast.'

'I know,' said Alfie, 'I know. It's a fucked up situation. I seem to attract them.'

'You still have to go back though, Alfie. You'll just have to avoid this ex of yours. She might not even still be there. But you need to go. You need to get this collar.' Hera paused for a sip of the drink the waiter had slipped unobtrusively onto the table. 'And that's not all. Your life mate is there too, Alfie. Carci see the future. That's why they're so dangerous. They never usually tell, but sometimes, when they're dying . . .'

Alfie remembered the Carci that had said he couldn't stay with the Amazon pack. 'I thought this message was from your priests?'

Hera looked down and shook her head.

'So did they say anything else? The Carci?'

Hera shrugged. 'Your destiny is waiting for you. Back where you were bitten. There is a lot you don't know about how you came to be.' She sniffed. 'They said a lot of that kind of stuff. But really, it was all about your life mate. How she's been waiting for you for eleven years. How you will return to her.'

'I don't believe in life mates.'

'Nor did I, until I met you.'

Alfie rubbed his temple. 'Don't, Hera. Some things are just more important than that.'

'I know, I know. Life mates. What garbage anyway. But I don't think the Carci care about what you believe, Alfie.'

'It makes no sense. Werewolves are known for being faithless. And I wasn't the most loyal man even before I was bitten.'

'Yes, well.'

'Did they tell you her name? This life mate of mine?' Because there was a moment when Alfie thought that maybe he'd got it wrong. Maybe the Carci were talking about someone else.

Hera said, 'Iris.'

To be continued in Mathilde Madden's novel *The Silver Collar*, Book One of The Silver Werewolf Trilogy

Broken Angel

Madelynne Ellis

Contents

1 **The Crossroads**

The speedometer was climbing. He'd topped the ton two blocks ago, when he'd shot the red light and headed up into the old quarter. Somehow, he felt safer among the winding cobblestones and chewed-up tarmac of the old city. He understood how it operated, knew all the sharp corners and the short cuts, the winding alleyways of Birdcage Walk and the Copse Road down by the canal. The wide avenues of the Heights made him feel too exposed, and what he didn't need right now was exposed. He'd only gone there for the book. Book! Huh, more like a pamphlet, and written in a cipher that made him dizzy just looking at it. He hoped it was worth all the trouble.

There were four, maybe five of them, all gaining fast, but he couldn't push the bike any harder. He was already risking a head-on collision. He might know this area, but places changed. Walls would appear overnight as if they'd always been there, because they were always made of the same yellow-grey stone. Still, he'd got himself into this mess. He'd been stupid, thought they were just some soft Lux gang seeing him off their turf, and he knew he could take on five of them. But instead of drawing knives and guns, he'd watched them morph, skin stretching and flexing, bones popping, elongating. He'd got on the bike fast – damn fast. Youkai! Bad shit! He wasn't sticking around to be soul food for a demon. He'd kicked the bike into action, left a treadmark on the one that got in the way, and hadn't looked back until he crossed the division bridge.

There'd been rumours about the youkai. How they

were on the rise, that they were showing themselves more, but he hadn't taken them seriously. Who had? The youkai were a fairytale parents used to keep their kids away from the crossroads. Fewer than a dozen people in the city had actually seen one, and they were mostly written off as delusional. They'd have been entirely dismissed if it weren't for the Talon. Them you took seriously. The Talon were nobody's idea of a joke. If they so much as suspected you were a demon, you were butchered meat. People stayed clear of them; people told tales about them, more tales than they did of the youkai, if truth were told. 'Little demons,' they yelled at their kids, 'the Talon'll come and get you.'

The bike was juddering beneath him, as he burned uphill towards the crossroads and the swinging iron gibbets. He could hear them clanking in the wind, swinging on their iron chains like the pendulum of a horrible alarm clock. Some nights he dreamt about those gibbets, how they'd burst open and the dead would spew out in their thousands to march through the city. Or was it the youkai? Demons or dead, it all added up to a nightmare.

Maybe the crossroads hadn't been such a good choice. He hadn't been thinking. Too late to turn back now; the only side street led straight into the canal. He'd just have to head down into the Cathedral Quarter by way of Steepleside.

He barely noticed them at first; they were so still, just two black pinpoints in a world of grey. He was almost on top of them before their presence actually sank in – two frozen marionettes, waiting, but not for him. The Talon. He caught the eyes of one as the bike rushed between them; they were glassy-green and cold, like a doll's. That's what the Lux called them, 'Dolls' or 'Talon's Dolls', though never to their faces, even the Lux weren't foolish enough for that.

He skidded into the corner, narrowly avoiding the

lich-gate and nearly ripping the knee out of his leathers. Somehow, he brought the bike to a halt by a stinking gibbet, after a one hundred and eighty degree spin that left a scar of rubber on the road. He was just in time to watch the show. One doll decapitated the leading youkai as he tried to pass between them.

The other three met similarly gruesome ends, their human skins torn from their filthy youkai hides, dying with shrieks of outrage, and a splatter of coppery dust, which seemed to hang in the air, floating, sinking.

An explosion of pain raked through his shoulders. Blaze jerked forwards in shock. There was just the lich-gate behind him, yet something had him, drew threads of fire across his back. It lifted him off the pavement, off the bike, rattling him so hard his eardrums throbbed. He kicked out, fighting the terror. The shadow of its wings darkened the side of the buildings. Great black angel's wings, their flapping accompanied by a majestic keening from beyond the lich-gate. Something else latched onto his ankle. One of the dolls had come to him. Her fingers wrapped around his leg just below the knee, gripping and pulling. Tendons and sinews stretched. 'Get the fuck off me! Get the fuck off.' He kicked harder, brought his head back sharply into the demon's face. Something crunched, but the wings just flapped harder and the keening wail rose an octave.

Steel slashed through the air beside him. It hit the youkai with a gristly smack. Acid burned through the tears in his jacket. Then he was falling ... falling in a cloud of crow feathers.

It released the boy, but despite the wound she'd opened in the winged youkai's side, Asha watched it soar out of reach. The slash should have taken off its legs. Any normal demon would have had the courtesy to die.

Irked, she wiped her blade clean across the front of her long skirt and sheathed it. At least she'd given the bastard something to think about, judging by the thick coppery-stain in the air. The alchemists would be out later with their sheets to collect it, armed with their curses and their shotguns. Blood Rain, they called it: highly desirable, highly addictive and highly illegal. Just a teaspoon on the tongue could make a love slave of anyone. Then there were the other side effects: stamina, insomnia and a desperate hunger for red meat.

She flicked her tongue into the air, then looked down at the boy.

He'd fallen on his front, so she gazed at his spiky blond hair and the torn back of his fringed jacket. Ten lacerations had scored through the leather and flesh, bitten deep into the muscle. His blood was slowly seeping through, but not too fast. He wouldn't bleed out.

'Asha.' Her partner clamped a gloved hand upon her shoulder. 'Is he all right? We should get off the street.'

Asha bent and dipped a finger into one of his wounds, then licked the blood from her finger. 'He'll live. But he's out cold, and he tastes of youkai.'

Jaku crouched beside her and stroked a hand through the boy's blond hair. 'The winged one ... I think it was Venom. He's probably poisoned him. Shame, he's a pretty one.' Asha shook her head at the glint in Jaku's eyes. What was it about her partner and blonds? He was forever mooning over their leader.

'Let him be.' She stood and searched the skies, but there was no sign of the youkai. 'Are you sure it was Venom? That doesn't make sense. He wouldn't normally risk exposing himself over a boy.'

'That would depend on the boy,' said Jaku, continuing to stroke the boy's head, though he made a show of checking his pulse when Asha scowled. 'It was him. He's distinctive; like a hooded cobra. Besides, how many youkai do you know that routinely show their wings?'

'The only youkai I know are dust on the breeze.' Her tone was sour. Normally, she prided herself on doing the job properly. The fact that the demons' captain had escaped didn't lessen her annoyance. 'What do we do with him?' she asked.

Jaku stood, lifting the boy. 'We take him to the archive with us. I know you're a cruel-hearted bitch, but he's too cute to leave for the Ghost Wind, and Talon will want to know why Venom thinks he's so important.'

The archive was dirty and dark, ingrained with a waxy miasma that permeated the skin. The archivist, Palter Rodgers, had visibly aged since Asha's last visit eight months earlier. He scowled as they forced their way past him, through aisles of books to a table near the centre of the cavernous building.

Asha swept the papers from the table and Jaku laid the boy on the cleared surface. Finally, she got a proper look at him. Jaku was right. He was pretty. His ash-blond hair was swept back from his face as if blown by the wind and then frozen into spikes. He was far too pale, though, mostly a result of the blood loss, but he looked like the nocturnal type, too.

Asha stroked a fingertip across his brow. A livid bruise was spreading across his cheek and around his right eye-socket. She continued down his nose to his sensual upturned mouth. There was an appealing symmetry about him, that made you want to stare, to touch, explore. He had a cute little flaw, where someone had taken a nick out of his jaw.

'I saw him first,' said Jaku, pressing a hand to the boy's blood-drenched T-shirt.

'I think you've been inhaling too much demon dust.' She slapped his hand away. 'What's this?' She slipped a wallet and a thin leather-bound book from the inner pocket of his jacket. 'Blaze.' Her eyes widened sceptically. 'It says his name's Blaze, and he's out of the Birdcage.' That much had been apparent from the kohl smeared around his eyes and the fringe of crows' feathers on his jacket. 'Not much cash, but take a look at this.' She held out the folio to Jaku. 'Reckon this might be what they were after? It's a copy of –'

'– Kell's Prophecy!' Palter Rodgers stretched over the table to snatch it from her hand. 'In sixty years of working here, I've never seen a copy.' He rubbed irritably at the ox-blood-coloured stain the boy's injures had caused on the cover. 'It's sacrilegious. Far too dangerous for the Talon or any boy to be walking the streets with.'

'But what is it?' Asha demanded.

'The forgotten chapter, the whole truth, ripped out of the Apostle's Dialogue by some pious fool in the fifteenth century.'

'Almost certainly what we came looking for, then.' Jaku held his hand out for the book, but Palter Rodgers clasped it to his body.

'It stays here,' he said.

Asha and Jaku exchanged glances.

'I think Talon might have an opinion on that.'

'Talon would agree with me. It should be kept locked up.'

'Nevertheless, we need to know its contents, particularly if they relate to the cycles of demon rule, and the storm that's brewing. I assume I can at least consult it in your presence?'

Asha patted him on the back. 'Go find out what we need. I can patch him up on my own.'

Jaku's lips formed a grim smile. 'Let's find ourselves a quiet spot.' He rounded Palter Rodgers up like a sheep and herded him down the nearest aisle of books. 'You can read it to me. I like a good story, and it'll save me getting my mucky fingers on it.' He waved his blood-stained gloves under Rodgers' nose. 'Shout if you need anything, Asha. And watch him if he comes round.'

Asha waited until they were out of sight, then turned back to her patient. He was stirring slightly, his lips forming silent words. 'What is it?' She leant over his body. 'Tell me.'

Blaze wasn't quite sure when he became conscious of the motion around him or of the cool press of fingertips against his brow. When he opened his eyes, she was leaning across him, her black hair tickling his neck, and her pale features frozen into perfection, like a painted porcelain mask, from which two green eyes peered.

'Where am I?' he asked, entranced by her cold loveliness, the slender arch of her eyebrows and her immensely long black eyelashes. She straightened, took a step back from the table upon which he was lying, and raised her palms to indicate the books. 'You're in the archive of the Blessed Brethren of the Deceased.' He could see that now, every surface of the vast hall was littered with books and papers. They stood in piles that reached to the first floor balcony, and from there, almost to the great domed glass roof.

Papers. He felt his pockets for the pamphlet, but it was gone. Lost during the fight or perhaps taken by the youkai or the Talon. 'Where's my stuff?' He swung his legs over the table edge and tried to sit. Pain shot up his spine and tightened like a knotted cord at the back of his neck. He doubled in agony and flopped ungracefully back onto the tabletop.

'You probably ought to stay flat.' Her tone was neutral, though there was a soothing burr to it. 'You've lost a lot of blood.' She reached over to touch him, but he warded her off. Loveliness aside, she was one of the Talon, and he didn't trust her. 'Hey, go easy. I'm just trying to help. You need stitches.'

Blaze drew himself up again, and this time managed to stay upright and face her. She was dressed head to foot in a fanciful black outfit that looked more suitable for a fairytale funeral than a sword fight. 'You're Talon,' he said, trying not to focus on the swell of her breasts beneath the veil of lace. 'You don't help anyone.'

Anger flickered through the air between them, though her face remained emotionless. 'The Talon protect people from the youkai.'

'So you say.' He watched her fingers curl into a fist. Her hands were pale and delicate; more, he imagined, like those of a pampered courtesan from the Heights than a trained killer, but he'd seen her in action. She was ruthless and precise.

'If we hadn't helped you outside, you'd be mincemeat by now.' She stepped forwards, so her long skirt brushed his knees, and he caught a faint scent of her perfume. It was dark, warm and musky with a slightly sharp base that brought to mind more images of a high-class whore.

'Maybe,' he said, just to see her reaction, but he provoked little more than a twitch of her black-painted lips. 'For all I know you're the reason they attacked. Outside the Talon, only a handful of people in the entire city have even seen a youkai.'

'Have seen a youkai uncloaked,' she corrected, looking him straight in the eyes. 'They walk among the populace in the guise of humans, biding their time.'

'Is that the truth, or a lie you use to ease your conscience after you massacre the innocent?'

Her eyes glittered with pale green fire. 'No demon is innocent. Maybe I should have let Venom have his way?'

'Likely I'd be dead.' He folded his arms across his chest

'You think so.' She tilted her head to one side and smiled wickedly. 'Actually, they like their meat fresh.' She licked her lips. 'And, preferably, alive and still kicking while they swallow.'

Blaze felt the smile drop from his lips. His limbs felt suddenly heavy, and he sagged, bumping his elbow against the tabletop.

She caught him, her grip firm around his arm and

helped him into a chair. 'Now, do you wish for my help, or shall I let you die of blood poisoning?'

'Depends on the cost.'

'No cost.' She stroked a cool hand across his brow, which seemed to soothe some of the angry pain still beating there.

'Everything comes at a price,' he said. 'Name yours or I'll have to forgo the offer.'

She shook her head clearly bemused. 'You're a strange man, Blaze Makaresh. Is this what living in the Birdcage does to you? Makes you wary of accepting any gift?'

He heard her words but a fog seemed to be roiling through his head again. He shut his eyes as he was drawn into its hazy reality.

'Hey, stay with me.' She shook him gently. He felt her palms press to his burning cheeks. 'Blaze,' she whispered. Her breath was warm against his lips. 'All right, you can pay me in kisses or eyelashes, your choice.' Her words seemed to drift to him across a hazy veil. A kiss, that would be nice, he thought.

A kiss before dying.

Her lips were soft against his, just a gentle, chaste pressure and not a real kiss like he wanted. Nevertheless, it seemed to suck him into a realm of clinging shadows, where the only sound was the monotonous drumming of his slowing heartbeat.

'You're not blacking out on me.' Her voice boomed inside his head, startling him into wakefulness. 'You're stronger than this. Snap out of it!' She smacked him hard across the cheek.

Blaze's eyes snapped open. He rubbed at the stinging mark. She was staring at him, her green eyes blazing and pointy little chin held high. 'Ouch!' he complained.

'Enough crap.' She grasped the cuff of his leather jacket and tugged. 'We need to get this stuff off you.' She peeled his T-shirt from him like a layer of skin. It was completely sodden with blood, and had matted to the flesh in places. White heat lanced through the base of his skull. Lifting his arms was pure agony.

'Couldn't you just have cut it off?'

'I can just see your reaction if I'd pulled a knife on you. Besides, you'll need something to get home in later.' She dropped the sodden black T-shirt to the floor, and then placed his arm around her shoulder. 'Stand up, please.' She turned the wooden chair around, and made him straddle it facing its spindly back.

'Verdict?'

'I'll tell you when I've cleaned it up.' She fetched a bowl of water and a cloth, and laid them out on the table along with a suture needle and a strand of silk thread she pulled out of the collar of her dress. 'Ready?' She moistened the cloth.

'I guess.' Blaze gritted his teeth as she wiped one small patch of crusted blood away from the first laceration, but it didn't sting as much as he expected. 'Have you a name?' He rested his head on his arms.

'Asha.'

'Mmm,' he said, silently rolling the name across his tongue. 'So, what made you join the Talon, Asha?'

'None of your business. Here, suck on this.' She offered him a square of dun-coloured resin.

'What is it?'

'It'll help with the pain. And it might keep you quiet.'

He nibbled a corner, then chewed the rest. It tasted of soil and acidic, overripe apples. It didn't seem to do much for the pain, but it did warm the area around his groin, although, that might have been the delicate brush of her fingers against his skin. He turned his head further, and strained to see her.

Asha wrung out the cloth, turning the water in the bowl red.

'You're hesitating.' He observed, as she dragged her

teeth over her bottom lip, so a teasing hint of pink showed through the black.

'Poison,' she said. 'Can't you smell it?'

Blaze shook his head.

'Like burned sugar and sex.'

He shook his head more decisively.

Asha peered over her shoulder. Two faint voices were drifting through the layers of dust and parchment from the back of the building. 'The best way is the old-fashioned way.' She rested her hands upon his back and leant close to him, treating him to a second draft of her exotic perfume. 'To suck it out.'

A grin stretched across his face. She might have been talking about cleaning a wound but that didn't stop his heart doing a little jump of excitement. 'Suck away,' he said, and it sounded dirty.

Asha was tempted to slap him again, except she knew it was the poison talking. Blood Rain wasn't the only demon-derived drug that drove up the libido. Sexual excess was the demons' main calling card. It was how they manipulated humans, how they insinuated them-selves into the lives and beds of the rich and influential. Considering his wounds and the blood he'd lost, it was no wonder he was succumbing so easily.

She tentatively pressed her tongue to the first of the ten long gashes and licked. The mixture of blood and poison tingled on her tongue. It tasted bitter, like Blood Rain, though the ripple of pleasure that flowed down her throat was sweet. She licked again, her tongue delving into the wound, and the taste became acrid. She spat it out, then returned to the wound and began to suck.

Beneath her, she felt him tremble, and his spine stiffen. 'Shh!' she soothed before tending the next gash. Her eyes closed. Her nipples rasped against the inside of her bodice. Desire quickened between her thighs.

'Drink it down,' said a voice from her memory. 'Drink it down, my pretty Asha.'

Cruel fingernails dug half-moon indents into the backs of her thighs. A second hand covered her mons and squeezed. 'Cast off your restraints. Let go, let go . . .'

'Ah!' She jerked away from him and stood panting, her back to the nearest bookshelf, the taste of youkai poison thick on her tongue. She wiped it off, first with her hands, and then by dragging her tongue across her coat cuff.

The poison shouldn't have affected her like that. She'd been exposed to enough Blood Rain to build some resistance.

Blaze lifted his head and looked at her. 'Finished?' His blue eyes were still bright, but they'd lost some of the feverish glaze.

Asha nodded. 'I just need to stitch you and put on some wound filler.' She produced a small pot from somewhere. 'It'll help seal the wounds and keep them clean.'

He nodded. 'I'm ready. I feel much better now my head's cleared a bit.'

Asha threaded the needle, and then pressed another cube of resin on him. 'Chew. This is gonna hurt.'

2 **Branded**

The bathroom was ingrained with a thick waxy residue. There were books stacked beneath the sinks, and every tile on the floor was cracked. Blaze flicked on the light, but despite a line of fixtures, only a single bulb blinked into life, giving everything a nicotine glow. The only window was barred and boarded. Blaze ignored the cubicles, figuring he'd as likely find more parchment as any sort of plumbing. One sink housed a spider, the other a colony of woodlice. The mirror was intact, though he had to rub a circle in the grime in order to get a reflection.

Astoundingly, he didn't look nearly as fucked as he felt. He didn't know how far he'd fallen, perhaps a few feet, but it must have been straight onto his head because that's where it hurt. He rolled his shoulders. The skin felt tight and they were still a bit tender, but otherwise not too bad. She'd done a good job of patching him up. He guessed he should thank her for that.

Blaze chased the spider away, and flung his blood-caked T-shirt into the sink. He ran the tap while he inspected the damage to his back. It was a mess of spidery stitches and putrid looking goop: herbal wound filler – yeah, it looked like blended mud and straw, and it smelled bad enough to believe it might actually work. Untreated demon wounds went gangrenous. He guessed he was thankful he'd been picked up by the Talon and not left to rot or been taken to some greedy back street alchemist. He had little enough as it was, there was no way he could afford to pay a doctor, and it was bloody hard to stitch your own back.

Blaze teased a few strands of hair forwards over his

face, and gave himself a wry smile. At least his hair wax was holding, and somehow that made everything more bearable. He took out his eyeliner and touched up the kohl around his eyes, ignoring the bruises.

The water in the sink had turned red by the time he'd finished. He turned off the tap, plunged his hands into the icy water and sluiced his T-shirt about a bit. He wasn't going to get it clean, but at least it'd get the worst of the blood out, and if he wore it back to front, maybe he could pass the slashes off as fashion.

Amazingly, the radiator in the corner was hot. Blaze hung the black fabric over its wide vents. With a bit of luck it'd be dry soon and he'd be able to pull it back on. The archive wasn't cold, but he felt exposed walking around naked from the waist up. Having finished on his back, Asha was now patching up his jacket. He guessed he was grateful the youkai hadn't shredded his trousers too. That would have been too much to take. Underwear wasn't a feature of his attire. Then again, maybe waking naked in Asha's arms wouldn't have been so bad. It might even have cracked a chip in her icy façade.

Blaze grinned at his reflection. The Talon were all like that, frozen automatons, moving with precise and deadly precision and never showing a flicker of emotion. But, the kiss, he'd felt her tremble. Oh, she was good at hiding it, but he'd felt her longing and frustration. She'd wanted to touch him. No – she had been touching him. He'd felt the tremble of her fingertips exploring the contours of his chest, the delicate peaks of his nipples, and the way she'd dressed his wounds had been far more intimate than was surely necessary. He didn't pretend to know anything about medicine, but he was sure it was normally gorier and less sensual. The way she'd drawn her tongue across his skin had sent shivers of pleasure straight down to his groin. Moreover, when she'd sucked – he covered his face with his hands and breathed out hard – well, it'd felt as if she was doing something infinitely more intimate.

There was still a warm tingle centred in his groin.

Blaze slumped back against the cubicle wall. Fuck the painkillers. They tasted like dried beetle dung. He knew the quickest way to get rid of a sore head.

He undid the buttons of his leather trousers, pushed one hand inside and closed his eyes. Rolling back time, he imagined himself waking on the table, not to the image of her face, but to the sight of her upthrust bottom. He slid a hand up her stockings, to the bare stretch of flesh between their tops and the lace edge of her knickers. One finger pushed inside and dipped into the moist heat of her sex. The smell of her need was thick in his nostrils as she sat back upon his face, covering his mouth and nose, and insistently rocked.

She tasted sweet on his tongue as he delved deep into her core. His head swam, light-headed from lack of oxygen, but that only made his cock throb harder and beg for a touch.

She peeled off her gloves next, revealing petite dainty white hands with blood-red nails. They circled his shaft, coaxing, teasing, and drawing long tremors of pleasure from his body.

His back arched against the cubicle wall as he thrust his cock harder into his coiled hand. 'Asha . . .' he hissed under his breath. 'Asha. Oh, Asha . . .'

His peak engulfed him. It jerked his head backwards, fire streaming up from his balls and pouring out of his cock. He sagged a little, smiling, breathing, high on adrenaline and endorphins.

Eventually, he opened his eyes and straightened his trousers. Next job was to track down what had happened to that pamphlet. He swung round to face the door, but only got half a step before a wave of nausea bent him double.

The next thing he knew, he was on the floor, shrieking in agony, his shoulders alive with pain. It was like razor blades scoring his skin, like the youkai shaking him again. Sickness choked him. His stomach heaved, cramping all his abdominal muscles. His eyes burned. Everything that could beat or thrum was doing so, and over it all a grating cacophony of cracked voices were singing him a lullaby.

'No,' he tried to yell, but what came out was a litany of words he couldn't comprehend.

He was vaguely aware that someone was hammering on the door.

Blaze dragged himself over to the sinks on his belly, and managed to pull himself onto his knees, then tentatively upright.

The reflection in the mirror was not his own. His eyes glowed like burnished copper. Strange runes traced across his skin, then dissolved into the flesh. One appeared repeatedly above his heart. When it finally faded, he sighed in relief, only to watch it bubble and remain as a raised scar.

'Talon witch.' He clasped the sink tight and pressed his face to the silvered glass. What the hell had she done to him?

The glow in his eyes began to fade and the echo of voices ebbed.

What had she given him in those painkillers? Or was this some side effect of the youkai poison?

He dug his thumbs into the top of his eye sockets, and only removed them once the wracking pain was completely gone.

Blaze stared at his reflection in the mirror. His irises were blue again. The mark on his chest remained, but the claw-marks and the stitches had vanished from his shoulders. He ran his fingertips over the new skin. What was going on? She'd said it would take weeks to heal, even with the aid of the poultice.

'Pah!' snorted Palter Rodgers. 'It's worth a small fortune, a big fortune to the right buyer. What other explanation do you need?'

'A less convenient one.' Jaku swiped Palter Rodgers' hand out of the way. 'Sit down and shut up, will you.'

Rodgers glared at him from beneath his bristly eyebrows, but shuffled backwards and took a chair in the corner.

Asha took Blaze's hand and gave it a squeeze. 'You're not in any trouble. It's just that we need to know. It's important to a lead we're following.'

'Asha.' Jaku silenced her.

'My grandmother.' Blaze felt the familiar prickle of tears sting his eyes, and resisted the urge to blink. He was not going to cry in front of two demon-killers and a weasely librarian. 'She died four months ago. It's taken a while to locate a copy.' It felt as if he was forcing the words around glass balls stuck in his throat. 'I just assumed it was something to do with my lineage. I never knew my parents, and she never mentioned them. I thought there'd be something when she died. A photograph, some letters, something, but there was just the adoption papers from the orphanage and a first birthday card with the title of that book written inside.

Palter Rodgers made a choking sound. 'Totally heartbreaking.'

Blaze gritted his teeth, though he was tempted to punch the old man. He'd come here when he'd first started looking for the book, this being the oldest document repository in the city, and been rudely turned away. After all he'd been through since then, he wasn't prepared to sit here and be mocked.

Jaku clamped a hand across the front of Palter Rodgers' face. 'I told you to shut up. If you interrupt again, I'll forcibly remove you.'

'It's my office.'

'Only for as long as Talon pays your wage.'

Rodgers just grunted. Jaku let go. His eyes were glittering. 'Ever had any problems with the youkai before?'

Blaze shook his head.

'First time?'

He nodded.

'So, you've no idea what this is?' Jaku lifted the pamphlet and ran his thumb tip along the edge of the paper. It flopped open on a page bearing an elaborate hand-drawn design. Unconsciously, Blaze raised his hand to his chest. Through the damp weave of his T-shirt, he could just trace the raised outline of the scar upon his chest. He wasn't sure. He'd have to check they were a match when he next got some privacy.

'No.' He shook his head. 'No. As I said, I barely had time to leaf through it.'

'The passages around it are written in the ancient tongue,' said Jaku. 'So, I can't read them, but this old fool claims to know a few words, and has shown me several translations by his forebears. It is part of an apocalyptic prophecy that foresees the return to darkness, when the demons' prince will wake from his thousand-year slumber and cast a shadow across the sun. It claims that the city will become a youkai paradise, a vast playground of cruelty, perversity and vice. However, his rebirth will encompass many stages, during which we will know him only by his mark.' He tapped a finger to the drawing. 'As I'm sure you'll appreciate, this prophecy gives the Talon much concern. The astrologers claim the stars are shifting, that the time of the awakening grows near . . .' He paused, his gaze focused upon Blaze, and slowly closed his mouth, but his thoughts ran on inside Blaze's mind. *And here you are, a child of unknown lineage, carrying an ancient manuscript that bears his mark, having already attracted the attention of the youkai captain.*

Blaze reached across and picked up the text. Jaku was

clearly suspicious. Hell, he was suspicious of himself. He had no idea what was going on, whether he was hearing the truth, or the doctrine of an elaborate scam. Except, he could think of nothing that they'd want from him. He had nothing besides his own body, which was theirs for the asking, and the right price.

Asha squeezed his hand again, reminding him of her presence. He pulled away from her grip. He couldn't trust them. For all he knew they'd given him something that was causing the pain, the seizures.

The candlelight was orange across the pages of the booklet. The ancient symbols danced before his eyes. They sunk into the paper, rearranged themselves on the page, like the marks that had appeared upon his skin, until they formed into a sentence he could read.

We will know him by his mark, and both youkai and bleeders will fall down before his gaze.

Startled, he dropped the book.

'What is it?' Asha pressed a hand to his shoulder and leant over him.

'Nothing.' He raised his hand to his throat and sought the slender chain he always wore. It wasn't there.

His surprise must have registered in his expression, for Jaku who had swooped down to retrieve the pamphlet, raised his perfectly curved eyebrows quizzically.

'My pendant's gone,' he blurted, standing up fast. 'It must have come off during the fight. I have to get it.'

'You can't.' Asha pushed her way between the two men 'It's suicide to step into the Ghost Wind.'

He tried to push her aside, but she was far stronger than she looked.

'Don't be a fool, Blaze.'

'Get out of my way.'

'Is a worthless trinket really worth the price of your soul?' said Palter Rodgers. He was reclining against the open door.

'It's not worthless,' Blaze snarled. He batted the edge

of the pamphlet. 'Besides this stupid book, it's the only connection I have to my family.'

'The love token they left you with at the orphanage?' Rodgers' face stretched into a malicious grin. Blaze rose to punch him, but Asha got there first. The archivist crumpled, winded, and she took his place on the threshold. 'It changes nothing. It's far too dangerous to go out. Wait until dawn.'

'The road will have been swept clean by then.' Rodgers' eyes glittered with spite. He coughed violently into his hand. 'Likely the dead will consider it rich pickings, normally all they reap is the gold teeth out of the unfortunates in the gibbets.'

'Get out of my way.' Blaze tried to force his way past Asha again.

Jaku touched the back of his neck, stilling his motion and causing prickles of electricity to shoot up his spine. Every hair on his body stood on end. 'I'll go. We have five minutes until the lich-gate opens. Plenty of time.'

'Jaku, no.' Asha shook her head, but she stepped aside to let him pass.

'I don't fear the dead, and I'm uninjured. My odds of getting back safely are better.'

'But.'

'We're wasting time.' Jaku pulled the archivist to his feet. 'Bring your keys, old man. You two stay here. If we're not back within six minutes, bolt yourselves inside this room and don't open the door until daybreak.'

'I know the drill,' said Asha. 'Go.'

The pair hurried away.

3 **Venom's Descent**

Blaze watched Asha close the door and put her back to the wood. She eyed him curiously, with her arms folded across her chest. 'Is your past really worth risking a man's life for?'

'I was quite happy to go myself.' He refused to feel guilty. Jaku had volunteered to go outside.

Asha dug her teeth into her bottom lip. 'You know we couldn't let you do that, even without the Ghost Wind.'

'Frightened I'll try to escape?'

The apprehensive flutter of her eyelashes confirmed the truth. He frowned at her, and she pushed away from the door to come to him. 'If we'd let you out, you'd have been on your bike and away. Don't try to deny it.'

Blaze rubbed his fingers across his knuckles, but didn't respond. Until this moment, he hadn't actually thought of escaping. He hadn't realised that he needed to. When had she switched roles from his saviour to his jailor? Maybe from the moment he stepped out of the bathroom, and they started discussing the blasted pamphlet.

He snatched it off the table.

Of course, now that he knew he was a prisoner, it dawned on him that her suspicions were right. If he'd reached his bike, he would have run. The pamphlet had told him little enough, and as he couldn't afford to pay someone to translate it for him, there was little point in keeping it. With nothing to bring him back, yes, he'd have run from the Talon. He was almost tempted to run now, except even if he got away from her, and evaded

Palter Rodgers, the gate guard, he still wouldn't reach the bike and get far enough down the road to outrun the dead.

Nobody got caught in the Ghost Wind and survived. It's icy grip strangled without mercy. It was clean and cold, the perfect way to murder. There wasn't a night that went past when some poor unfortunate didn't find himself at the mercy of the chill windborne horde.

He glanced warily at the tiny skylight above Palter Rodgers' desk. The wind was already picking up outside; another few minutes and clawed fingers would be rattling the window frames. He spared a glance for Asha. Her features had tightened into the mask-like expression she'd presented when he'd first seen her. She'd withdrawn, was probably hiding her fear for her partner in the only way she knew how.

Blaze resumed his seat, and turned the pamphlet in his hands. The cover was blotched and worn in places, but surprisingly tactile. It had a distinctive smell too, a malty, acidic odour that had little in common with normal leather. He wondered if the others had noticed it too. It was almost ... like bacon cooked in cider with a hint of something nefarious. Rat, maybe.

He traced his thumb along the spine and it fell open in his palm at the image of the sigil. From what he recalled, the version on his chest was far cruder than the picture in the book, which was comprised of many delicate swirls.

Blaze looked down at his T-shirt as if he could see the pattern burnt onto his skin through the cloth. What was that supposed to mean? That he'd be responsible for waking some ages old demon prince? Not bloody likely. It didn't make sense after what had happened earlier either. Why attack him? Why not ask for a quiet word? Were the two incidents even connected? There'd been rumours enough about the youkai recently. Maybe they were just hungry. Maybe he'd seemed like an easy mark.

The sigil on his chest burned, bringing with it a sharp flash of pain.

He must have winced, because Asha was suddenly kneeling by his side.

'How are you feeling?' She pressed her hand to his brow. The mask replaced with motherly concern. 'I can give you more painkillers if the effect is wearing off.'

Blaze tightened his grip on the booklet, so the colour bled out of his thumbs. 'I'm fine,' he growled. No sooner were the words spoken, than the thrumming in his hindbrain started again. Blinded by the pain, he clasped her arm for support.

'Blaze. I think I ought to check the poultice is working. You don't look so good.' Her free hand tugged at the bottom of his damp T-shirt.

'No!' He clapped a hand over hers, preventing her from revealing any more of his chest. 'I'm fine. It's fine. Just a twinge.' He managed a pained smile.

She sat back on her haunches and eyed him quizzically, but didn't let go of his T-shirt even when he removed his hand from hers. 'I think we have wildly different concepts of fine. The fake smile isn't convincing me.' She tugged again at the black cloth, this time exposing a three-inch band of flesh around his midriff.

'Really, Asha – leave it!'

She lowered her eyelashes a moment in response, then her brows furrowed and her green eyes bore into him. 'Don't be so stupid.'

He stared into the crystal fire of her eyes, and almost backed down. Only the thought of having to try to explain the mark upon his chest and his miraculously healed shoulder blades prevented him.

'Blaze.' She leant into him. So close, he could smell the scent of her body beneath her perfume. 'You're hot. Burning up. There's something wrong with the wound.' She slid her hand below the fabric and up his side towards his back.

Wild panic fluttered in his chest beside the flaring heat of the pulsing sigil. Her hands felt icy against his skin. To distract her, he did the only thing that came into his head. He kissed her. Hard.

For a moment, he felt her shock: a sharp intake of breath, a clenching of all the muscles in her back. Then instead of pushing him away and slapping him, she was kissing him back.

Her tongue played against the seam of his lips, igniting both passion and terror. He wanted her, had known that almost from the moment he'd woken. Perhaps before that, but she was out of his league. Talon – you didn't mess. This was wrong. There'd be payback. She was his jailor. The thought just excited him more. Unable to stop himself, Blaze pressed his tongue into her mouth. His moans mingled with hers. The globes of her bottom fitted neatly into his hands as she straddled his lap and rocked against the bulge of his cock. Like splashes of heaven, her kisses rained upon his face. He felt disorientated, shivery, but the earlier pain dwindled to a pinpoint. It flared again, white-hot when she squeezed his nipple, but in a good way, a way that made his cock thicken and buck.

Her underwear rasped against the zip of his trousers as she writhed upon his lap, urging him to loose his cock with the rock of her hips. Both her hands were beneath his shirt. They roved across his freshly healed skin, which tingled with each touch. Where his skin had been cold, now it was hot, as if the heat of her soul was seeping into him wherever their bodies made contact. No way was this natural.

Blaze looked at her in wonder. A slender line of perspiration peppered her brow. There was a glazed sheen to her eyes. 'Asha!' He put his hand out to stop her, but didn't push. He wasn't sure if she was even aware of his resistance. She was gazing at him as though he was out of focus. 'Asha, there's something wrong. The poison you drew...' Would it be this slow acting? He hadn't a clue about youkai poisons beyond what she'd told him, but he didn't think this was simply down to lust. 'I think we have to stop.'

Blaze stretched away from her, and took refuge in the depths of the sofa, but it was no use. It simply put him in a more vulnerable position.

Asha tore at the waistband of his leather jeans. The fly gave, revealing his rapidly hardening cock. It bucked as if begging attention. Blaze gulped down a deep breath while he watched Asha lick her lips. Then her mouth closed, soft and eager, over the ruddy helm, and he was hers. He couldn't stop her. The pleasure was so intense, he could do little more than groan and clench his fists. In his mind, he knotted his fingers in her hair, held her still so he could watch his cock slide in and out as he fucked her mouth with quick deep strokes and watched her lipstick smear. Her tongue teased the sensitive eye. He was going to walk away with black lip prints all along the shaft. Just that thought was enough to draw him that bit closer to coming. 'Asha, please...' His control was fraying, his reservations melting away.

The sigil on his chest flared white-hot again and seemed to writhe in time with their motion. It hurt, but her lullaby of poisonous kisses somehow overrode everything, and turned his words of denial into gasps of surrender.

'Asha!' Jaku's shadow fell across them both. Blaze raised his hands to ward off an attack, but instead Jaku's hands closed around Asha's waist, and lifted her from him.

She kicked and flailed, caught Jaku hard across the face as she twisted. In return, he spritzed her with a fine mist, which seemed to snap her from her trance. The glaze fell from her eyes. She blinked rapidly, turned her head and saw him, spread out before her like a banquet.

Asha's mouth fell open, but she made no sound, just blushed high across her cheekbones and turned away. Blaze expected Jaku to say something, but he simply gave him a look of profound pity that sliced to the quick. 'Your pendant wasn't there,' he said.

Blaze blinked uncertainly. Fuck the pendant. Why wasn't he asking what was going on? Was this some sort of regular occurrence?

'I couldn't bring in your bike either.' Jaku turned his head away from Blaze and watched Asha hurry to the back of the office. 'Not enough time.'

'Sure.' Blaze zipped himself up and stood. Clearly, he was missing something. The question was who to ask? Asha had hidden herself behind the mountain of paper on Rodgers' desk, so when Jaku walked back into the main archive, he followed.

He caught up with him halfway down the central aisle of books, where Jaku had balanced a compact mirror and was busy wiping blood-splatter from his pale face.

'Sorry about your stuff,' he said without turning. 'Somebody took it. Maybe Venom came back, I don't know.'

Nor did Blaze. He couldn't think of a single reason why anyone would want his pendant. It was as Palter Rodgers had noted, 'a worthless love token'.

Blaze rocked from one foot to the other while he watched the strange man retouch his lipstick. He made several abortive starts before he finally asked straight out: 'What just happened in there?'

'If you don't know, you're even more naive than you look.'

'I didn't mean that, I meant the rest. All the stuff you didn't say.'

Jaku shrugged. 'She's not my girlfriend.'

'And . . .'

Jaku arched one perfectly plucked eyebrow. 'And, it

was probably the youkai poison she sucked from you taking effect. Nearly all of them have a similar effect to Blood Rain.' He stowed his cosmetics. 'Seduction is their trademark. It's how they win influence.'

'That still doesn't answer my question.'

Jaku ran his tongue across his too white teeth. 'Fine, if you want it straight.' His lips curved into a nasty smirk. 'You're pretty, she's a slut, and she likes the hit she gets off the stuff. She didn't need to lick the wounds clean. The poultice would have worked just as well on it's own. A little slower perhaps, but fine.'

'Are you suggesting she's an addict?' The very idea seemed ridiculous. How could a member of the Talon – the demon defence league – be addicted to a youkai poison? How could that be OK? Besides, he'd met Blood Rain addicts before, and she'd didn't fit the profile. They were all either high-flyers from the Heights, or else slum-rats desperate to escape the limits of their own skins.

Jaku made no response. He pulled a chair up to a nearby table and sat down with his long skirts fanned out around him.

Blaze cautiously followed, and recognised it as the table he'd woken upon. He scooped up his slashed jacket from the floor. Most of the blood on it had dried, so that when he shook it, flakes fluttered to the floor like crimson butterflies.

'I thought you were supposed to hate demons.'

'We hunt them,' Jaku replied. He pulled out the pamphlet he'd taken from Palter Rodgers' office. 'I'm not sure love or hate comes into it. It's mostly a matter of pride. But if we're still talking Blood Rain, you'd have to ask Talon about that. I'm sure he sees advantages in her indulgence.'

Blaze pulled on his jacket. Half the decorative crows' feathers had come out and there was a tear in the cuff in addition to the rips across the back. He plucked at the gash in irritation. Talon! 'Talon's a person?'

'Something like that.' Jaku sucked his lips into a pout while his gaze roved across Blaze's body. 'He'll love you.'

Blaze thrust his hands into his pockets, feeling distinctly uncomfortable. He didn't intend to meet him. Come morning, he was getting out of here, no matter what.

Alone in the office, Asha slumped across Palter Rodgers' desk. What had just happened? She could still feel the youkai poison flowing through her veins, luring her into oblivion with promises of pleasure, if only she'd pinch her tight nipples or slip a hand beneath her skirts and touch her needy clit. She dared not look up for fear of finding Blaze still spread out for her on the sofa, his tight black T-shirt half raised and his cock peeping eagerly from his fly.

The half-choked, yielding sounds of his groans still filled her ears. He'd been putty in her hands; pliable, malleable, with a precious hint of resistance, that made her think he hadn't been quite so into it as his body. He'd wanted her though, wanted her despite being torn half-open by Venom.

'Stop it!' Asha slammed her fist into the wall of books piled upon the desktop. Manuscripts and folios scattered across the carpet. She stared unseeingly at the destruction, anger beating a rapid cadence behind her eyes, but still her fingers stretched out to trace an imaginary path down his body.

His taste was in her mouth: musky and slightly bitter. Her tongue traced the imaginary head of his cock. Next time ... oh, hell yes ... next time; she'd take him the whole way, until he spilled his seed into her mouth.

Asha clamped a hand across her mouth. 'No!' She seized a paper knife and jabbed it into the blotter. 'Stop it! Get out of my head.' She'd never dreamt Venom's poison would be this potent. If she'd even suspected, she'd have left the herbal goop to do its thing and stayed clear of the wound. Jaku thought he knew it all, but Jaku was wrong. There was a lot Jaku didn't know.

Asha sank back into the chair, the paper knife still clamped tightly in her hand. Fucking Blood Rain. She hated what it did, what Talon did. She despised being a passive little sex slave. One day, she was going to bind him in his own chair, scratch her nails down his thighs and pull his hair. She'd feed him Blood Rain off a silver spoon, and then line up volunteers to fuck him. But she wouldn't let them. She'd make him sweat; writhe until he was truly begging. Then she would have him. Oh boy, would she have him.

Of course, she'd have to get Jaku out of the way first. Her partner was far too enamoured of their sadistic leader. The thought of Talon sprawled half-naked in his blasted throne like some feudal lord made her grind her teeth. She'd stood enough of him, really, but things were going to change. Soon.

She scored his name into the blotter, then crossed it out. 'Damn him.' She stabbed repeatedly at the paper until she'd obliterated the name and dug several chunks of wood from the desk. If only his existence was so easily destroyed, but he was nigh on invulnerable, dressed in charms and wards, his very being bolstered with alchemy. 'Damn him, damn his soul.' He ruined everything. Twisted and destroyed everything. She'd considered running before today, but how? There was no easy route out of the City, and staying within his reach would be like running into the Ghost Wind – suicide.

An image of Blaze pierced her thoughts again, but this time it brought a smile with it. Talon would hate that he'd had no control over the encounter. Maybe that in itself made it worth the embarrassment. She supposed she'd have to seek Blaze out and apologise, make it clear that it was a one-off mistake. Then again, she'd rather enjoyed the feel of his lips brushing against her own, even if he did taste of youkai. She wondered what tale

Jaku was busy spinning him. Her partner only saw what he wanted to, never the whole truth – that she was trapped.

Something wet slapped the side of her face.

Asha jerked upright. The rattly skylight had blown open, and heavy raindrops were winding their way in through the gap. Her first thought was for a pole with which to close it, her second that it was already too late.

Palter Rodgers stood in the doorway watching her. His studious lined face, waxy and drawn, and his head tilted at an odd angle.

'What is it?' she asked.

He opened his mouth but instead of a string of protests at the mess she'd made of his desk, the only sound that emerged was a mournful groan.

'Hellfire! Jaku!' she screamed. The dead were in the building, had crept inside while her mind was elsewhere.

She planted a boot into Palter Rodgers' stomach, and he crumpled. The paper knife she left protruding from his left eye socket. He'd only just crossed over, a few more minutes and it wouldn't have been so easy. 'Jaku . . . Jaku . . . Blaze.'

Asha skidded to a halt in the central archive between the two tallest aisles of books, relieved to find the two men apparently fine. They were standing by the table where they'd first laid Blaze, with their backs to her, looking up at the domed glass roof.

A shadow swept across the floor. Like a startled mouse, Asha froze. Once it had passed, she edged towards the men and turned her gaze skywards.

Torches on the second floor balcony cast glittering streaks across the metal frame. Most of the glass panels were stained the same inky shade as the night sky, and dotted with silver depictions of the constellations, but near the centre, two figures circled in a timeless dance, an ageless red-robed priest, and a dark winged youkai.

The shadow beyond the glass moved with considerable speed. It circled, then vanished behind the illustration. For a moment, everything was still. Her ears strained for a sound. Then, a dull thud shook the glass.

Splinter lines spread from the point of impact like frosted cobwebs. Another thump echoed around the hall. Then the dome shattered.

Asha raised her arms, as splintered glass fell like crystal raindrops. One, scored a line across her cheekbone, others stung her arms.

Above, a black shape dropped through the hole in the dome. It hung in the air a moment, before its wings spread, and blotted out the stars. They were black, except for a single plume of green near the base of each wing.

'Venom!' She wasn't sure if the cry was hers or Jaku's. Either way, the youkai captain should have been home nursing his wounds, not targeting them.

Asha gripped her sword hilt, that she didn't recall drawing. There was further hammering coming from the direction of the archive door. It slowly petered out, only to be followed by the yawn of aged hinges. The Ghost Wind rushed along the aisles, bruising her cheeks with its icy chill. The dead were marching on them, to the beat of a war drum. Youkai poured through the hole in the glass roof.

'Run!' Jaku shoved her towards the rear of the building. Blaze was already ahead, his hands raised to protect his head. Venom swooped down behind him. For the second time that day, she cleaved his flesh, this time catching him between his wings. He screeched in agony, turned and swiped at her, sending her hurtling into a towering pile of books.

Jaku was between them in a flash. He jabbed with his glaive, and successfully pinned the youkai captain to a bookcase through one wing.

'Is there another exit?' Blaze yelled, as he pulled her free of the books.

'Only through a window into the Death Ward.' She

stared at Venom's face. It was the first time she'd seen him close-up. His demon visage was a twisted parody of a human face, part man, part snake. His eyes elongated, with hardly any whites. The huge irises putrid green. He opened his mouth and this time his voice was shrill and full of menace.

'Shit! I thought the only way in there was through the gate.' Blaze tugged at her clothing, urging her to move.

Jaku caught up with them, minus his halberd, and herded them up the aisle from the rear. 'The only official way in is through the lich-gate, but these buildings once belonged to the Death Stewards, or Copse men. They didn't mind overlooking the dead.'

Asha glanced back nervously in time to see Venom draw the pole-arm from his perforated wing and hurl it at them. 'Fuck!' yelled Blaze, succinctly expressing her own thoughts. It missed and skittered harmlessly along the floor. Jaku scooped it up.

'Move!' he shoved them both hard, and they ploughed over the busted door, into the bathroom.

Asha was in first. She plunged her sword up through the ribs of a walking corpse, before her mind had properly registered its presence. It screamed. The metal blade hissed as both dissolved into a pungent pile of ash.

Blaze doubled over the sink, his face stretched into an expression of terror, and retched.

'Help!' Jaku grasped the top of the door and lifted it back into place. 'Now the window, Asha.'

She shook her head. The square window was barred. There was no way through without a hacksaw and a lot more time.

'Hold the door.'

They swapped places. Asha pressed her whole weight against the splintered wood, while Jaku charged across to the window and tugged at the iron bars. 'Bugger!' he swore.

Through the door, Asha could hear the rumble of

guttural laughter and choral voices raised in blasphemous praise. 'Quickly,' she begged. If just a few of them pushed their weight against the wood, it would fall, trapping her beneath their marching footsteps. 'Jaku!' The desperation rang in her voice.

He jammed the glaive's haft through the bars and pushed, but though they creaked, they didn't shift.

'Jaku!'

Blaze sprinted to the window, still wiping spittle from his lips. He elbowed Jaku out of the way, took hold of the bars with both hands, and wrenched. The strain turned his cheeks ruddy and the tendons in his slender neck bulged. With an eerie creaking groan the metal rivets gave and shot free of the plaster. Blaze landed on his back holding the bars.

Jaku immediately pulled himself into the window space and kicked out the boards. He jumped through, and Blaze followed.

'Asha,' they both called, peering back through the hole at her.

She released the pressure on the door and ran. A blast of air hit her legs as the door landed behind her. She didn't look back, just leapt head first into the black maw.

The world tumbled around her. She hit the earth and rolled, finally coming to rest on her back facing the sky. Everything was white, white with fog, and white with the crackle of frost under foot.

The men seized each of her wrists and helped her upright.

'We'd better keep moving,' said Jaku. He glanced back at the building. 'This is holy ground. It might keep the demons at bay, but it won't stop the dead.'

4 Death Ward

Blaze clasped Asha's cold hand tightly. Everything he'd ever heard about the Death Ward was bad. People didn't even come here for funerals anymore. They held a wake elsewhere and entrusted their loved ones to the Copse men, who escorted them to their proper place beyond the gate and prayed that when the Ghost Wind blew they didn't come back to visit.

'Let go.' Asha shook off his tight grip. She looked at him with narrowed eyes.

So this was how it was going to be, was it? Pretend the incident in the office never happened and favour him with her icy Talon reserve. He couldn't say he was surprised.

'I take it your shoulders are much better.' She dug her teeth into her bottom lip, then realising what she was doing, forced herself to stop.

'Er – yes. Reckon you're a good doctor.' He tried to sound light-hearted but it came out strained, and he was forced to look away. The way her hands had roved across his skin, she surely already knew his wounds had mended. It wasn't exactly normal to tear iron bars from walls, either.

Actually, he was a little perturbed by that himself. Normally he had trouble tearing a hole in a newspaper, let alone freeing himself from jail.

Jaku was eyeing him peculiarly too. 'We ought to get going.' He turned a full circle, so that his coat-skirt flared out around him, and seemed to pinpoint a landmark in the billowing mist. 'We'll be fine here as long as the Ghost Wind blows, but it's probably best if we don't stand around.'

He led them a short distance, between twin grave-stones and past lines of thigh-high iron railings. The frosty ground crunched with each footstep. Every now and then, the fog would peel back a little and they'd catch a glimpse of a shambling figure or a view across a clearing. Across one such stretch, they left a trail of footprints and crushed ice-flowers.

Blaze fell into step with Jaku. 'Have you been here before?'

'Many times,' the demon-hunter replied. 'My family were Copse men. I don't fear the dead, but I respect them. Don't worry. There are ways out of here. Paths that lead below the city.'

'And you *know* this for sure?' said Asha.

Jaku nodded. 'Trust me.'

They reached another fence, this one slightly higher and decorated with an eagle and snake motif. Instead of passing it by, they followed its border until they reached a gate. Jaku beckoned them inside and closed the iron gate behind them. At the centre of the enclosure stood a high marble vault, carved with fluted columns and hung with leering gargoyles. The most grotesque sat guarding the stone door.

Jaku tugged off his leather glove with his teeth and pressed his fingers into its gaping mouth.

'This crypt belongs to my family,' he explained, while obviously fighting the urge to wince. 'Only the blood of a living member of the line will open the door. I'm the last. When I die, no one will be able to pass within, and I'll be buried out here, to act as my family's guardian for all eternity.'

'Sounds like a raw deal,' said Blaze.

Jaku glared at him.

'Hey, I meant no offence.' Blaze raised his hands and backed away a little. 'I just meant that it didn't sound like much of a fun job.'

Asha clasped his shoulder, which made him start.

'Jaku is only the last of his line because he chooses to be. There's nothing to stop him fathering a child.'

'Why don't you?'

Jaku pulled his hand from the gargoyle's mouth. It was dripping blood, but he clasped it to his chest and turned away before they could examine it too closely.

The vault ground open and he stepped into the darkness.

'Because that would involve more intimacy with a woman than he cares for. Isn't that obvious?' Asha patted Blaze across the back, and he remembered to wince. She walked past him, stopped in the doorway and turned her head to look back at him. 'You needn't pretend,' she hissed. 'You taste of youkai magic and you're starting to smell of it. Once we're free of this mess, you're going to tell me what you know, or I'm going to live up to those Talon stories you've heard.' She smiled, showing her perfect white teeth.

Blaze swallowed. Somehow, he didn't think he'd survive the process.

'Get inside,' Jaku called. 'It won't stay open forever.'

Blaze ducked his head and followed Asha into the tomb.

The interior of the mausoleum was surprising clean and scentless. The narrow entranceway widened after a few feet into a heptagonal chamber, where Jaku had lit a hurricane lantern that hung from the ceiling. For want of a bandage, he'd pulled his leather glove back on. He was busy lighting a wooden torch when they reached him.

Blaze peered into several of the deep cubbyholes that lined four of the walls. 'No bodies,' he remarked.

'They're out walking, as they have no guardian to protect them yet.' Jaku's low voice echoed off the stonework. 'We'd best make sure we're gone by the time they return.' He opened a door, which led onto a spiral stair. 'There are two levels below this. The lowest opens into the city catacombs, but the way is warded with old magic. I *should* be able to get us through. Wait here, and don't touch anything.'

The moment the door closed, Asha grabbed Blaze. 'Since we've got a moment,' she hissed. She backed him against a wall and pinned his hands above his head. 'Talk to me,' she growled into his face. 'Tell me what happened in Rodgers' office. Why did you kiss me? Why is Venom chasing you? What's this all this about?'

Alarmed, Blaze shook his head. 'I don't know. I swear it.'

'Show me your back.' She didn't wait for him to turn, just spun him around and wrenched up his jacket and T-shirt as far as they would go. 'Aah!' She jerked him forwards into the cold stone wall as her fingertips traced over the smooth skin of his shoulders. 'How? There's not even a mark.'

'I don't know.' He pressed his cheek to the cool granite, feeling sickly hot again. He didn't have any answers for her. All he knew was that her touch was making his temperature rise.

Asha continued to rub her palms across the tight muscles of his back as if trying to find a single defect. He shivered, as the strange caress roused further heat in his loins. His cock slowly thickened, and the memory of her mouth forming a perfect O around his shaft returned with vivid clarity.

Blaze pushed her off and turned around. 'I swear, I don't know, but stop.' He held her at arm's-length, his hand pressed to her abdomen just below her breasts. He was aware of her breathing, shallow like his own. She was looking at him, her expression starting to glaze again.

'There's this as well,' he blurted. He didn't know what was happening, but maybe they could make sense of it together if they trusted each other.

His stomach was already showing, so he only had to

pull the black fabric a little higher to show her the brand upon his skin. 'It happened in the bathroom, the same time my skin healed. I didn't know if it was something you'd done, or if it was a result of the attack or what. It's why I kissed you. You were so insistent on checking my wounds. It was the only thing I could think of to distract you.

She traced her fingertip over the symbol on his chest. It sent shivers of pleasure rippling through his abdomen. His next breath came out sharp. 'Careful,' he gasped. She didn't remove her hand, just kept her palm pressed to the sigil.

'I take it you don't normally tear iron bars off walls.'

'No.'

'What are you feeling?'

Blaze shook his head. He couldn't put it into words, and wasn't sure if he wanted to. He certainly didn't want to share the fantasy running through his head about how he longed to lift her skirt, reverse their positions and fuck her until every vestige of her mask cracked, her skin turned ruddy and their bodies smelled of sex and each other.

'Tell me.'

He could hardly breath, let alone speak.

'Pain?' Her hand slid down his front from his breastbone to the sensitive space between his naval and his groin. 'Pleasure?'

Even her words were like a caress. Blaze trembled. His balls felt heavy and tight, just the way they had when she'd fellated him. 'Careful! Careful!' he whimpered. 'Last time it hurt.' He grit his teeth.

Asha kept her hand still, although it remained in contact with his naked skin. 'Then tell me what you're feeling?'

'Fire. Burning.' He had to spit the words out. His mouth felt parched and he could feel his temperature spiralling upwards. His eyes snapped open. 'Touch me,

Asha.' He wrenched open his fly with one hand and dragged her palm down to his crotch with the other. 'Please. I need you for this ... I don't understand it, but I need you.'

'What do you mean?' she demanded, although her soft palm closed around his aching shaft.

Blaze just sighed in relief as her thumb rubbed a lingering caress across the head of his cock, and pleasure raced along the shaft like a stream of sparklers. He didn't understand, but he knew he needed to come.

His eyes fluttered, then rolled upwards into his head.

It was raining ash and feathers: great black feathers. The sky was distorted, coloured a yellow-tinged metallic grey, and all the clouds had creepy blood-red linings. He was naked on the cathedral steps ... no ... the roof. For a split-second, he was disorientated, then he spread his arms wide. Lightning struck the roof. It crackled along the apex and poured into him until he was full of fire and light. His whole body was ablaze.

It was the most excruciating and ecstatic experience of his life.

Almost consumed, he was suddenly snatched back from the flames and trapped again within his own body. Asha was staring at him, her hand still curled around his cock, although she was no longer caressing him. Steam was pouring off his body.

'Venom's done something to you,' she gasped. Then she turned and fled down the spiral stair.

Blaze pushed his still hard cock into his trousers and zipped up. It wasn't until he heard a second thump from below that he realised she'd run into trouble.

The steps were steep and narrow, only half the width of his feet. They emerged into a cobble-stoned chamber lit by a single torch held in a wall sconce. Asha had her back to him. Her sword had dissolved back in the bathroom so she'd drawn her off-hand weapon, a long handled knife. He watched her dance around a shadowy opponent he momentarily mistook for Jaku until he realised the other man was slumped on the far side of the chamber clutching his abdomen. 'Help her,' he yelled. 'Don't just stand there like a fucking lemon.'

Blaze charged forwards in response, then froze again when he realised he didn't own a weapon, and fists against a skeleton wasn't going to gain him anything other than broken knuckles. He looked left, right. There were bodies incarcerated upright in pockets in the walls. He ran to the nearest, which was clutching some sort of halberd, and tugged at the haft. It didn't budge, so he braced his foot against the wall between the skeletons legs and tried again. This time it gave and he stumbled backwards, the corpse walking with him.

'Holy shit!' The foetid stink of the flesh still clinging to it made his stomach heave, but it was already empty.

He tore at the wooden pole and kicked at the skeleton's ankles so that they spun in an increasingly manic dance. He couldn't see what was happening to Asha, although he'd glimpsed enough of her opponent to know he was probably better off. At least the bastard thing he was wrestling with didn't have a crown and a demonic glare. He kicked it in the groin, which seemed to work despite the absence of genitals.

The skeleton bent double, perhaps reacting instinctively to a memory of pain. Blaze raised the halberd, but the blow never connected. Mid-stroke a clap of pain tore through the left side of his brain. Temporarily blind, Blaze dropped to his knees and clutched his head.

Someone was screaming inside his skull. The pressure was intense. It gnawed at the back of his eyeballs and seared lines across his scalp. Blaze clasped and released clumps of his hair. He tore at the stone earth, tried to scream but it felt as though his vocal chords had been cut. Then everything began to pulse and dance, and his whole world became one massive breath of despair.

The sound of hard pellets hitting even harder surfaces penetrated the red haze of his existence. Slowly, the pain collapsed in on itself, fading away until it was no more than a memory.

'Blaze?'

He uncurled cautiously. The torch was still spitting out its bitter orange light, but the floor was now peppered with shards of splintered white bone. 'What happened?' he gasped.

'You did.' Jaku was still slumped against the far wall. 'I don't know what you are. Maybe it's best I don't, but for now I'm grateful.' He nodded towards Asha, who was flat on her back.

Blaze rushed to her side. She was limp in his arms when he lifted her, although her only visible wound was the cut across her right cheek she'd sustained when the glass roof had collapsed. 'Asha, Asha . . .' He cradled her, kissed her and ran his tongue along the wound. 'Wake up, Asha.' He looked back at Jaku in despair. 'What's wrong with her?'

Jaku pushed himself to his feet, leaning heavily on his glaive. 'The force of the blast knocked her off her feet.' He fumbled into the pocket of his long coat. 'Here, try this.'

Blaze caught the vial, which he recognised as the thing Jaku had spritzed her with in Palter Rodgers' office. He pulled the stopper out and flicked some into her face. 'What is it?'

'Holy water,' said Jaku, and his lips stretched into a smile that showed all his pearly-white teeth. 'Probably best you don't get it on your skin.'

'Why?' He hesitated with the bottle.

'Not her. She'll be fine. You.'

Asha sat up, coughing, and batted away Blaze's attempt to hold her. 'I'm fine.'

'Why's it bad if it touches my skin and not hers?'

Jaku hobbled towards the exit.

Asha ran to him and pressed her hand to where he clutched his side.

'I'll be fine, nothing a few stitches won't fix,' he said, although he briefly accepted her support. 'Fetch some of those bone splinters, and bring him.' He tilted his head towards Blaze. 'He's blown the seal, so lets get on before my family get back. They'll have felt the ripple.

'What are you implying with the holy water?' Blaze overheard her ask.

Jaku scowled. 'You don't need me to spell it out, Asha. You know what he is. You've tasted him. And you know why I'm not saying it.'

'Because we'll have to act.'

Their eyes met, and he nodded. Then they both turned and looked at Blaze.

5 **Blood Rush**

Asha avoided meeting Blaze's eyes, although she allowed him to slip his hand into hers once she'd put her knife away. It was true. She did know what he was, or at least what he was becoming. She was also wise enough not to voice her opinion. Jaku was right, while it remained unspoken they could keep working together, say it aloud and everything would have to change. They were the Talon. They slaughtered demons. They didn't befriend them. They didn't defend them. They didn't hold hands with them and they certainly didn't long for them in the way she longed for Blaze. She wanted to feel his lips on her again, his hands roving over her skin, coaxing, caressing, exploring and flooding her body with his warmth. She squeezed his fingers tight. Then again, maybe she was still just feeling the effects of Venom's poison, but the way her heart seemed to clench at the thought of parting with him suggested otherwise. Still, it was something she was going to have to face before the night was out.

They plunged through the crypt door, all three together. The ragged edges of the broken seal feathered against her skin like thousands of stinging tentacles. She shrugged off the residual effects of the magic. It was harmless, just looking for a route through which to earth itself, although the tingling didn't help curb her lust.

Her bodice chafed her erect nipples.

The catacombs beyond were murky and lined with phosphorescent algae. Several of the passageways were flooded. They struggled along with the single torch Blaze brought from the tomb, while Jaku's breathing grew more ragged with each step.

It was hard to tell if he was paler than normal, due to his heavy make-up and the green tinge that the algae gave to everything. After about ten minutes, she stopped them. 'Jaku,' she pleaded. 'Let me patch you up.' The front of his coat was sticky with blood.

'Not here. A little further on.' His words punctuated the air in staccato bursts. 'I'll be fine. Keep moving.'

She didn't like it but she let him lead. Jaku was stubborn to the core, and maybe there was a room not far with space to move and better light. Besides, she knew he hated anyone peeling back the layers of his feminine guise. Undressing, even just unfastening his clothing in front of Blaze would be absolute torture. The only people, men, who got to see Jaku naked were the ones he took to bed, and even they were rare. Actually, she wasn't sure even they got to undress him.

She had a sudden image of Jaku on his back, his long skirts pushed up, lace knickers caught around his thighs and a faceless man kneeling between his legs, one hand upon Jaku's pale white knee. Lust wrenched at her insides, she breathed out sharply, shocked by just how erotic, how charged she found the concept of a hand upon his knee, prying open his legs. Venom's poison was obviously still having an effect. She'd never considered her partner in such a way before.

'Get it under control, Asha,' she whispered to herself. 'Now really isn't the time. Next, you'll be imagining the two of them together.' Her head turned to Blaze, then Jaku. No! That way madness lay.

She stumbled, causing Jaku to groan.

Damn it! When would the blasted tunnels end? They all needed to rest, and she wanted a chance to talk to Blaze alone. She had to make sure he understood just how much danger he was in.

He leant a little closer to her as they rounded a sharp

corner, and the sweet-musky scent of his skin caused her senses to perk. Her body reacted with a tight, welcoming flutter deep in her abdomen. Asha stared at him. His eyes glittered with black magic in the half-light. Her lips parted in anticipation. This was crazy. They couldn't continue like this, but the draw to him was incredibly strong, like the draw she felt towards Talon when he powdered her skin with Blood Rain.

The thought of her dangerous lover immediately sobered her thoughts. Hell! What were they doing? They couldn't lead Blaze back to the cathedral. Talon would slaughter him. He tortured youkai for fun. He didn't baby-sit half-breeds, especially half-breeds that might turn out to be more than that. What if he was the avatar of the prophesied youkai prince? Talon wouldn't thank them for bringing him into their headquarters, even if the secret of its location was extremely badly kept.

She stopped dead in her tracks.

The two men jerked to a halt either side of her.

'What is it?' asked Blaze. There were dark smudges of concern below his eyes.

'Enough! We're stopping.'

'No,' Jaku croaked, though he sagged a little at the knees. 'There's a place we can stop ... a room ... round the next corner...'

Asha mentally assessed the distance – two hundred yards, perhaps. 'All right, but no further, and once we get there, no more pretending. We need to sort this out.'

Judging by their expressions, they both realised what she meant.

It took ages to stumble those last few yards, but eventually they made it, and the dingy passageway opened out into a cellar. A short staircase climbed to a door, beyond which lay a windowless alchemy lab.

Blaze used the sputtering torch to light several rows of stubby candles that littered one worktop, then jammed the torch inside a metal bucket.

Asha helped Jaku to the table and he slumped against it while she worked the cricks out of her shoulder.

Every surface bar the table was crammed with glassware: flasks, test tubes, boiling tubes and row upon row of coloured liquids in stoppered bottles. There was an athanor in one corner and a set of brass scales in another. The skeletal remains of some bird of prey hung from the ceiling in a ghastly parody of life.

Asha ran her finger along one of the worktops. It came away coated with grime. 'What is this place, something to do with the Copse men?

'Maggot's,' said Jaku. He raised his head slightly to look at her, though he had his upper body pressed to the tabletop. 'We're on Hangover Street, just off Steepleside.'

'I know this place,' Blaze sniffed at the contents of a cobalt-blue bottle. 'My gran used to come here, but it's been boarded up for years.'

'Uh-huh,' Jaku croaked. He slithered off the table and landed on his back with a thump.

'Damn it!' Asha rushed across to her comrade. 'Jaku,' she pressed her hand to his brow, then his throat. His pulse was weak and flighty. She tore open the buttons of his coat and pushed up his shirt, to reveal a layer of white cotton, now stained scarlet. 'Jaku, you fool. Blaze, find me some scissors.'

She heard him pull out several drawers, but when he came over, he was carrying a knife. 'Best I could do,' he apologised.

'Whatever! Cut this.' She held up a bloody patch of linen for him to slice though. The incision made, she tore apart the cloth to reach the wound. Jaku made a sobbing noise in the back of his throat. 'I'm sorry,' she soothed. 'Blaze, bring one of the candles.'

Asha pulled the same suture needle she'd used to mend Blaze from her collar, threaded it and waved it through the candle flame. 'Hold the wound closed, while I sew.'

'Not him.'

'Ignore him,' said Asha.

Blaze clamped the bloody wound with his fingers. It wasn't deep, just smooth and bleeding profusely. Jaku grit his teeth in response to the touch and closed his eyes. His breathing was ragged and wheezy. Each time the thread pulled through his skin he let out an uncomfortable hiss.

'Feed him the resin. It's in my right pocket.' Blaze delved inside her pocket, and found the painkillers, but Jaku just snapped his teeth when he tried to feed him it.

'Jaku!' Asha jabbed him with the needle a final time, then tied a knot. She shoved Blaze out of the way and stuffed four meaty chunks of resin into Jaku's mouth. He didn't try to bite her, but he did glower menacingly. 'You'll thank me for it later,' she hissed.

'I hate this stuff.' He spat at least half of it out. 'I'd rather use Blaze's method.'

'What method?'

'Wanking. That's right isn't it?' He turned to Blaze, who turned his back and walked away. Jaku's black lips spread into a heartless grin. 'You didn't really believe he was killing cockroaches.'

'Shut up! Rest.' She rolled him onto an old straw mat in the corner.

Jaku arched his perfectly plucked eyebrows. 'Then again, maybe I should just get him to come over and lick it for me. His spit's worked wonders on your cheek.'

The instinctive reaction to check her cheek luckily overrode her urge to hit him. A punch-up with her injured partner wouldn't be clever. Asha carefully traced the gash on her cheek. Where it had been a long tender line a few minutes ago, it was now just a dried up scab of about half the length.

'He snuck a taste while you were out cold.'

'Go to sleep, Jaku.' She pushed his head down. 'We'll move again, come dawn. The dead won't bother us then.'

She didn't mention the demons. She hoped for all their sakes that they'd reach safety before they were tracked down, although, they could probably home in on Blaze. He stank of their magic. Besides, where was safe, exactly?

'Fuck!' yelled Blaze, succinctly expressing her own thoughts.

Blaze stared dazedly at his hands. He'd come to the sink to wash Jaku's blood from them, only to find his skin was already absorbing it. To hide his shock and a certain amount of physical revulsion, he turned on the tap regardless. The pipes squealed and knocked in protest. All that came out was a brief splutter of brackish goop. So, maybe it was just as well he no longer needed to clean his hands.

Asha pushed her hands into the sink alongside his.

'It's not working,' he said. She was standing far too close to him, so their hips pressed together. He itched to touch her, but there was no point in dwelling on what couldn't be. They'd already decided he was no longer on their side. Blaze pushed his hands into his jacket pockets. He'd been stupid. He'd got caught up in the moment, forgotten that they were Talon, that she was his jailor.

'I think it's time I went,' he said.

Asha wiped her bloody fingers down the skirt of her coat, leaving shiny smears on the black fabric. 'You can't. It's too dangerous.' She opened her heavily kohl-lined eyes extra wide and stared at him.

Blaze apprehensively licked his lips and sneaked a look in Jaku's direction. Thankfully, he appeared to be sleeping. 'I can get home from here. It's not that far.' He somehow willed himself from her side and towards the door they'd come through.

Asha darted in front of him. 'Wait!' She held up her hand to stop him. 'There's probably a youkai welcoming party waiting for you. You barely survived the first time

Venom got hold of you. Do you really want to face him alone?

Blaze shrugged. 'The alternative doesn't seem much better. I can hardly hope for any better treatment at the cathedral. I don't know what's happening to me, but you're both making it obvious you think I'm one of them.' He kicked at the nearby table leg. 'Maybe you're right. I don't know what's happening, so it's probably better all round if I go.'

'No.' Asha raised her hand and touched his arm. 'Please, Blaze. Trust me.'

He wanted to. It would make everything so much simpler. Just her touch made him tremble and his resolve waver. 'You heard what Palter Rodgers said about the prophecy. If I'm tied up with that, Talon's not just going to sit back and give me sanctuary. He'll lop my head off or use me as a bartering tool.'

'It'll be all right. I can talk to him, Blaze.'

'Really? Will it?'

'Yes,' she said decisively, but her eyes told him differently. She was just scared of the consequences of letting him go. 'At least get some rest before you run. Maybe if we look at the pamphlet again we'll find something . . .'

He was almost tempted. Maybe they would find the answers he needed in there; then again, maybe all he'd find was a ticket to his own funeral. 'No.' If he was going, it had to be now, before Jaku woke.

'Please, Blaze,' she said again. This time she pressed her hand to his cheek. The simple touch seemed to sear a pathway straight to his loins. He wanted to grab her in that moment, to throw her onto the tabletop and wet his hand inside her knickers. Instead, he remained absolutely still and breathless.

He heard her swallow. She let her finger slide down his cheek, her own face downcast. Her little finger brushed the edge of his mouth and then ran across the plump surface of his lower lip.

'Don't,' he said, though desire tugged at him. 'You'll only make things more complicated.'

'What if I say, I can't let you go without . . .' Her words petered out. She glanced warily at Jaku.

'Without what?' he said bending towards her, now seeking out her liquid eyes. 'Without what?'

She smiled, shook her head sadly. 'You're right, you'd better go. But you'd better hit me first, give me an alibi.'

Blaze recoiled in horror. He couldn't hit her. Oh, he knew she was a warrior, tougher than he was and far more lethal, but there was something fragile about her too, and he wanted to kiss her, not hit her. Besides, to make it look real, he'd have to knock her out. Blaze shook his head. He remembered her body, warm and soft in his arms, the taste of her lips and the smell of her hair. 'I can't.'

'Then I can't let you leave.' She drew her knife and took five paces backwards until she blocked the doorway. 'Hit me, and do it hard, or you'll have to stay.'

'Asha, get out of my way.'

'Make me. Your punch will be nothing compared with what I'll face from Talon if you don't.'

His mind raced. He couldn't hit her. Just couldn't. She wasn't his enemy. He briefly contemplated leaping onto the workbench and attempting to wade through the alchemical junk to the boarded up window and kicking his way out. They'd used one window as an escape route, why not another. Only thinking about it, he wasn't actually sure where the window was. He couldn't even tell where the shop doorway had been, and the noise of smashing the boards would definitely wake Jaku.

'All right, you win.' He raised his hands in surrender and walked forwards until his stomach pressed against the blade. Cautiously, Asha lowered the knife.

'Don't try anything.'

'What's to try?' He took another step closer, intending to somehow edge around her.

'Blaze,' she said in a low growl.

He ignored the tone of her voice and sought the truth in her gaze instead. There was no hostility in the green depths, just a few wary shadows and the same crazy sense of longing he felt himself.

He was still going, but he couldn't leave her like this.

Blaze grabbed her wrists, and pushed her back against the aged door. Her pulse was strong beneath his fingertips. It raced just like his heart. Sod the plan. He just wanted to kiss her.

The kiss was sleek and salty.

Asha fought against his grip. She wanted him, but she didn't want him to hold her, not like this. The bruising press of his fingers on her inner wrists reminded her too vividly of Talon. She wanted to be able to touch, to push her hands inside his T-shirt and rove all over his chest. She wanted to feel his nipples, his navel, the knotted muscles of his back and the soft space between his ear and his jaw. She wanted to lick him there, and feel the tremors it brought run down his neck.

She didn't know if it was the poison, years of Blood Rain kicks, or just the scent of him at that moment that was making her feel this way, but she did know she no longer cared. Maybe it was none of those things, just the simple thought of saying goodbye, having only just found him.

For so long, sex had been tied up in knots of deceit and fear, enmeshed in anger and resentment. Talon didn't love her. He loved the control he had over her, that he had over them all. He was forever playing on their desires and kinks, tempting them to lust after what they couldn't have. Jaku accused her of being a sex slave and an addict, but he'd have traded his soul for a single kiss from Talon.

Asha longed for so much more. What she wanted was someone she could trust, rely on and allow herself to love. Maybe Blaze was that person. He certainly wanted her body and soul. That was clear just from the way he kissed.

They pulled apart for air. Blaze smeared a second kiss across her face. He nibbled along the edge of her jaw and licked over her pulse point.

'Let go. I want to touch you.' She fought against his hold, driving her lower body against his in the process.

He forced a leg between hers. 'Not yet.' Blaze rubbed his face against her breasts, luxuriating in the feel of the sumptuous fabric against his cheek. He unfastened the top button with his teeth, exposing the black, boned corset beneath, and the mesh of lace covering the top of her breasts. 'I wish I had the time to unwrap you.'

Finally, he released her hands as he slid onto his knees. Asha pushed her fingers into his spiky hair. It was curiously soft, despite the wax or whatever it was holding it aloft. She pulled and scrunched handfuls of the blond strands. Meanwhile, his hands were on her ankles, tracing the curves of the bones. Slowly, his touch climbed the length of her boots to her calves. One finger edged inside the leather. 'No time,' he hissed beneath his breath, 'or I'd have you naked apart from these.'

The admission planted a vivid image of her spread out upon a great baroque bed; her legs spread wide for him, and every inch of her body buff naked, except for her tightly laced boots. She wanted time for that too.

Blaze's hands pushed higher. He found the seams of her stockings and traced them up to their lacy tops. From there, it was just a few hand spans until he was teasing the dark curls escaping the wisp of fabric covering her mons.

His tongue rasped against the silk.

Asha cried out at his touch. Her hips rolled with longing. 'Oh, yes!' She clutched his head to her body and begged for more in a language of mewls and purrs.

Blaze sucked her clit through the fabric, until she was drowning in sweat and clutching the door handle for support; her legs ready to buckle beneath her.

'Come for me,' he said into her pussy.

'Not yet,' she whimpered. 'I want you to come too.'

Blaze rose to his feet. He pulled the scrap of her knickers aside and slid his fingers between her open thighs, and into her liquid heat.

He lifted her.

Asha wound her legs around his waist and rubbed her slit against the hummock beneath his leather trousers. Somehow, they managed to get them open between them and down his thighs.

His cock sprang up eagerly. It dipped into her entrance. Then they were locked in an ageless, bumping, grinding union.

Asha closed her eyes and gave herself up to the pleasure. The smell of him, musky, yet sweet like cinnamon, was intoxicating. She was drunk on his scent. It was no ordinary youkai perfume, but something uniquely him. She wanted to cocoon herself in that smell and let it seep into her skin. She was buzzing. Her clit was getting all the attention it needed from the up-thrust of his cock.

It took her by surprise when he peeled them away from the support of the door and carried her to the table. He lowered her onto the surface of the table and opened her up again with two, then three stiff fingers.

'What's wrong?' she asked.

Blaze laughed. He pulled her from the tabletop and turned her around. 'Nothing, absolutely nothing.' He urged her back onto the table, kneeling with her bum exposed. 'Nice.' His palm warmed her rear. One finger wriggled into the crease between her cheeks, touched her anus and then slipped around until his knuckles ground against her clit.

'Blaze.' She felt herself blush.

'Hmm.' He licked her firmly between her exposed cheeks.

Talon had tortured her with such shameful taboos, but having Blaze do it, was very different. He made it sensual, not crude.

His tongue dabbed at her hole, while his fingers worked her clit. 'You taste good,' he murmured. 'But I've something else for you now.' His cock bucked against her thigh, leaving sticky dots. He pulled her back, towards his hips, so her upper body lay flat against the table, and spread her arms out wide, until they lay like two stacked crosses. 'Ready.' He pushed inside her again, filling her with his length.

Asha caught a brief glimpse of their reflections in the surface of the weedy fish tank. Her eyes were luminous and glinted like emeralds. Her hair was plastered to her cheek on one side and sticking up on the other. Blaze's eyes were closed, but the sigil on his chest glowed with pale-blue flames.

'Asha ... Asha,' he murmured her name into her dark hair. He bucked faster, harder. Her orgasm was building fast. It swept up suddenly like a hot geyser. It started in her sex, then prickled along her back and fluttered against her scalp.

She felt Blaze's body arch away from hers as he came inside her. The hot splashes wet her skin. Several hit her face. Confused, she tried to turn, but he still held her wrists.

Blaze's screams echoed around the tiny room.

Crimson dots splattered across the table and the rows of dirty glassware. Blood ran into her eyes until her long eyelashes were thick with it and glued closed. 'Blaze,' she screamed adding her voice to his.

The feel of her body pulsing around his cock, drawing him in, was the final push he needed. He'd been riding close to the edge for so long, had failed to reach climax too many times tonight. It's what he'd been craving since he'd awakened with her above him. Now her orgasm sucked at his cock. His hips pumped in painful need. Fate was sweeping him along.

The horizon was dark.

Normally, the world fell silent when he came. This time there was noise, overwhelming noise: drums and static, and the grim wails of the damned. He was standing in the Ghost Wind. The sky was grey and red. Youkai poured through the open gates of the swinging gibbets and the dead performed a macabre opera.

Blaze rode his orgasm to the brink of insanity. The final noise was his own keening as the bittersweet spike overwhelmed him.

Lines of fire streamed down his back. The skin blistered, then split like overripe fruit. He screamed in ecstasy and pain. The muscles of his back strained and stretched. He looked down. The sigil on his chest glowed with a ghastly green flame while Asha writhed beneath him in a pool of blood. He didn't understand what was happening. Something brushed the back of his thigh. Blaze turned sharply but found himself off balance and chasing his own shadow. He stumbled, fell, and landed in a pool of feathers. He had wings. Great black feathery wings. He strained to see them, his voice still raised in horror and confusion.

Jaku reared awkwardly from the mat in the corner. He fumbled with his glaive, but there was no room to swing it. Blaze scrambled away from him but merely backed himself up against the cupboards.

'No, Jaku, no!' Asha was between them, her clothes tattered and heavy with blood. She kicked the pole-arm from his grasp.

'We're taking him in,' Jaku growled. He plucked a slender silver pin from his cuff. 'Move.'

She threw herself onto Blaze. The weight of her body

seemed to crush the air from his chest. She smeared kisses across his bloodied face, entwined herself around his limbs. The trace of her fingers across his feathers brought the urgency of their union back with renewed vigour.

Jaku's face loomed closer. 'Relax,' said his voice. Fear, said his eyes.

Asha had him pinned. He couldn't move.

Blaze felt only the tiniest prick, just a single sharp jab against his neck. Then the world went dark and still.

6. Caged

He woke to darkness, on a cold stone floor with a thumping headache, and a painful lump below his left ear where Jaku had slid the needle into his neck.

'Hello.' He stood up and looked around, but could make out little beyond the reach of his hands. Most of his clothes were missing. He was left with just his trousers, and even they were open around his waist. The wings were gone too, but he was pretty sure he hadn't imagined them, as he could feel a strange pattern etched into his back. The sigil on his chest was glowing with a faint blue edge.

Blaze zipped up and took a hesitant step forwards. The stone was cold against his bare feet. 'Hello! Where am I?' Another pace and he hit the bars.

Shocked, he ran his hand up and down the dull metal surface. The friction left his hand tingling and sent a shivery charge down his spine. They'd obviously had some kind of ward put on them.

'Asha!'

Where was he? Had she brought him here? All he remembered was her squirming against him and Jaku's shiny black eyes getting closer and closer.

He tried to bend the bars, use his strength the way he had to get them out of the archive, but nothing budged; the magic just raised all the hairs on his body. 'Asha,' he screamed loudly, this time, and his voiced echoed.

'I'm afraid Asha is indisposed,' said a distant, melodic male voice. 'Perhaps I can help.'

A faint blue globe leapt out of the darkness several metres away, revealing a single hazy figure slowly approaching. His cage was in some sort of cavernous stone hall. The roof soared above them, several storeys high. The cathedral, he realised. Of course, where else would they take him? Which meant this – he stopped to look at the figure approaching – was presumably Talon.

The man who stopped five paces back from the bars was not what he expected. For starters, unlike his marionettes, he was blond, with long tresses bound in hundreds of tiny braids, each adorned with a sliver of jade, bloodstone or bone. His narrow expressive face was also devoid of any make-up.

'Blaze Makaresh, the demon's proxy.' He smiled, and cruel light flared in his vivid blue eyes. 'Welcome, we have much to discuss.'

Blaze recoiled from his aggressively sexual poise. He was naked apart from a long slender silver chain, which held a key against his chest, and a pair of hip-hugging trousers. A tattoo of thorns girdled his slender hips.

'Ah, do I make you nervous?' Talon laughed. He stretched out a hand towards the bars, a chain hung from the tip of his index finger. 'I believe this is yours. Put it on.'

His pendant! The one he'd lost when Venom attacked, or one very similar.

Blaze seized it and stared at the twisted silver spiral and it's delicate green heart. 'How?' he demanded. How had it come to be here?

'I pulled a few strings,' said Talon dismissively. He turned his back on the cage. 'Now, put it on and maybe I'll let you out to play.'

Blaze slipped the chain around his neck, too relieved to have it back to question its reappearance, or wonder why Talon was so eager for him to put it on.

'Don't try anything, demon boy.' Talon walked *through* the bars and into the cell. Blaze backed away sharply. He touched the metal bars, which were still as solid as ever. 'Give me your hand,' said Talon, extending his.

Tentatively, Blaze held it out. Talon grasped it firmly and tugged him closer. He was surprisingly strong despite his slender appearance and Blaze found himself clasped in his arms. One of Talon's long nails scratched a path across his cheek inside his trousers.

'She has good taste. I'll give her that. It wouldn't do for you to have been ugly. Of course, now she's had you,' he ran a finger up Blaze's throat and beneath his chin, 'I'll have to do the same.'

'Get off me.' Blaze shoved Talon hard in the chest, but all he succeeded in doing was backing himself up against the bars.'

Talon laughed. 'Aw, how sweet.' The mocking turn of his voice turned icy. 'I'll have fun with you later. Now, as I said, it's time for a little group discussion.'

The hall was suddenly awash with light. Bright blue globes lit every column. A ring of black clothed figures surrounded the cage: Talon's dolls in all their theatrical finery.

Blaze searched the ring and found Asha and Jaku together, but neither of their expressions was friendly. Jaku's was hard, and his eyes glittered with an intense hatred. Asha simply looked through him. She'd changed her outfit, and looked as perfect now as when he'd first encountered her. The other dolls merely regarded him with cold indifference. If they were fascinated with the beast they had captured, he couldn't read it in their eyes.

'Come here, Asha, Jaku.' Talon's voice rang loud and clear. The pair immediately stepped out of the circle and up onto the dais.

Blaze pressed his body to the bars and tried to reach her. 'Asha, what happened?' he demanded. Why had she agreed to bring him here? What had they done to her? Asha stopped just shy of his reach. She didn't look at him. When he tried desperately to touch her with just his fingertips, Jaku stepped between them and batted his hand out of the way.

'Youkai slime,' he cursed. 'We should have sent you straight back to hell. Look what you've done to her.'

'I'm not a demon!' Blaze cried, cutting him off.

'Oh, but you are.' Talon traced a crimson nail across his shoulder. 'The prophecy is quite clear on that, Burning Prince. We've been waiting for you. And thanks to Asha, we have you.'

Blaze glared at her, but there was still no response, not even a nervous press of her teeth into her plump lower lip. Her eyes were just blank emotionless mirrors. 'What have you done to her?' he demanded.

'Not me,' said Talon. 'Not this time. She absorbed far too much of your blood, not to mention what other fluids you drowned her in. It's taken hours to calm her.' He rolled his hips against Blaze's bottom. 'If you understand what I mean.' He puffed a strand of Blaze's spiky hair aside and his hot breath tickled Blaze's ear. 'I should be angry with you, but I understand it had to be her.'

'Get off me. What are you talking about?'

'The prophecy: ages of riddles boiled down to a single chance encounter – brilliant! Totally unpredictable!' Talon sounded genuine amused. He chuckled, causing his long braids to whip Blaze's shoulders. 'Asha's special amongst us,' he continued. 'Can you not see it?'

Blaze looked again at the circle of painted dolls surrounding the cage. They were virtually identical, dressed in black and lace. The only variations between them were minor differences in the way they dressed their hair, or in flashes of colour, like Jaku's neon blue sash. Eye colour, he wondered. Asha had such beautiful eyes.

'Let me give you a clue.' Talon took Blaze's hand and placed it over his crotch. Blaze recoiled at the feel of the other man's erection hard beneath his hand, but Talon held him firm. 'What do you feel?' he demanded.

'Nothing, let go.'

'Tell me what you feel.' Talon's blue eyes drowned him with their intensity. 'It's not a trick.'

'Your cock,' he spat.

'Exactly.' Talon released his hold. 'Exactly that.'

'She's the only woman,' he blurted, finally seeing what had been obvious from the start if he'd only opened his eyes and ignored the paint and the costumes. 'But the image, the nicknames, why?'

Talon laughed again, and this time it was bitter and sadistic. 'Well, it filters out most of the undesirable applicants.' His mouth stretched into a wide grin and his tongue played across his lips. 'Also, it amuses me to have them dress this way. Better this than hairy chests, hairy legs and the persistent stink of sweat and testosterone.'

'Like the idea of a cock nestled in panties, do you?' said Blaze.

Talon thrust his hand inside the back of Blaze's trousers again and pushed a finger into the channel between his cheeks. 'I think you know the answer to that already, pretty boy. And don't even imagine I'd find it an insult.'

Blaze pushed him away again. Far from wanting to smack him every time he touched him, Talon's touch sent fizzles of lust racing through his limbs. They kept saying youkai were all about sex, that it was how they controlled and manipulated everything. Nobody had ever mentioned that it rendered them constantly turned on. But then, nobody had ever spent much time talking to the youkai. The Talon just butchered them and everyone else lived in a state of perpetual fear of their arrival. Not that he was a demon. He wasn't!

He wanted to laugh but found himself shaking his head. How could he be their prince? He knew nothing about them, and their current leader had virtually ripped him apart. He guessed he could rationalize it as jealousy, but really, Venom had nothing to worry about. OK, so, he'd blown a few skeletons to smithereens and briefly grown a pair of wings, but now he was stuck in a Talon prison with a sadistic mastermind. No, the only person that needed to worry was him. 'I thought you wanted to talk,' he barked at Talon.

The slender man pursed his lips. 'You know, on seconds thoughts, I'm not so sure we need to. How about I just issue a statement?' He swept his braided hair back from his shoulders and raised his hand. 'One book,' the pamphlet appeared in his hand out of thin air, 'one prophecy and one fledgling demon prince. I trust you'll excuse me if I divert the course of history. You see if anyone's going to create a paradise of perversity on earth, it's going to be me, not some dull boy from the Birdcage. Which is why having you locked in a box is so delicious.' He leered at Blaze, who shook his head in disbelief.

'You're crazy.'

'Asha, come join us.' Talon held out his hand and pulled her through the bars of the cage, then one by one the lights in the hall went out, until they were standing beneath a lone blue spotlight. 'Why don't you taste him,' he sighed into her ear. 'I know you want to. You've been longing for his essence ever since you returned.' He let her dark hair fall through his fingers. 'I'm quite distraught by your abandonment.' He mocked sadness, then his lips thinned, and twisted into an evil sneer. 'But you'll give me a final gift, won't you, Asha?' He retreated to the opposite side of the cage and slouched with his back to the bars. 'Milk him for me. Make him mine.'

Blaze backed away, but there wasn't far he could go without circling round towards Talon, or pressing himself against the ensorcelled bars, and no matter how hard he pushed they wouldn't give to let him pass through the way they had for others.

Asha's face remained emotionless as she moved towards him. Only in the very depths of her eyes could he find any hint of human frailty. Was this the same woman he'd made frantic love to earlier, the same woman who'd licked his wounds clean, and who'd threatened to take his head if he really was a demon? 'Asha,' he whispered to her, but her expression remained vacant.

'His arms, Jaku,' said Talon.

Manacles snapped closed around his wrists and fastened him to the enchanted bars. He struggled, but all he could do was move up and down and kick.

Asha extended a hand towards the sigil on his chest. 'Don't touch me,' he snapped. He kicked out, trying to keep her away. Then he saw that the sigil blazing on his chest was also burnt into her palm.

What had happened in Maggot's shop, had he contaminated her in some way when he'd given in to his lust? He should have run as he'd intended too. Damn it! He'd been so stupid, and he had so many questions, but he could see there'd be no answers until Talon was done with his entertainment.

Their skin touched. The two sigils pressed together and glowed with an eerie orange light. It spread up across his chest and along Asha's arm, growing stronger as it travelled, and turning bronze, then green. The glow reached his loins and it felt as though he was sucked into readiness by a soft-mouthed whore. Before him, Asha was trembling. Her expression no longer empty but glazed with resignation and fear, and hopeless lustfulness. Had he really done this to her?

'Don't be so heartless,' Talon goaded. 'Can't you see the lady's gagging for it? You've got her into this state, it's only fit you slake her lust.'

'Let me,' she said, and she moved her hand to his fly. 'Let me give you pleasure.' Her fingernails traced shivery pathways down his thighs and she dropped to her knees. Blaze struggled awkwardly against the bars, pushing himself onto tiptoes to keep out of her reach, but her dainty hand wrapped firmly around his straining cock. Her lips encircled the head and drew him down deep.

He didn't want to respond. He wanted to be unmoved and deny Talon his pleasure, but he couldn't resist her skill, and nor could he forget it was her on her knees attending him. Asha – he wanted her. Longed to push inside her again and feel her body compelling him towards ecstasy. He closed his eyes, but the darkness didn't help, it just concentrated the sensation and made him ache for her. It left him too open to the whims of his imagination. His dreams had been so vivid recently he didn't think they were a safe place to go.

Instead, he forced himself to look across the cage at Talon, who was mirroring his position against the bars. The slender man was intently focused on the bobbing of Asha's head, so intently focused that his own hips followed her rhythm.

'Are you still there, Jaku?' Talon asked.

The demon-hunter appeared at the bars. 'My liege.'

Talon smirked at the title. 'Go help your partner.'

Jaku hesitated, looking both hurt and angry. The notion that he'd refuse to pleasure another man had never occurred to him. Still, his expression was bitter.

'For me, Jaku. For me. You'll get your reward later.'

'Truly?'

Talon beckoned him closer. 'Come.' He pushed his hand through the bars and closed it around the back of Jaku's head, then pulled him close and kissed him through the space between the bars. 'Now serve me well.'

Blaze followed Jaku's movement around the cage perimeter, until he vanished behind his back. 'Don't touch me,' he said when he felt Jaku's large hands snake across his hips.

'It brings me no pleasure, believe me.' He tugged Blaze's trousers down to his knees.

'But it'll bring you much, later,' said Talon.

Blaze's gaze flickered across to him. He was still mirroring his pose, only now he'd unfastened the fly of his trousers, so that his long straight cock was clearly visible. Like his slender hips, it too was inked with barbed thorns. The sight of that rearing shaft filled him with apprehension, but also caused a sharp peak of pleasure to tighten in his balls.

Asha's mouth still worked its magic.

He winced as Jaku's tongue stroked into the tender cleft between his buttocks, but his protest soon changed to a whimper of enjoyment. The gentle but insistent licking dabbed repetitively at his anal whorl, blowing away preconceptions of pain and distaste. It was exquisite agony, delicious in its very intensity. He rocked his hips, gave himself up to the sensations which assailed him front and back. 'Ah, yes,' he sighed. He couldn't fight any longer. The fever was in his blood. He wanted this too much. He needed to come like other people needed to scratch an itch. He couldn't resist. Fine, he'd come for Talon's bloody pleasure, if that's what he wanted. There was no shame in it on his part.

He looked across the cage again, but to his surprise, Talon was no longer there.

'Miss me?' said a voice behind him. He felt the press of a body against his back, where moments before he'd felt only the caress of metal bars. Something hot and hard, not Jaku's tongue, pushed insistently between his buttocks. The channel was wet and slippery and yielded easily to the pressure. Talon's cock slid in the wetness and prodded against his virgin hole.

'You can't be a youkai prince and be vanilla,' Talon hissed into his ear. 'Perversity is in their blood. So, let me initiate you by shedding my seed in your bowels.' Talon's fingers danced menacingly across Blaze's stomach. His body shifted, wiry steel flexing against Blaze's back.

Blaze tensed, but his cock fluttered in anticipation of what came next.

'Oh, fuck!' he moaned. There was no escape. He was

manacled and Asha had already rendered his balls high and heavy, with the dance of her tongue around his shaft. He was tingling with the need for release. The promise of more bittersweet sensations was too much to grasp. 'Don't,' he whimpered. His eyes filled with tears of confusion. The salt stung his eyes, but he refused to blink. Blinking would release the flood and no matter what, he wasn't going to cry. He wasn't going to give Talon that pleasure. Except, unable to wipe them away, he couldn't stop them falling.

Talon caught one precious droplet as it rolled down his cheek and licked it off his finger. 'Beautiful,' he sighed. He caught another. This he transferred to a goblet held by Jaku, which was already encrusted on the inside with a suspicious looking powder. 'Blood Rain,' Talon confirmed. 'Your demon essence, distilled from your wing wounds.' The tear hit the powder, causing a faint hiss as they combined. 'Just one more ingredient to collect. I don't think I'll have to wait long, do you?' He wriggled his hips and his cock nuzzled into Blaze's back passage. His flat belly tensed, but his cock leapt at the intrusion and wept tears of its own that Asha licked from the eye with eager flicks of her tongue. 'Yes,' she gasped around his shaft. There was a dark entreaty in her eyes. It goaded him to offer himself up to the pleasure presented, and to accept what came. She shifted on her knees and pulled her skirts from beneath them. Her hand moved below the hemline and came to rest between the apex of her thighs.

The image of her frantically frigging her clit as she sucked him was too much. He thrust deep into her mouth and pulled back, impaling himself on Talon's waiting cock, which squeezed past his tight sphincter, opening him and violating him. There was no pain, just an overwhelming sense of fullness and desperate urgency. Sensations flooded over him, as he penetrated and in turn was possessed. Every pulse of pleasure, every lick was magnified as Talon's cock slid smoothly in and out of his willing anus, until he was shaking and begging incoherently for more. More pleasure, more excess.

There was no blackout this time, no escape into that other realm, no darkling sky and eerie cacophony to save him, just here and now, sandwiched between Talon and Asha.

The sigil on his chest flared white hot, and writhed, as if a connection had been short-circuited but still sought a point of ignition.

Not even the sight of Asha's hand working frantically at her clit tipped him over. He'd never thought he'd long for the gaudy dreamscape. She came with a sharp cry, releasing him from her mouth in the process. Blaze's cock flexed urgently in the cold air, seeking warmth again, but she fell back and gave herself up to the fluttery joy.

The sensation in his rear grew sharper, now undiluted by the coaxing of her tongue upon his cock. Talon surged into him. With each thrust, it felt like he was pushing right through Blaze's arse and into his cock. There was no resisting his rhythm. It was overwhelming in its simple delight. Blaze's body jerked with pleasure. Words spilled incoherently from his tongue. 'Asha, suck me,' he begged as his cock twitched with increasing urgency.

His whole body flexed. He was going to come, all too aware of what was around him.

As he skirted closer and closer to the edge, Blaze's thoughts began to clarify. The last time he'd climaxed had been when everything changed. The spilling of his seed had brought clouds of agony and his wings. Would the next peak provide his one chance of freedom, or simply trap him in a small cell with a pair of feathery pinions. A bird in a cage.

Did he care?

'Asha!' Talon barked over his shoulder.

She rose onto her knees again immediately, still panting with the aftershocks of her own orgasm. Her lips closed over his glans again with a smile.

The first judder hit him, hard. His spine arched and he hit his head against Talon's brow. The other man grunted in annoyance and slapped his arse, but Blaze was already too far gone. He moaned and jerked helplessly as streamers of come pumped from his body onto Asha's waiting tongue, while he felt Talon come inside him.

He watched the pearlescent drops dribble down her chin.

'Ah, don't waste it!' Talon offered her the golden goblet, and she spat his semen into the effervescent mixture it contained. 'Excellent,' he said and he wiped his wet cock across Blaze's arse.

His head strangely clear, Blaze fought against the grip of the manacles. Asha pressed a hand to his thigh. She winked.

Blaze stared at her. For just a moment, her eyes seemed clear. 'Trust me,' she mouthed. Then the vacant expression was back. She rose, pressed her body close to his, and sought his lips. A drop of something cold hit his tongue. It was both sweet and sour. His eyes widened in shock.

'Let him be, you voracious harpy.' Talon pulled her off him. 'I have what I need. Come.' He pulled her through the bars again, which seemed to ripple as they passed.

Blaze held the liquid on his tongue, not daring to swallow, but at the last moment, her hand snagged around the chain of his pendant. It snapped. He swallowed automatically, and almost cried out, but then he remembered her words. 'Trust me.' It was his only option. His head felt cloudy.

'Don't fly off now, will you?' Talon joked. He loosened the manacles with a snap of his fingertips, then extended a hand towards a figure on the steps. 'Jaku.' He pulled the man to his side, leaving Asha stumbling behind them. 'Goodbye, Blaze Makaresh,' he called. 'Your execution is at dawn.'

Dawn. Dawn. If felt as if he'd been chasing the blasted sunrise all night.

Blaze sagged onto the cage floor, feeling drowsy. Hadn't the sun risen yet?

7 Force Change

Asha sat on the bottom step of the dais and watched Talon hurry away with Jaku. He was too preoccupied with his new demon-cordial to notice her hanging back. Too used to seeing her high on Blood Rain to realise that this time she was faking it. Oh, she'd certainly been woozy and sex crazed when they'd arrived back with Blaze, but that had worn off when she'd come. Now, he no longer controlled her. All the bonds were broken. This time, she really was leaving, and she was taking Blaze with her.

The remaining light blinked out once Talon left the hall. Still cautious, Asha rolled onto her stomach and slithered back up the steps to the top of the dais. She wasn't sure if he'd posted guards.

'Blaze.' She pushed her hand between the solid bars and clasped his foot. She felt him jump, then twist around to see her. His face pressed to the bars a little above hers. 'Did you swallow?' she asked.

He hesitated, sought her gaze, then nodded.

Asha sighed in relief. 'Good. A few minutes and you should be able to break out.'

'Hang on,' he hissed. He dragged his hand through bhis blond hair. 'What's going on? What have you given me?'

'Sometimes we have to be discreet. It's a test we use in the Heights, when clients want to check out potential lovers. It forces the change.'

He pulled back from the bars. 'Why? Are you crazy?' Accepting the truth was hard enough without transforming in the citadel of his enemy.

'Shhh!' she hissed frantically, waving him back to the bars. 'Not too loud. Changing now is the only thing that will keep you alive. I was with Talon while he went through the prophecy. He has no problem reading that stuff. Not all the parts have been fulfilled yet, if they had you'd be able to change at will. Your pendant,' she held the snapped chain up to him, but pulled it out of reach when he tried to grab it. 'It's an inhibitor. Am I right, you've worn it since birth?'

Blaze nodded. 'I told you, it's my one connection to my family.'

'Oh, Blaze. It's far more than that. It's how your ancestors have kept their bloodline hidden. This would all have happened the first time you had sex if you hadn't been wearing that thing. Your grandmother knew. She has trying to keep you safe. You're powerless while you're wearing it. I reckon Venom knew, that's why he attacked.'

'So you're saying I'd have been youkai all along except for that?'

Asha reached out to him and squeezed his wrist. 'You're not a demon. You're a good man.'

'Is that how you rationalise it?'

'Let's not argue now, there's no time. Talon doesn't just want to kill you. He's planning to usurp you. All this,' she spread her arm out to encompass the room, 'it's not enough anymore. He wants absolute control of the City, the Heights, everything. He doesn't see why he can't divert the prophecy a little and rewrite it as Talon rule instead of Demon rule. That's why he wanted your essence.'

Blaze pressed forward again and grasped the bars with both hands, causing the metal to glint and spark. 'I don't want to rule anything, Asha.'

'I know,' she reassured him, also rising from her knees. 'I've got a plan, but first we need to get out of the cathedral. I'm sorry I brought you here, but Jaku left me no choice. He'd have killed you there and then if I hadn't agreed. Perhaps me also. He's convinced I'm tainted.' She rubbed at her hand.

Blaze lifted his hand to his neck and traced the tender lump where Jaku had jabbed him earlier. 'Poison,' she said. 'His speciality.'

Blaze nodded and wrenched the bars again, causing another shower of sparks. 'How much longer do we have to wait for this force change thing to work?'

Asha shrugged. 'A few seconds.' She'd barely finished speaking before his eyes rolled back into his skull, and his skin began to stretch.

She'd seen youkai transform before, but it had never been this personal. His bones shifted, tendons bulged, then the lines of colour on his back seemed to lift off the skin and solidify into bone and feathers.

'Blaze, are you all right?' she asked when his shape stabilised. She touched the edge of one of the feathers and he shivered in response.

'Careful.' He flexed them as much as the cramped space would allow. 'That feels a little too good. Do it too often and all I'll care about is having you here on the floor.'

She pulled her hand back. 'Can you break out?'

'Stand back.'

She'd expected him to bend the bars again, but instead he simply knelt in the centre of the cell with his hands pressed to his head as if to prevent his skull cracking open.

The ward splintered slowly. Fracture lines ran up the bars, like cracks in a glacier. Slivers popped out and fizzed as they burned up. Finally, the whole cage shattered and dispersed in an explosion of deafening fireworks.

The hall doors immediately swung inwards, admitting scores of black-clad guards. She'd been right. Talon hadn't trusted the cage alone to hold him.

She grabbed Blaze's hand and tugged him towards the cathedral's great door, hoping to flee down the steps onto the concourse outside and cross the canal, but Blaze stopped running a few paces from the dais.

'No, not that way.' A row of Talon's dolls already formed a defensive wall of pole-arms they'd never cross. He wrapped an arm around her middle and sprang skywards. For a moment, she thought they would simply fall, then his wings spread wide and began to beat. They soared upwards to the rafters. Shouts of alarm and dismay followed them. Someone loosed an arrow. It zipped past, but others were lining up to take shots.

Blaze dived towards the circular stained glass window high above the great door. 'Brace yourself,' he shouted. 'We're going through.'

He was copying Venom, she realised, wishing for a second that he hadn't seen the winged youkai's descent into the archive earlier that night, but their passage through the glass was less destructive. Blaze shattered a single rose-tinted pane with his thoughts, and they were out.

Asha stared at Blaze in wonderment. His abilities were strengthening, becoming increasingly refined. How long before his humanity fell away and he transformed into the monster he was destined to become? She knew Talon planned to change things, but he hadn't bargained on Blaze still being alive.

He'd be after them soon. Already the rest of the dolls were pouring down the cathedral steps.

Blaze swept high over the white marble plaza, borne on the dawn breeze.

Asha clasped him tightly around the waist, trying not to get in the way of the beating wings that fanned air across her face. The world below seemed scaled down to the size of a child's model. They hovered above the quayside, where the streetlights still glowed like strands of faerie lights.

'Where to now?' Blaze asked. The first rays of the morning sun caught in his blond hair, bleaching it snowy-white. He laughed. 'This is fun.'

'Don't get carried away,' she warned, although his smile was infectious. Asha closed her eyes as he swooped over the rooftops of the Cathedral Quarter, feeling distinctly queasy. She had a plan, but how much of it should she reveal? What if she told him and he didn't consent? She wouldn't 'persuade' him alone.

'The Sidings off Steepleside,' she said, her decision made. She chewed her lips as they followed the blue-black ribbon of the canal to the north. She wasn't going to explain, she was just going to go ahead and do. Suki would help. Blaze might still be gentle and beautiful now, but it wouldn't last, and the youkai were an abomination not meant for this world. She had to act before he led them straight into the Second Age of Darkness.

The pendant alone wasn't enough to keep him stable. She clasped it tight within her hand. It was too easily removed, or lost. Venom had proved that when he'd torn it from Blaze's neck and let it fall onto the street where the dead had picked it up, and promptly bartered it with Talon for she dreaded to think what.

Regardless, this was the only way. She had to mark Blaze with the symbol in a more permanent fashion.

The Sidings were deserted as they swooped across the weed-strewn cobbles towards the rusty humped back of the former engine sheds. Suki's workshop was the last on the right, just a few steps from the blackened shell of the former station. There'd been no trains for years, what little traffic left the City now went out of the Heights. Asha glanced warily at the line of old carriages that stood halfway down the platform. There were too many rumours about this place for her to feel comfortable. They'd had too many run-ins with the youkai out here. She tried several times to get Suki to move, but the rent was cheap, and out here, she was away from Talon's clutches.

Blaze glanced about nervously, his black angel's wings fanning slowly behind them. She almost reached out to touch the ebony feathers, then remembered what he'd said about them being sensitive. Maybe that piece of knowledge would come in useful. She wondered if it was true for all demons.

'Isn't this youkai central?' he asked.

A crazy part of her wanted to laugh at him. Why worry about the youkai when you were destined to become their prince?

'We're not stopping long.' She grabbed his hand and tugged him across the yard. Blaze found himself a flat piece of stone to stand on while she rapped on the door. The long toes of his bare feet curled slightly against the concrete as they waited for a response.

Boots! She'd forgotten all about them. Really, her escape plan had been terrible. It was a miracle they'd actually got out.

The sound of bolts being drawn drew her attention back to the door. It opened a fraction then shut again.

'Suki.' Asha hammered on the steel. 'I need a favour.'

The door opened again, revealing a tiny sprite of a woman with cropped pink hair that was matted and stuck up at angles. Last night's make-up was still smudged across her face. 'That's normally what you come for. You're not one to drop round for coffee.'

She turned her head, saw Blaze and blinked. 'You've changed partners and sides by the look of it.'

'Looks are deceiving.' Asha pushed her way into the building, forcing her friend to back down the corridor.

'Please tell me he doesn't have wings.' Suki rubbed at her mascara-encrusted eyelashes.

'Sorry.' Asha pulled Blaze inside and shut the door. She then shoved him into the kitchen, and marched Suki into the workroom.

'Is he ... youkai?' Her friend edged nervously up against the leather dentist chair in the centre of the room.

'It's complicated and I don't have time. Can you tattoo him for me?'

'What! Are you marking them now instead of killing them? Has Talon completely lost his grip on reality?'

'Blaze is a special case. He's human. If we mark him with this symbol,' she thrust the pendant towards Suki, 'we can stop the curse, and prevent him becoming one of them.'

'Right...' Suki drawled although she accepted the pendant, even held it aloft so that it caught the light. 'Look, I'm not being funny, but are you sure about this, and doesn't he need to be in human form before I do this?'

Asha pinched the bridge of her nose, suddenly incredibly tired. She'd had too much sex and no sleep. The weariness was slowly creeping along her limbs.

'Please, Suki. You're my last hope. Jaku's deserted me. He's off playing at being Talon's whore or something.'

'I thought that was your role.'

'I quit.'

A grin spread across Suki's face. 'About bloody time.' The smile twisted into a grimace. 'Ah ... I get it. You're running. OK.' She scrunched a handful of pink hair. 'Lose the wings and I'll do it.'

Asha hurried back towards the kitchen. She kept forgetting he couldn't shift at will like other youkai.

'Do you have a pill that does it?' Suki whispered. 'I know you have stuff that makes them show their true forms.'

Asha shook her head. 'No, I've never needed one. Normally if they grow wings, I just hack their heads off.' She looked at Suki. 'Not an option today. I want him to survive.'

Suki raised her hands. 'Hey, I'm sure you've got it all worked out.'

Asha scowled.

OK, so what's worked before?'

She shrugged. 'Last time they just sort of disappeared of their own accord.'

'Like the spell wore off or something?'

'Or something. But we don't have time to sit around. I need to get this done and get out of here before the rest of the crew show up.' She sucked her lower lip into her mouth and bowed her head. Her only clue was that his transformations seemed to be triggered by sex.

Sex – the youkai calling card. It made sense, given everything that had happened and the urgency with which Talon had pressed the pendant upon him.

Asha grasped the door handle and took a deep breath 'OK, cunning plan number one. Fuck him until his wings fall off.'

Blaze stumbled about the gloomy kitchen in search of a lamp or a light switch. He didn't know what Asha was up to, but he knew he didn't care for being left in the dark in either sense of the word. He was half tempted to sneak back into the hall and eavesdrop, half tempted to simply take off. What stopped him was his rumbling stomach. When had he last eaten? He vaguely recalled dunking a biscuit into the sugary tea Asha had forced on him back in the archive. Before that, he couldn't recall.

Eventually he found food, a meagre choice of bread, cheese and half-plucked poultry. He ate the bread without thinking, then picked at the bird. Why couldn't they have flown straight out of the City? Talon wouldn't follow them into the wastelands. The only people who went there were the merchants, and they had the sense to travel in convoy, and only as far as Kazra. He had no idea where the shuttles out of the Heights went, maybe some idyllic paradise.

'Come on, Asha,' he mumbled between mouthfuls. He wanted to go outside again, flex his wings and soar on the breeze.

Blaze found a chair, but the wings made it difficult to sit, so he leant against the pan rack instead, and poked at his new appendages in curiosity. He brushed a finger along the tips of his feathers as Asha had done in the cathedral. Delight shivered through his body in response, just as it had when she'd done it. He did it again and pleasure knotted in his groin. Enough of that, or he'd be shooting in his pants.

The kitchen door opened, casting a beam of light across the floor. Asha froze barely over the threshold. Her heavily made-up eyes widened in alarm. 'What are you doing?' She sprinted towards him and snatched the bird from his hands. From between her breasts, she produced a black handkerchief and wiped his mouth. 'Shit, shit, shit! What are you thinking? You're eating raw fucking meat.'

Blaze warded her off and wiped his mouth with the back of his hand. It came away bloody. Strangely, he didn't feel reviled by the sight. He licked his fingers.

'I thought you said he was human.' the pink pixie sidled into the room behind Asha carrying a lantern.

'He is.'

'Barely. I've seen gargoyles with more manners.'

Asha clasped his hands and pulled them away from his lips. 'Do you trust me, Blaze?'

The question made him suspicious, resentful. They'd been through enough together.

'Should I?'

Asha wet her lips. 'Yes.' She entwined her fingers with his. 'Come next door.'

He let her lead him, but followed warily.

The workroom was part dentist's, part art studio. He wasn't sure what he was seeing at first, until Suki picked up a slender bamboo stylus.

'Why are we here?' Between the sigil and the wings, he really didn't need further decoration.

On the periphery of his vision, he saw Suki move. Something light swung in her grasp. His focus seemed to shift of its own accord, and zoom in on the swinging chain – his pendant.

The ink, the persuasion, all the unspoken words suddenly made sense. 'No!' He shoved Asha away. 'No!' He wouldn't lie still and let her bind him. His skin crawled at the thought of being trapped in only one form, though he barely had any concept of being anything else.

Asha extended a hand to soothe him, but when he batted it away, she curled her fingers into his biceps instead. While he struggled, her other hand clasped the leather around his waist. They wrestled like pit fighters, neither willing to let go. He tried to sweep her leg, but ended up wrong footing himself. He might be stronger, but she was swift and trained as a killer, and didn't have a set of wings she wasn't used to.

Asha locked his arm. 'Be still or I'll knock you out.'

Be still! He almost laughed. He wasn't just some boy out of the Birdcage anymore, he was a youkai prince, and he wasn't bound by the physical.

His head throbbed as he concentrated his energies.

Asha yelped. Her grasp slackened then fell away altogether. Blaze turned to find blood pouring from her nose and fear in her eyes. 'This isn't you.' She shook her head, a palm pressed to her bleeding nose.

He reached out to touch her, his emotions in turmoil. He didn't like to see her hurt and know that he was the cause, but at the same time, she was acting as his enemy. 'Don't push me,' he hissed. His gaze fixed on the bright red river flowing down her arm. The urge to lick it from her skin was too strong. Blaze bent and drew his tongue along her arm. The taste was cloying and sweet. He wanted more – a taste of her flesh. The urge to bite almost overwhelmed him.

A shadow streaked across the wall. Blaze raised his arms, but Suki jumped onto his back. She plucked two fistfuls of feathers from his wings, while fighting for purchase.

It should have hurt, but instead of pain, pleasure lanced along his spine like savage lightning. Each rough stroke, each tear of her nails brought trance inducing ecstasy. He'd never felt the like. Desire pulsed through him. Every feather stood erect. He closed his eyes with the intensity of it, forgetting Asha and her blood streaked face.

'I don't know what you're doing, but keep doing it,' Asha hissed.

'Please,' he whimpered. It wasn't a plea for mercy. This was clearly the reason the youkai rarely showed their wings. It made them too vulnerable. You couldn't function like this, at the mercy of your body's pleasure response, a little rough play capable of shattering rational thought. Suki was playing him like a harp.

Blaze's mouth fell slack, while his throat tightened around squeals of bliss. It was as if he'd grown a hundred cocks and each was being fellated. His actual cock was as erect as his wings.

Despite Suki clawing at his back, Blaze rubbed himself against Asha. He backed her against the wall and pressed his tongue deep into her mouth. The kiss tasted of her blood, thick and familiar, and salty. Good.

She clawed at his arms, but the bite of her nails only added to the pleasure he felt at having his wings tugged.

He jammed a hand between their bodies and loosened his fly. His cock sprang free, arching towards her as if seeking a home. However, pressing it against her wasn't enough.

Blaze fumbled with her skirts. There was blood running freely down his arms where she'd scratched him.

Her thighs were sticky with sweat and arousal. He ripped through her lacy knickers and wet his fingers in the heat of her sex. Asha whimpered beneath him as he jammed two fingers into her and used his thumb to work her clit.

Seeing her jerk and open for him still wasn't enough. His lips felt bee stung with need. He needed to taste her, devour her. Only by doing so, would he reach his true youkai form.

The sigil smouldered against his skin.

'Don't deny me. Open for me.' He nudged Asha's thighs apart with his knee and added a third finger to the two already twisting in and out of her hole.

'Blaze, no,' she sobbed. 'We don't have time for this. We need to act before it's too late.'

'Nonsense.' He pulled his fingers free of her pussy, with a sticky pop, and pushed them into her mouth instead to silence her protests.

Asha sucked at them, her tongue curved around his finger. Her eyes were wide with fear and longing. 'Asha,' he moaned. 'Don't deny me.' He pulled his fingers out slowly. She didn't scream, just looked at him, her dark eyes wild with terror.

Blaze loosened the hooks of her blouse and pulled the edges apart to reveal the skin of her throat. A delicate film of sweat gleamed across the surface of her bust, pushed into plumpness by her bodice. He licked a line across the plump swell, then scooped one globe from her bodice and sucked the nipple deep into his mouth.

'Ah,' she squealed, falling back against the support of the wall, her breathing light and rapid. Her head twisted from side to side, causing her long hair to cascade across her breasts in ebony waves. He teased the nipple with his teeth, desperate to bite, and even more eager to get inside her.

Blaze let his trousers drop. He hitched up her skirt to her waist, and with barely a wiggle, his cock butted between her thighs and into her vulva.

She gave a hoarse gasp as he gave her his length.

Blaze dug his fingers into her thighs. He hitched one up around his hip, so he could slide in and out more smoothly. He fucked her with long punishing jerks of his hips that made her whole body shake and brought his orgasm on fast.

Suki still tugged at his back. Blaze revelled in the overload of pleasurable sensations. Fireworks traversed his back with flighty fingers, jets of pleasure shot forward into his cock. His orgasm tightened like a fist clenched inside him.

Asha sobbed her orgasm into his shoulder as he sucked hard at her neck aiming to bruise. She continued to whimper as the muscles of her sex sucked him deeper. He looked her in the eyes, seeing right into the depths of her green gaze as she panted and shook. Her orgasm reduced to weak erratic shudders, she crushed her head against his jerking shoulder.

The surprise of her teeth, sharp against his neck, stole his breath. His climax swelled, and burst like a nova.

'Oh, yes!' His legs buckled, even as his cock still pulsed. He collapsed onto his knees, cock shiny with ejaculate.

Asha stroked a hand through his hair.

Behind him, Suki shrieked. He felt her jerk away from his body and turned to see what was causing her alarm.

She was standing holding handfuls of his feathers, which she dropped the moment their eyes met. There were more feathers on the floor behind him, and more still falling. His wings were exposed to their white gleaming bones, which crumbled even as he watched, leaving behind an inky impression across his back and a fine white powder on the floor.

Enraged, he turned back to Asha, an accusation already on his lips. She'd known, or suspected. Screwing him had been part of the plan all along.

Her eyes were wide and bright. 'I'm sorry,' she said, right before toppling him backwards onto the floor with the weight of her body. She straddled his head, pinned his arms, and muffled his curses with her sex.

The remains of her lacy knickers pressed against his mouth and nose, silenced him as effectively as a gag. The lack of oxygen made his thoughts fuzzy. He couldn't focus his mind. Another figure straddled his legs. Suki's fingers danced over his stomach like icicles, if icicles could be hot, as well as cold.

The first needle bit into his skin. After that, it punctured him in an endlessly repetitive motion, until the angular jabs and sweep of the ink brush blended into one numb ache. Each time he struggled, Asha pressed down more firmly over his mouth and nose restricting his air supply. The only way to get her to rise again was to work his tongue against her swollen clit.

'Hurry,' she harried Suki. 'It doesn't need to be artistic, just accurate.'

'Do you want to do it?'

He felt Asha shaking her head.

'Right, then let me do my thing. It's not a quick job, it's intricate.'

Time lost its meaning after that. He struggled, fought for breath and licked again. Eventually, Asha came. It was still several steady ticks of the clock before she rose to her feet.

Blaze sat abruptly, feeling woozy, his face smeared with her pussy juice, and his lower abdomen bloody. A layer of white gauze covered the tattoo, but couldn't quite hide the swirls of ink beneath. Suki was cleaning her tools.

'I'm sorry,' Asha said, hardly daring to meet his gaze. She extended a hand towards him. Blaze ignored it. Anger burned in his veins, animal and vengeful, but when he saw her bite her lip, his rage seemed to evaporate.

He was in his own skin, his own mind, and he wasn't

craving flesh and blood. The marks he'd left around her neck were already livid. Blaze stretched out his hand and clasped hers. 'Thank you.'

Instead of pulling him up, she straddled his lap and smothered him. Blaze pushed her back a fraction to look at her face. Tears glittered in her eyelashes. He kissed them away, feeling strangely passive, content to remain in her embrace. His lips found hers and they kissed long and deep. It felt like a first kiss, fluttery and full of promise, but there was a bitter sting laced in with the sweetness.

'Sorry to break it up,' Suki interrupted. She faced them twirling a stylus between her ink-stained fingertips. 'But how long are you planning on sticking around, and what am I supposed to do with all these feathers?'

'Sell them as quills,' suggested Asha.

'Turn them into a demon duvet.' Blaze yawned. 'Then you can sleep under me.' His gaze fixed firmly on Asha, who pursed her lips.

Suki gaze a loud tut. 'I'm going to make some drinks.' She reached the hall just as the hammering started.

'Time's up.' Asha leapt to her feet and tugged Blaze onto his.

'Out.' Suki hissed. 'Up the stairs.'

They scrambled out of the skylight in the bedroom onto the corrugated roof.

'This way.' The sidings were crawling with Talon's dolls. 'Fuck!' Asha whisked him towards the back of the building. 'We'll make for the tunnels. It's our only hope.'

8 Subway Shuffle

At the rear of the building, they slid down onto the back of a decrepit coalbunker. There was no sign of anyone else. Talon had probably guessed at her whereabouts from the direction of their flight. He was taking a big risk bringing such a large group out here. If there were any youkai around here, they'd be out within seconds to defend their territory.

She rather hoped they would fight, then maybe they could sneak away unobserved.

The ground at the back of the sidings was all rolling wasteland, pitted with rubble and brambles. No way she could drag Blaze across it barefoot. He was struggling enough on concrete. The platform was the only option.

'We've got to run for it.' She took Blaze's hand and gave it a squeeze. He looked shattered, in need of bed rest and a few square meals. As well as the blood, he now had coal dust smeared up his arms.

'Sure.' He rubbed his nose leaving a dirty smear.

Asha wet her thumb and wiped it off. 'OK, just keep heading for the tunnel and don't stop no matter what. If we get through there, I don't think they'll follow us. The wasteland's too dangerous.' She deliberately stopped herself thinking about what that meant for them. They'd work something out.

They slipped through the shadows as far as the platform without incident. The old station buildings still smelled of charred wood. Candy wrappers and windborne weeds chased across the tarmac as they ran for the tunnel.

'Halt!'

'Just keep running,' Asha gasped.

The tunnel was pitch-black just a few yards into its maw. She stuck to the railway lines, but soon found the way blocked by a carriage. Blaze caught up with her. 'Climb up.' He scuttled up onto the couplings and tried the door. It gave without much effort. 'Come on.' He stretched a hand out towards her and pulled her up.

'Let me.' Asha pushed ahead, leading with her sword arm. She'd managed to re-equip at the cathedral.

A light flickered on overhead, as if the carriage had sensed their presence and was trying to make them welcome. The interior was a gaudy mix of purple checks and orange gingham. Once it might have been plush, now it was threadbare and streaked with mould, an unloved relic of a former age.

More lights blinked on as they sprinted along the central aisle. The glass door at the end squeaked aside ahead of their arrival, revealing another identical carriage and the promise of more beyond.

She counted off another three while her ears strained for the sound of pursuit. They never made it as far as the fifth.

The door ahead swooshed open when they were still in the middle of the carriage. Asha stopped short, panting for breath and sensing danger. 'Blaze,' she whispered, and glanced back at him. He had his hand pushed inside his waistband, obviously trying to stop it chafing the fragile surface of the tattoo. Two spots of raw colour streaked his cheekbones. 'Take my knife.'

She felt him ease it from its sheath. She didn't know how good he'd be in a fight, but it looked more threatening than being unarmed.

Slowly, cautiously, they advanced again, when the enemy revealed himself, Asha gasped. It was not Talon as she'd expected, or even her former partner, but the corrupt vision of Venom's youkai hide. His eyes stretched in diagonal slits, from a slender pointy nose to almost the base of his eyebrows. Coloured blotches ran from that same pointy nose into his hairline at the centre of an impressive widow's peak, like the diamond marking of a snake.

He immediately dropped to one knee with his head bowed. 'My prince. This way.' He gestured to the carriage beyond.

'No! Don't trust him.' Asha's free hand closed hard around Blaze's wrist. 'You're not one of them.'

Venom looked up at them from under his scaly eyebrows. 'He's not one of you either, Talon witch.' The bright green of his eyes glittered with a luminescent flare. 'Do you really think you can thwart destiny? Your arrogance truly knows no bounds.'

Blaze strained to see around her, but Asha pushed him firmly back. Venom laughed. 'Come.' He rose to his feet. 'It's your only choice if you want to live.' He was staring over their shoulders at the door they'd just passed through. Asha turned sharply. Talon was standing in the doorway.

A low-level chatter gnawed inside his skull. Blaze clutched the metal ears of the nearest chair back. He didn't know whom to trust. There was a blond vision of sadism behind him and the youkai who'd nearly killed him ahead.

'Venom,' he hissed.

'My liege.' The sibilant words of his subject echoed inside his aching head. His vision blurred. When his focus returned, they were standing above the town. The sky was black and ash swirled in the air like snow. Above, the moon lay full, behind a red filter. 'The Blood Moon,' Venom's voice confirmed. 'It rises just once in an aeon. It awaits your ascension.'

The sigil on his chest smouldered until the smell of

burning flesh made him claw at it in anger. He felt his
sinews stretch and pop beneath his skin, but his wings
couldn't break through.

'The witch, what has she done to you?' Venom's rage
lanced through his cranium.

What had she done?

Venom wrenched at his trousers, laying bare the
tender surface of the tattoo. 'No!' He ripped a claw
through the skin. 'She won't prevent it. The Blood Moon
comes.'

Blaze screamed. Venom's words echoed in his head.
The Blood Moon. The Blood Moon. There was a blur of
motion beside him. He was still on the train, pinned
against the chair by Asha's slender frame. He didn't
know what had happened in his absence but the front
of her dress was torn, so that her right leg was exposed
from ankle to mid-thigh. Both Venom and Talon had
closed in on them. Asha was holding them at bay with
her sword and its metal sheath, one either side. They
appeared to have reached a stalemate, neither of them
prepared to make the next move.

'Asha, my treasure,' Talon's whispered persuasively.
The same voice he'd used to control her back in the
cathedral. 'Deliver him unto me.' Blaze felt her stiffen.

'Stay back.' She tilted her chin upwards, her jaw set in
a determined frown.

Venom also edged a fraction closer. 'My prince,' he
begged. Blaze felt himself pulled in by the words and his
low husky tone. When his stomach muscles twitched, he
knew that had not Asha interfered with his destiny and
had Suki brand him with ink, then he'd have flown to
the demon's side without hesitation. Even now, it was a
struggle just to remain still. The demon blood sang in his
veins.

Blaze searched the carriage for an escape route. The
window behind him consisted of two panes of solid
glass. He doubted it would break. The door behind

Venom swished open. Jaku crept across the threshold silent as death. While they'd been stuck here, he'd obviously found a way to sneak around outside. He was dressed in vivid scarlet brocade overlaid with shimmering netting that captured the light, which then scintillated amongst a thousand beads. Clearly, his new status as chief concubine had demanded something more showy.

Jaku levelled his glaive like a battering ram. His mouth set in a thin resolute moue. Then he charged.

It was no more than six paces from the door to Venom's back, but time seemed to slow inexplicably as Blaze watched Jaku sprint. At the very last moment, Venom seemed to sense the danger and twisted upon the spot. He put his hands out, but too late. Jaku ploughed straight into him, ramming the glaive home and forcing him backwards off his feet.

Lightning fast, Asha shoved Blaze into the seats. He cracked his head against the window and landed on the purple plush, causing a plume of choking mould spores to puff into the air.

Talon was not so quick as Asha. Venom toppled onto him, still driven by Jaku's rage, causing him to stagger under the combined weight of the two men.

Metal scraped gratingly against other metal. Magic flared and dissipated in a kaleidoscopic shower of sparks. Blaze rolled beneath the table clutching his ears, to block out the din of power and rage. A war of words in the ancient tongue spilled into the present. The magic alive: writhing, gasping and hungry lit the carriage like a beacon. Venom cursed. Talon's words scarred the air with lines of fire.

Then total, annihilating silence.

The three men dropped to their knees almost level with the table. The mould spores slowly drifted downwards, turning the air a hazy shade of pink.

Jaku inhaled a deep lungful and fell coughing to the

floor, his hands clutched to his lace-covered throat. He lay choking and twitching, his eyes streaming. Unaffected by the spores, Venom clutched his stomach where the glaive pierced him front to back. He stared at Blaze, the viridian light slowly departing from his eyes. 'I would have served you, my liege.' His solid form frayed. He shimmered, and then crumbled into heaps of coppery dust. Blaze extended a hand but he was already gone.

Talon, apparently also immune to the spores, sat back on his haunches. For a moment, he seemed victorious, then he opened his mouth and blood welled from his throat. Five deep wounds punctured his chest and throat from the demon's cruel talons. 'Asha,' he gurgled, barely audible. His hand locked around her ankle. 'Give me your strength.' His eyes rolled into his head.

Asha's arm flopped limply, punching Blaze into alertness. As she faded, Talon's wounds began to knit. Dancing lights flickered across his skin, like a circus of fireflies. He was stealing her strength, using her life-force to replenish his own.

Blaze launched himself from beneath the table. 'No! Leave her!' He snatched Jaku's glaive from Venom's powdered remains, and stabbed downwards with all his strength. The point bit deep. Talon howled in protest, but there were no charms or runes marked upon his flesh left to save him. His eyes opened wide and shone accusingly at Blaze.

'You won't win, Blaze Makaresh.' His words rattled hollowly. He was already a cipher of death.

Blaze released the pole-arm from his grasp, and numbly watched the glitter-glow fade from Talon's skin. When the last blinked out, his sucking breaths rasped no more. He felt no sorrow or elation, just an empty numbness, as if he'd cut away part of his soul.

Asha's hand closed around his wrist. She still lay sprawled across the table, but she'd managed to turn herself around. Whatever Talon had done had taken its toll. She looked almost corpse-like under the sharp electric glare, her skin sallow and clammy. He felt a wave of hatred. Briefly, his anger overwhelmed him and he kicked at Talon's body. Ending his life wasn't enough. He wanted to undo his very existence.

'Blaze.' Her voice washed over him like a soft balm, it salved the pain he barely realised he felt. She swung herself into a sitting position, and gingerly lowered her feet onto the floor. It took effort to stand. He saw her wobble, but with steely determination she summoned her will. 'There's no time to linger.' He noticed she avoided knocking the fixtures, presumably for fear of releasing another plume of noxious spores. Her gaze rested on Talon. No hint of sadness or remorse showed in her face. The mask was firmly back in place. 'Come.'

Taking his hand, she led him past Jaku, incapacitated by choking, his eyes shining with hatred. He felt her hesitate, but only for a moment.

They found a way out onto the rail track at the head of the train, and fled deep into the tunnel. His limbs felt weary and stretched. The adrenaline haze was gone, and the future looked bleak, but he held her hand tight, felt her warmth and believed.

Epilogue

The overhead light blinked on and off. On the carriage floor, something stirred amidst the silence of death. Talon opened his eyes.

There was no sign of his former lover and her new pet, or of his new one, and not even a trace of coppery dust on the carpet, although the weapon that had ended Venom's life remained.

Talon stood and his dark reflection peered back at him from the window. His blond hair hung loose from its braids and blood matted the ends, turning the golden strands red. He leant closer to the glass. His eyes had changed too. He couldn't determine their colour, but their shape was more elongated, and the pupils slit like a cat's.

He remembered dying!

Had his alchemy saved him, the runes that scarred his body or the magic he'd woven with Blaze's essence?

He stretched and two snowy wings fanned from his back. Venom's blood stirred in his veins. He wasn't revived. He was reborn. Reborn for a purpose.

He remembered the Blood Moon.

The city would fall to him tonight.

Falling Dancer

Anne Tourney

1

The first few days after a Release feel like coming home from a holiday in hell. You wander around your apartment, blinking at your furniture, and your furniture blinks back at you, stunned and light-bleached. You suck down black coffee, but caffeine can't jolt your nerves out of their numbness. The bliss of having your body back makes you treat yourself like a newborn baby, coddling yourself, cocooning yourself in quilts. When your cat whisks against your calves, your skin screams at the feathery contact. You ache in that deep, throbbing core between your legs the way you would after a three-day sex binge.

You tell yourself for the thousandth time that you will never, ever do this again.

Last night's Release just about killed me. The lost spirit tore through me with a need so monstrous that it left me crumpled up on the floor of an abandoned department store, whimpering and shaking, the aftermath shuddering through bone and muscle, through heart and brain. When it was over, I led the poor girl out of the maze of smashed display cases and mannequin parts, back to the apartment where I left her in her roommates' care. I was sceptical about whether a couple of strung-out anorexics could nurse their semi-conscious friend back to health, but I had no desire to take in another stray. These days it's all I can do to take care of myself.

I call myself an exorcist. I'm really more like a co-dependent for fallen angels.

In a hungover trance, I stir salt into my coffee instead of sugar. I drink it anyway. The milky morning light makes everything look faintly blessed, even the stack of porn DVDs on my TV set. Those movies are reminders of my last bout with celibacy, when I swore I'd never screw up another guy's head by asking him to believe in things that only the damned should comprehend.

The only trace of my last job is the black backpack that I shrugged off in the middle of the floor thirteen hours ago. The pack holds my kit: a knife, a chalice, a few sacred books, a vial of water that I hope is still holy. Cheesy stage props, for the most part, but they work on some of the older Fallen Ones, and the mortals find them damn convincing. Later I'll have my librarian buddy Max get the stuff blessed again, the way a businessman gets his suits dry-cleaned after a conference, but for now I don't want to lay eyes or hands on that crap.

The toaster is the only reflecting surface in my apartment. I use it as a mirror to put on my make-up while I suck down the last of my saltwater coffee. My hair looks like an electrocuted raven's feathers, and the white tufts around my temples are starting to show – I make a mental note to set up an appointment at the salon. Premature white is an occupational hazard; I keep my colourist busy. My shift at the bar starts at seven, but fortunately the place is only a few blocks from my apartment. Walking in fresh air wakes me up a bit, but I'm still groggy as I dig around in my purse for the keys to the dive.

The Ofice is affectionately known by its regulars as the 'Office' or, better yet, 'The Orifice'. A gaggle of night staff from Saint Stephen's is already waiting outside, smoking in their scrubs, swapping stories about last night's freak show at the ER. The guy who presented with an apple lodged in his ass – did he hook up with Eve last night and think he'd find the Garden of Eden in his rectum? And that redhead who came in by bus, all wild-eyed and screaming, what a hottie! They gave her enough Haldol to tranquilise an elephant, but it still couldn't knock her out.

With a shift in the light, the nurses become bird-human hybrids, vultures with human heads, straight from a Hieronymous Bosch triptych. The cackle and caw of a world I wish I didn't know so well fills the air. The cries of relief begin before I can open the door.

'Kelda! Yo, Kel!'

'About time you showed your cute arse around here.'

'Need vodka – stat.'

I'm twenty minutes late, but the gang doesn't give me too much shit. I've poured them all a few free screwdrivers and Bloody Marys in my day. Refusing to look at anyone until I'm safely within dim light, I unlock the door, and the nurses file in like obedient schoolchildren after a fire drill. The Ofice (one of the customers told me that the name means 'Snakepit' in Greek, and I've never doubted the appropriateness of that), is dark inside, and smells of cigarette smoke ineffectively masked with Pine-sol.

The crowd assume their usual posts at the bar, except for one of the ER docs. Sander hangs back with me, a tall form in jeans and a white T-shirt, hair still damp; he's the only one who bothered to take a shower before they flocked over here. I wonder, as I inhale the clean smell of him – not just clean skin, but a clean soul – if I should feel flattered by his effort at hygiene. Though Sander doesn't have Speak, he's clear enough to see through. He would say it's the purity of science, but it feels more like a mask hiding the face of innocence, to me.

'Interesting case last night, the redhead,' Sander begins.

Sander never makes small talk or offers backstory; he just dives in as if our exchanges were one long, private conversation held in bed after a long night. Whenever he does this, a patch of skin between my breasts tingles like the imprint of a kiss.

'Really? What happened?'

I'm still digging around in my bag, pretending to look for my cash register keys, which are tucked safely in my palm. I'd rather Sander didn't know what his shower-fresh aura does to me on a morning like this, how much I wish I could go back to his place with him and lie on a bed covered with cool, milk-white cotton sheets, in a room that I've always imagined to be as pure as the inside of a chapel, though in reality, it's probably a typical bachelor's festering den.

'Ambulance brought in a woman who'd fallen eleven storeys through a canvas awning, and landed on her back on the sidewalk. The concrete should've snapped her spine in half, but there's not a scratch on her.'

Unlike a lot of the other ER docs I've met, Sander never resorts to slang, or slapping a tag like 'jumper' on a woman who fell from the top of a building. He never mistakes the bodies that he heals, or the deaths he witnesses, for the spirit inside the shell.

For us, it's just another day at work, Sander once said. For the patients and their families, that trip to the ER could be the night that changes everything they ever knew.

I think that was the morning I looked at him, sitting across the bar, his lean biceps framing a tomato juice with lime, and thought that Sander and I were either going to end up being immortal soulmates or doomed fuckbuddies.

Alas, we haven't become either. But I still glance at him sideways as I'm pouring drinks, or steal glances at the packed muscle of his arse under his scrub pants, and dream.

'What do you think saved her? Was she high on something?'

'Nope. Her blood alcohol level was normal. Tox screen came back negative. If I weren't an atheist, I'd say it had to be divine intervention.'

'You sure it was divine?'

'Are you saying there's another kind?'

'Buddy, if you only knew.'

Sander gives me an odd look. He has tawny, light-brown eyes, feline eyes. In a man who's so disciplined, so utterly civilised, those feral eyes drive me crazy. I let myself have one long drink of his golden gaze. Too long to keep my heart from going into overdrive, but brief enough to keep that look from turning into a touch.

'I get the feeling there's a lot more to you than what I see behind the bar,' Sander says.

I smile with one corner of my mouth. 'You'd be right.'

'Do you think you'd ever show me?' he asks, in a voice too low for any of the nurses to hear. No matter how much those guys wash their hands at work, their minds are always in the gutter, and their lust for dirty gossip is legendary.

Seconds tick by. I'm lining up a row of free cocktails for the nurses, amends for being late. The bar owner would strangle me if he knew I was doing this; on the other hand, he'd strangle me if any of his hospital clients complained about me being late all the time. The hospital staff keep us in business; the rest of the day, we get nothing but a few retired state employees nursing a single draught beer for hours.

'Maybe,' I tell him.

I turn away to pass out the drinks. That 'maybe' took a hell of a lot of discipline. I feel like I deserve a medal. There aren't any awards for abstinence in a life like mine. Too bad, because I feel like I'm always denying myself something: sleepy Saturday morning sex; alcohol and other forms of intoxication; nights of sweaty, ecstatic dancing with strangers who get closer than lovers in the primal collisions we share to music.

A couple of nurses at the other end of the bar are talking about the falling redhead. Fitch, a hairy gorilla of a guy with a skull like a cue-ball, is chatting with Amy, a pretty blonde whose Tinkerbell body hides a power-house of strength and focus. I've heard that she can hold down an acute psychotic with one hand while starting an IV on a cancer patient with another.

'She told me she worked as a dancer,' Fitch says. 'I believe it. I can see that bod swinging on a pole.'

Amy rolls her eyes. 'Or a meathook. You're such a perv. It's probably the dancing that held her together when she fell. Sure as hell wasn't booze or drugs. I just wonder why she jumped in the first place.'

Fitch's massive shoulders rise in a shrug. 'Maybe there's something new on the streets. Some kind of junk we haven't heard of yet. Makes strippers think they can fly. She definitely wasn't suicidal. It was all I could do to keep her in the room until the doc could discharge her. Sander wanted to admit her, but she wasn't having any of that. Would have been like trying to admit a cougar. Talk about energy – she was on a high all her own.'

The tiny hairs on the back of my neck stand straight up, as if they were charged with static. I don't want to listen, but I do.

'Did anyone ever claim her?' Amy asks.

'Nah. She left alone. No purse, no ID, no clothes. We gave her a gown and a pair of scrub pants, and she bailed, crazy as ever. Didn't want to hang around for a psych consult.'

'Can't say I blame her. Did she say where she was going?'

'Said she had a lot of "catching up" to do. What exactly do exotic dancers catch up on?'

'Same stuff as the rest of us girls. Paying bills. Doing laundry. Cheating on their boyfriends.'

'No boyfriend in this case,' Fitch smirks. 'I asked. Said she was unattached. She dances at a club called the Ninth Circle.'

'Never heard of it,' Amy says. 'Hey, Kel, have you heard of the Ninth Circle?'

'Yeah. It's my apartment building.' I hand Fitch and Amy their drinks. They make a perfunctory grab for their wallets. 'These are on the house, guys.'

'Kelda doesn't hang out at strip clubs,' Fitch says. 'Under all those tats and the black leather and studs, she leads the life of a Catholic schoolgirl.'

'Catholic schoolgirls get around a lot more than I do.'

No need to tell Fitch that I've not only been to the Ninth Circle, I used to dance there, in a former life. I lasted a few weeks before I made the switch to dyke bars. The girls tip better, and they don't expect to see you crawl.

'So Kel, are you dating anyone these days?' Fitch asks, eyeballing my cleavage.

'What do you think?'

I flick the bar towel at him and strut away, twitching my arse. There were times when I thought I could go for a hot, sweaty roll with that big, beefy body of his. It would be like fucking a bald bear. But lately I'm grateful for those rare mornings when I can slip into bed alone and lose myself for hours in dreamless sleep.

Another wave of night-shift employees, mostly paramedics, crowds into the bar, and I'm suddenly swamped. I catch Sander watching me work, but I don't watch back. Sometimes I wonder how much those golden eyes see.

'Kelda!' Amy shouts down the bar. 'Wanna go to the Ninth Circle with me tonight? You can be my date; Fitch will be our beard.'

Those microscopic hairs do their dance again. No. I don't want to go back to the Ninth Circle. I don't need the flashbacks, and most of all, I don't need the grief of another job, especially after last night.

I don't need it. But I want it.

Why?

I wipe the bar with the damp towel, painting dark circles on the wood. One circle inside another, coiled, endless. There's never any end to this. That's why I can't break free.

'Not in this lifetime,' I shout back.

The Fallen One roamed the city all night, after they finally let her out of that maze of pain where they claimed they needed to fix her. They kept prodding her new body for fractured places, sliding her into machines to photograph her skeleton, drawing her blood to test it for poisons. She wanted to claw and kick herself free, but she'd waited too long for this body to risk letting them keep it.

What a body! What a windfall of muscle and bone! And the skin – she can't stop touching her new skin, the silk hills and smooth valleys, the lightly furred notch between her thighs. Hair the same colour as the hair she once had, the red of alchemy, its heavy ends brushing the small of her supple new back. With this body, she'll take hearts and souls the way she's longed to for so many years.

She finally finds a place to rest, a shelter marked with the blinking green letters M-O-T-E-L. The withered old man at the front desk demands money. Like a dying dragon, he spills smoke in and out of his nostrils, staring at the dark tips of her breasts under the thin hospital gown. He's hungry, but he's got nothing that she wants. She slides her tongue across her lower lip, making him a promise that she has no intention of keeping, and he hands her a key.

Behind the door of her room, she strips off the gown and pants and throws them in a corner. Naked, alone with her new fleshform, she stands in front of the mirror over the sink and inspects herself in the speckled glass. No flaws, not a single one. Apple-firm breasts rise above a taut belly. A long, lean waist widens gently into narrow hips, and the heart of her pelvis is crested by a delicate swirl of copper hair, slightly darker than the skeins that glide across her white shoulders and down her straight back. The legs are her favourite – the thighs are taut and strong, tapering into calves shaped like two halves of a slender heart.

Her feet make her frown. The toes curl against each other in twisted patterns, the arches look warped and double-broken. Callouses rim her heels like hooves.

But the feet aren't important. They'll take her wherever she wants to go. The coiled strength in her legs will carry her into the air; her arms are powerful enough to capture any lover she wants.

She wants them all. Every breathing, warm, blood-rich body that was denied to her for so long. Through all those centuries that she spent reuniting parted lovers – her punishment for letting herself fall – she was never allowed to touch or taste the fruit, herself. Temptation was the water that she drowned in, parched, flailing, but never allowed to drink or save herself.

Now she'll drink. She'll drink all she wants, then more, until every cell of her gorgeous new fleshform glows with pleasure, and the gaps between the shards of her spirit are filled with fire.

The girl she occupied left a map for her to follow. Memories, words, visions. A pit called the Ninth Circle, where she danced like a demon in secret, on the nights when she wasn't with her lover, or rehearsing in her studio. When the hulking, bald nurse at the hospital asked her what she did for a living (as if the limbo she'd existed in could be called 'living'), she said she was a dancer. She traced the map in her mind to the Ninth Circle, and when she named the place for him, his pupils dilated with an animal's hunger.

Those chicks are insane, he said, his voice a growl of admiration.

She smiled. He wanted to rip her naked body apart,

gobble the pink, juicy meat between her legs. The desire in his massive body raged through the sterile box of a room, but she wasn't ready. She hadn't even named herself yet.

The circle of yellow plastic on her wrist has a tag stamped with blue letters that spell the name 'Jane Doe'. No. That's not who she is. Jane Doe is the shadow of a multitude of lost, invisible souls.

Amara. That's more like it. Long, long ago she knew a slavegirl named Amara with molten skin and a sex like lava. Lust engulfed anyone who looked at her, and her lovers were too many to count. Back then, she wasn't strong enough to steal the slavegirl's body, but now she can take her name. *Amara.* It meant 'eternal' in Sanskrit. The slavegirl had been too dull to know what her name meant, much less have an inkling of how long, how horrifying an eternity could be.

The new Amara tosses her hair, making the strands whip her cheeks and chest like a mass of silken snakes. The ballerina's innocence is already vanishing from her face – once pure, the blue eyes are darkening to violet. Soon they'll be nearly black, twin purple pits in the snowy heart of a stolen face. Everything the ballerina denied herself, Amara will grab with the greed of a thousand lost years. A soul that's been hovering for so long can never be fully fed.

She touches her breasts, lifts their satin weight, touches the tips, which are small and pale as pearls. Under her fingers, the nipples darken and harden into dusky new buds. The flat silk surrounding them rises into scalloped rings. Using her nails, her palms, her forearms, Amara paints sensations across her skin – shivers, shudders, a deep electric throb. Desire used to haunt her like a shadow; now the ghost is coming to life again in stolen flesh.

Nestled between the tight outer wings of her sex is a tiny knot. Touching it sends a tremor through Amara's body. She circles the kernel, rubs it, strokes it into stiffness. Faster. Faster. Her inner flesh unfolds. Wetness seeps down her thighs. She pants like a running jackal. With her other hand, she enters the hole at her sex's heart, two fingers thrusting up and down in a simulated fuck. Her eyes widen in the mirror: two empty wells fill with wonder. This is what she's wanted forever; this is what the mortals give up their souls for. Something infinitesimally small, yet infinitely huge – the ripple that crests in a wave of joy.

A harsh, guttural moan comes from Amara's mouth, peaking in a raw, trilling squeal as she rides her first climax. Her hips thrust forwards, her spine arches. Her fingers curve into claws, arching over the back of the chair. She wants to rake her smooth belly until it bleeds – pain, so harsh and pure, could only make this glory sweeter – but even in the midst of her high, she knows better than to damage herself. Instead, she braces herself against the flimsy motel chair to keep from falling to the floor.

When the orgasm finally dies, Amara looks at her reflection again as she catches her breath. Her pupils, fully dilated, are black voids. The remains of a snarl twists her angelic mouth. She smiles at herself. The smile is triumphant. She owns the ballerina's body now; the possession is complete.

How can she ever get enough of this?

She will never, ever let this fleshform go.

'Kel! Can I get another draft?'

One of the old guys at the end of the bar waves his empty mug at me. I tap my watch.

'I'm off shift, Stan. Jack has you covered.'

My surly replacement, an ex-con, gives me the hairy eyeball.

'Hey. It's your job, buddy. Go take care of Stan.'

It's three o'clock, and I'm done with the Ofice for the

day. I shove the dishtowel in Jack's huge hand and go to the back room to get my backpack. The ER staff are long gone by now, replaced by a trio of regular, former public clerks who've retired into a career of sipping draught beer and plugging the jukebox with Patsy Cline. Unlike a lot of the bartenders, I don't hang around after I've done my time; I just throw down my towel, wave to the boys and go.

An early dusk turns the afternoon sinister. Masses of clouds, charged with dark threats, gather over the mountains. A few fat raindrops smack my cheeks. This new spirit, whoever she is, must be loving the weather. Every Fallen One adores a storm.

I plug my ears, blast NIN on my iPod, hoping music will drown my thoughts as I walk the six blocks home. Not every Fallen One is my responsibility. I try to tell myself that, but it doesn't work very well. I've already given up trying to resist.

The huge oaks guarding the courtyard of my building usher me into the gloom of the Granada's elegant decay. I love the old girl, the gently disintegrating lady. Some architect back in the 1920s created her from a fantasy of Moorish arches and courtyards, and she clings to the dream of exoticism the way an old woman refuses to give up her politically incorrect mink stole.

Halfway through the courtyard, I stop. There's a guy sitting on the steps that lead up to the arched double doors. He's all soot and shadows – black hair, pale mouth, blacker eyes, bruised by insomnia. Jagged cheekbones, asymmetrical nose. I wonder who broke that fine nose for him. As he watches me approaching, his nostrils flicker. The muscles in his shoulders and long legs tense.

I tense up, too. I listen. He's got Speak, though he doesn't know how to use it; I feel words forming behind those eyes. His Speak is strong enough to drown out Trent Reznor's voice in my ears. Something in this stranger is already reaching for me. This is where I should squint up at the Granada, claim to be lost and run.

Too late. He knows who I am. I flick off my iPod and let my backpack slide from my shoulder. Hell, it's not every day you find another black sheep sitting on your doorstep.

'Who are you?'

'My name's Brendan.'

'What do you want?'

'I don't want anything. I need your help.'

I stare down at him, hands on my hips, until he stands, too. He's tall, way taller than I am, shoulders wide under his battered leather jacket. Along with the busted nose, he's got a prize of a scar along his jaw, bisecting his lower lip. Apparently he used to mix it up, but there's no violence in him now, only a yearning confusion. I can't help noticing his hands, the beautifully functional fingers, their tips tapping ghost scales along his hard thighs. My guess is that he's a musician with a misspent youth. My favourite vice. I'm screwed.

'Practising your scales?' I nod at his dancing digits.

He offers me a ghost of a smile. 'Yeah. I'm a club pianist. Jazz composer in my daydreams. Are you the woman I'm looking for?'

Damn, don't I wish. He's got a fierce obsession cooking in that dark head of his, but whatever he needs from me has got nothing to do with the visions that are taking shape in my sex-starved imagination. He's big enough that he could plant me against a wall, holding me high while he pushed into me, our hips merging. I feel my spine flattened, my head banging against the plaster while he gives it to me rough, watching me all the while with those black, black eyes.

I hope Brendan doesn't have See as well as Speak. If he does, he's staring at a pornographic panorama of the two of us naked and sweat-filmed, my legs wrapped around his waist as he surges into me, my nails clawing the paper off my bedroom wall.

'I'm the woman you're looking for,' I sigh. 'Want to go for a coffee?'

'Coffee's the last thing I need right now. I've been jacked up on caffeine all night.'

'Vanilla milkshake, then. Whatever. I assumed you wanted to talk.'

'I don't want to be around people. My head's too fucked up.'

His eyes shift back and forth. His fingers are still playing their nervous tune. He catches me looking at his hands and shoves them in the pockets of his jacket.

'Fine. We'll talk right here. You aren't coming upstairs with me.'

I plant my butt on the stone steps. He sits down again and bites his lower lip. I'm already in lust with his full, soft mouth, the only vulnerable point in that arrangement of rough angles.

'So talk. I'm wiped out from work; I need a nap.' Desire sharpens my edges, especially when it's so clearly destined to go nowhere.

He rests his elbows on his knees, thighs spread at an angle. His fingers intertwine, the knuckles knitting together like the pieces of a Chinese puzzle.

'My girlfriend tried to kill herself last night, but she didn't die. She jumped out of an eleventh-storey window, but she's still alive. Crazy, right?'

The words come out in a half-choked rush, then stop.

'Not necessarily.'

He breathes deep, lets the breath leak through pursed lips. His fingers, for a moment, rest. 'One of the nurses at the hospital told me you might understand.'

Great. Nurses are giving out my name and address to the loved ones of the possessed. Next thing you know they'll be passing out my business card at the ER registration desk.

'I might. Tell me.'

'I don't know where to start,' he says, with a ragged laugh.

'The beginning works.'

He closes his eyes, sooty lashes sweeping over his cheeks. *I want to tell you everything, but I'm so freaked out I think my head's going to explode.*

I let myself touch his arm. The heat of his thoughts almost scorches my hand. If his extremities are that hot, the inside of his head must be a roiling furnace.

'It's OK, Brendan. Tell me anything. Your girlfriend's favourite colour. What she did for a living. Start with her name.'

'Lia. Her name is – was, might still be – Lia. She was a dancer in the city ballet. Wanted to be a choreographer. Her favourite colour was china blue. She was the most beautiful woman I've ever seen.'

'What does she look like?' I ask, though Lia is already coming to me, a lithe and lovely girl-woman, flowing copper hair, a heart the essence of innocence. Soul-food for the damned. I already know that Lia somehow ended up standing on the rooftop of a tall building, falling into a swan dive, colliding with something much more deadly than a concrete sidewalk.

'Redhead. Exquisite. Graceful as a deer. But that wasn't why I loved her. She was just ... pure. The world's shit couldn't touch her; it was like she was protected from anything hard or dark or ugly. I was a wreck when I met Lia. She saved me. All of me. My career, my body, my soul.'

'You make her sound like an angel.'

'She was. God, she really was.'

I could tell him that he's sorely mistaken, but I'm not that much of a bitch. Black sheep like Brendan are always looking for a shepherdess to take them by the hand and guide them through their inner wreckage. Onto a flesh-and-blood female with her own swarm of conflicts, they project the spirit of divinity. Meanwhile, the poor co-dependent girl thinks she's pulled her lover out of hell. Her ego soars, then takes a nosedive. Her soul shrinks into itself, profoundly misunderstood.

I knew I should have called in sick this morning, spent the day recovering from that bastard of a Release last night. Wouldn't have mattered, though. Brendan would have found his way to me. They always do.

'Is it possible,' I say, as delicately as I can, 'that Lia had issues you didn't know about?'

'Issues?'

His face is a blank. Men, even men with Speak, are so dense sometimes.

'Problems. Mental health concerns. Fucked-upness. Whatever you want to call it.'

'Well, yeah. She was seeing a psychiatrist. But that was mostly about her career. She didn't want to dance anymore.'

'A dancer who doesn't want to dance? That must have been a downer for her.'

He nods. 'It was. She'd lost something.'

'Did she ever tell you what it was?'

'No. That's what the shrink was trying to help her figure out. He had her trying some meds. They seemed to make things worse. She got vague. Lost whatever motivation she had. I tried to help her out of it by writing her some music, a dance she could choreograph. The ballet world was getting to her; she wanted to strike out on her own, but she was scared.'

'Is that why she tried to kill herself? Fear?'

Brendan shakes his head. 'Hell if I know. I wasn't with her when it happened. I was playing at a bar downtown when I found out that she'd jumped. Left in the middle of the set, got to the ER as fast as I could. She was there. But she wasn't. That ... *woman* ... she wasn't Lia.'

He shudders, his mouth twisting as if he'd tasted something foul. His beautiful hands clasp each other, clench, then dangle. I want to take one of them, caress the palm, squeeze the fingers, bring them to my mouth and lightly kiss each one. But that would be fake comfort. We're all naked when we enter the flesh world, and even more naked when we enter its invisible twin.

'We can find her,' I tell him. 'The question is, do you really want to?'

He turns his head to look at me. 'That's all I want. I want her back.'

But his Speak says, *I really don't know.*

2

Amara is trying to forget who she was, but a thousand years of exclusion gouged a deep wound in her memory, and the gash is still fiercely raw. She keeps hearing the whispered words *Er Shaghryn*, the name she had before. Er Shaghryn ... The Lost. She sees herself in a thick, dark forest, pushing her way through the thicket of thorns. She used her hands as invisible hatchets to chop the branches as she moved. Sheaves of brambles fell away, leaving a clear path for lovers to follow. Saving lovers wasn't her passion; it was her work until her curse finally ended, or until eternity skidded to a halt, whichever came first.

It was always the stupidest lovers who had to be saved – mortals with thick, earthbound bodies and thicker minds – it was a miracle they ever found each other in the first place. They never saw their guide walking ahead of them; they thought their genius or their desire brought them together. No gratitude for a minor fallen spirit, who was invisible except in the results of her work.

How long has it been, since a mortal saw me, and stopped in his tracks, his heart stalled with lust?

Amara shakes her head, neck whipping back and forth, until dizziness erases that name and its ugly freight from her mind. Er Shaghryn. Like all the others, the multitude of Fallen Ones, she had a name planted on her being. All her gorgeous, alluring mysteries were stripped away, replaced by a duty that she never wanted.

Music throbs through the cramped room, alien but ancient, the beat of blood. Mortal girls brush past Amara.

They bump her with their bodies, testing her, trying to feel who she is with their limited flesh. Their painted eyes shoot poison. She sucks in their hatred and shoots it back; they shrink away as if they've been shot.

'Who's that new bitch?' asks a girl with spun-gold hair, loud enough for Amara to hear.

'Fresh meat,' laughs her friend. They stroll out together, arms around each other's waists, leaving Amara alone in the dressing room.

She undulates in front of the smoky mirror, runs her hands up and down the sleek gift. *Fresh meat.* If only those two whores knew how right they were. Fresh, succulent, fragrant meat – Amara has craved a solid form for so long that she can hardly remember feeling anything else. Tonight she'll start crafting new memories, lush and dark, damp and dangerous as jungle undergrowth.

Brendan is dreaming about me. He doesn't know why, and tomorrow there won't be anything left but a hard-on and a sheepish memory. But I'm naked as dawn in his mind right now, my sins cleansed by the clear water of his subconscious.

I let myself slip into the dream with him. I'm breaking and entering – it's not right to show up uninvited in someone else's sleep, but when I see his rangy body tossing and twisting, I can't stop myself. His eyes dart back and forth under closed lids. Scraps of jazz and memories of loose-hipped women from the clubs drift through his mind, before his unconscious settles on an image of me. He shakes his head, slings an arm across his face. Moans something that sounds like a refusal. I know he's ready, even if he doesn't.

Whether he knows it, whether he wants it, Brendan and I are already lovers.

Restlessly he strokes his penis; I nudge his hand away and take his half-hard cock into my mouth. I don't mess around – this is a fast, hungry deep-throat. He swells to full erection, filling my mouth, glans butting the back of my throat, hips driving the shaft even deeper down. Because it's a dream, I can breathe through the mass of his cock. I could swallow him forever. I bury my nose in the crisp nest of his pubic hair. I cradle the firm weight of his balls in one hand, using one finger to prod his anus. Most men I've known won't admit how much they like this, except in dreams. His ass tightens at first, but soon he loosens up for me, lets me take him that way while I keep sucking with all the hunger of my loneliness.

I like to fill my lovers, in their dreams. Claim every hole. It's a trick I learnt from the Fallen Ones: seek every empty space, and take possession of it. Full occupation is the only way to go.

Brendan groans. If he were awake, he'd be clutching handfuls of my hair right now, but in his sleep, he grabs the sheets as his ass lifts off the mattress. My finger pushes in past the tight, ringed sphincter, as his shaft swells one more time, then throbs. He cries out as if something's being torn away from him, and yes, if I'm brutally honest, I'd have to admit that I'm stealing. As his climax dies, he softens in my mouth, slips out along my lips. When I break into a dream, I can pick up scents, but not flavours. I don't know anything about the way he tastes, only about the way he feels. He holds back, resists, and then lets himself plummet.

Brendan has an innocent soul. The inside of Brendan's head is probably a lot less cluttered and dangerous than his girlfriend's is. Was.

No, *is*. I can't give up on Lia, even though I'm already craving her boyfriend like a street drunk dreaming of strawberry wine. I have to believe that she's still in that limbo where souls go when they've been occupied by a lost and craven fallen angel. That bleak space, fogged with the chalky haze of half-consciousness, is shared by people in comas, and people who are dying slowly but can't, for whatever reason, let go.

In other words, that limbo is worse than hell. At least hell, as it was described to me by a Fundamentalist foster mother who was convinced that hell was my birthplace, is crowded by souls that have a few juicy stories to tell, and can still gasp them out while they burn.

Today was my day off. I spent it at the library – not the downtown public library, where the books gather dust while the patrons fight over computer terminals – but a small private library that's related, in some apocryphal way, to a seminary downtown. It's a room without windows, except for a cracked skylight that filters light through dusty glass. The walls are lined with books from floor to ceiling; leather-bound tomes that haven't seen sunlight since the foundation of the building was laid. I have to wear a dust mask when I work at the library, and my access depends on the mood swings of a cranky ex-priest named Max who has the only key, but that's OK. Those books are my soul food. Those mouldering texts are the feast I return to again and again, not just to nourish my mind, but to track down Fallen Ones.

I know a few exorcists who swear by the internet as a research source. But aside from a flock of underage cam girls, I've never found any fallen angels online.

My brain still rumbling with Latin, Greek and primordial tongues as old as human memory, I light a few candles around my apartment and put on a CD of Gregorian chants to keep myself in an ecclesiastical state of mind. I'm not religious, but since I rent headspace in the shadows of the Church, I like to stay on its good side.

I strip off my jeans and tank top and panties and slip into a white satin robe whose hem whisks the curve of my arse. The kimono isn't my usual style. I bought it on impulse at a Victoria's Secret in the mall, when I had a sudden and bizarre impulse to feel pure and innocent again ... if I ever was. Sometimes this work leaves me feeling grimy, and not just because I've been rolling around in dust and mould at the theology-geek library.

Sitting on the floor in lotus position, surrounded by candles and devout male voices, I close my eyes. I don't look forward to this part. That first attempt to find the Fallen One takes a lot out of me, and I never know who I'm going to contact. There's a lot of psychic static out there, a lot of restless, needy souls stuck in a perpetual half-life. As I'm easing into my visualisation, trying to find the gate to Purgatory, someone knocks on my door.

'Shit. Not now.' I open my eyes and glare at the door, willing the moron to disappear.

He, she, or it knocks again. Loudly, then louder still. It's a guy. Only a masculine fist could make that kind of racket.

I unwind my legs and stand up. I throw the door open, obscenities forming on my lips. The fist, poised to pound again, almost clocks me in the nose. I'm about ready to grab that fist and throw the bastard over my shoulder when I see who the hand is attached to.

'Sander!' Relief, and an unasked-for spark of sexual excitement, sends my voice up an octave. 'What are you doing, beating my door down like a freaking maniac?'

His eyes are circled with shadows and his mouth is soft and moist. He's wearing a button-down shirt and a pair of jeans that look like they've been slept in for days, and the lean lines of his jaw are blurred by stubble. As ragged as he looks, I'm acutely aware of the fact that I'm naked under my robe. Suddenly I'm all hungry skin.

'I'm sorry, Kel. I didn't mean to scare you. I'm not all that sane tonight.'

Not all that sober, either, judging from the way he smells. The booze is seeping from his pores. I stand back to let him come in. He grips my shoulders for balance as he staggers into my living room. His hands burn an imprint into my flesh that lingers after he's collapsed onto my loveseat. He looks around, taking in the candles, my little altar, my books and chalice.

'What are you doing here? Having some kind of ritual?'

'Ritual, yes. In the past tense. I was right in the middle of it when you started banging my door down. You scared the shit out of the goat I was about to sacrifice. What's going on, anyway? You look like hell.'

His answering laugh is a hollow rattle. 'Yeah, well. I think I went there last night.'

I start to lower myself onto the loveseat beside him, then I remember that I'm all but naked, and I sit primly in an armchair across the room. My shrine separates us, keeping me safe. Or maybe I should say, it's keeping Sander safe.

'Tell me what happened.'

Sander shakes his head. His dark blond hair, usually combed like a Boy Scout's, sticks up in shaggy tufts, as if he's been clutching his skull, trying to hold something in or keep something out.

'If I knew what happened last night, you'd be the first person I'd tell,' he says.

'Why's that?' I ask warily.

'Because you *get* this bullshit. I don't.'

Poor Sander. I've always known he has a tough time accepting the possibility that the concrete realities he deals with every day – broken bones, slashed flesh, blood, pain – point to anything other than themselves. Someone, or something, threw open a door for him last night and he's having a devil of a time closing it.

'I'll ignore the word "bullshit," since I know you didn't come here for a philosophical debate. Just describe what you remember.'

He sighs. 'After the bar yesterday, I went back to my place. I was off call, and I figured I'd just go home and fall into a coma, like I usually do. I never have a problem sleeping. I don't even dream.'

Sander starts to shake. The shaking begins in his lean shoulders and ripples all the way down to his hands.

'But yesterday, you did dream,' I prompt him. 'Was it about that redhead at the ER?'

Golden eyes, bloodshot and bleary, stare at me. 'I knew you'd know. God, I knew you'd know. I dreamt she was in my bed, naked, straddling my cock, riding me. At first it was this incredible turn-on. Then it morphed into the fuck from hell. She wanted something from me. Not just sex – the sex was a pretext. She was there to take everything I have, everything that makes me who I am.'

'How did the dream end?'

'That's the problem. It didn't end. I don't remember waking up. Next thing I knew, I was sitting at a table in a club. A titty bar. It wasn't your typical club, the kind of place where you go with your buddies; this place was evil. The girls looked like monsters. I was so drunk, their faces were warped. And the music ... it was drums. Nothing but drums. Like something out of a National Geographic documentary. Primitive. Terrifying.'

Ah, yes. The Ninth Circle. I know exactly where Sander went and who led him there. But there's a lot of stuff I still don't know about this Fallen One, so I pretend to be totally ignorant.

'You don't drink,' I remind him. 'How did you get shitfaced?'

'I have no idea. This morning I found an empty pint of Jack Daniels on the floor under my bed. Apparently I bought it, swallowed it and got plastered on it, but I don't even remember taking the first sip. You know what the weirdest part is?'

'What?'

He gives that vacant laugh again. 'I've got a breathalyser in my apartment. I won it as a door prize at a buddy's bachelor party. I tested myself on it when I got home. I blew nothing. From a physiological standpoint, I wasn't even buzzed. How the hell do I make sense of that?'

'We'll get to sense. Maybe. Start with the club.'

'No. I don't want to talk about the club until I've figured out how I got there. I want to know how I went from points A to B to C.' Sander straightens up on the couch, chops the air with his hand as if he were slashing marks on a number line.

'Sure you do. But let's do this my way first. Forget about linear time for a second. Let's talk in scenes. Was the redhead at the club?'

'Yes. Oh, yes. Right there in my face, dancing for me, as if I were the only guy in the place, and she was my personal sex slave. She didn't move like the other girls; she moved like a serpent, like some kind of concubine. Making these motions with her hands and her hips that mesmerised me. She started off standing over me, then lowered herself little by little, until her, uh, pubic area was parallel with my eyes. She wore a skimpy gold G-string that kept catching the light. Back and forth. Up and down. Grinding in directions I'd never even thought of. I felt like a snake being charmed.'

'Sounds like every heterosexual male's fantasy, being seduced by your own personal stripper. Right up there with the girl-girl threesome.'

Sander shudders. 'God, no. She wasn't seducing me, Kelda, she was pulling something out of me. It was a nightmare. I wanted to get out of there – never mind how I'd ended up there in the first place – but I might as well have been under conscious sedation. Awake, but incapable of moving. I'm amazed I can remember it at all.'

'You said she was pulling something out of you. What do you think she was taking?'

'I don't know how to say it without sounding like

some sort of New Age freak.' Sander looks at my shrine, then glances at me and throws me an apologetic smile. 'That's not what I meant.'

'I know what you meant. You don't know how to describe what happened in any way that your scientific education would help you explain.'

'Right. I want to find a clinical term for last night. The closest I can come is a fugue state. It's like part of me disappeared and met up with the rest of me later, with all kinds of wild stories to tell. But people in fugue states usually don't remember anything. I have these shreds of memory that just . . . bleed.'

'I'm going to make us some tea.'

I get up and walk to the kitchen. I walk fast, not because I'm jonesing for chamomile, but because I can't stand to see Sander looking like a husk. Maybe I've never acknowledged how important Sander's sanity is to me. In a world wracked by spirits and their combative energies, where the alien vowels of ancient languages echo along corridors of memory too murky to recollect, Sander's enlightened mind is an oasis. Now, sitting on my loveseat with his back hunched, his head hanging between his shoulder blades, he's lost that clarity. He's lost, period, in the primeval forest where the Irrational keeps enlightenment perpetually at bay.

Even in his hollowed state, I want him. One more thing I've never admitted to myself – how often I've wished that Sander and I could be lovers. 'Normal' lovers. The kind who lie around in bed on Sunday mornings, languidly fucking till noon, then share the newspaper before drifting out for a late lunch and an afternoon of furniture shopping at Ikea.

I reach into the cupboard and pretend to grope around for the tea while I think about what I'm going to say next. How much is he ready to hear? I do a bit of role-play in my head, imagine how I would define 'glamouring' for a twenty-first century doctor. *Glamouring*: the stage of possession when a Fallen One lures a mortal into a state of vulnerability, in which they are open to losing all of their energy, their will. Whatever makes me what I am, as Sander said. Glamouring isn't any fun, but compared to full-blown possession, it's a honeymoon.

I'm filling the kettle with water and trying to think of how to describe this soul sodomy in clinical terms, when Sander steps into the kitchen. I know he's going to touch me. My body goes tense. Before I can think too much about whether I want this – I already know I want this, I just don't think I should – he slips his arms around me from behind.

'I needed you tonight,' he says into my ear.

'For what?' My hand freezes over the sink, kettle suspended.

'For sense.'

'All those years of medical training and you're looking for sense from me?'

'You understand this shit. I don't.'

I don't know if the rasp in his voice comes from a night spent silently screaming, or from lust. Judging by the way he clings to me, and the hardness that's pressing into the small of my back, it's a blend of both.

I flash back to the first time I saw Sander, strolling out of the ER at nine o'clock on a Sunday morning. I'd been waiting for him out by the smoking shack. I needed to talk to him about a patient he'd seen the night before, an eighteen-year-old football hero who'd fallen into a coma and emerged as a monster his family couldn't recognise. When I saw Sander, I all but forgot about the kid. I'd never met a man whose mind was so radiantly clear, so still. No Speak at all, and for once, that was a blessing. On top of that, he was hot, even after pulling two consecutive shifts, even in his bloodied scrubs, with forty-eight hours worth of beard, he looked like the angel Gabriel, wiped out after wrestling with Jacob all night.

I don't need Speak to know what Sander wants to do;

I've got enough juice left that I can recognise lust and hunger and desperation when I feel them surging in on me.

'I don't think you're looking for sense right now, Sander.'

He reaches over to turn off the gas burner under the kettle.

'Not anymore.' He nuzzles the nape of my neck, lips grazing the fine stalks of those tiny hairs, sending streaks of electricity down my spinal cord.

'This is a bad idea. Seriously. If you want to talk, let's talk, but I can't do this.'

'Can't? Or don't want to?'

He answers his own question by untying the sash of my kimono and sliding his hand across my breasts. My nipples go stone-hard. My back arches against him. He planes my belly with the palm of his hand, strokes my waist from breast to hip.

'Can't. We're too different.'

'How?' He's pulling me into his warm, solid torso. His heart throbs under his ribs, or maybe that's my heart, and I just can't tell the difference anymore.

'You wrestle with mortals. I wrestle with . . .'

My words die as his fingers touch the sleek fur between my thighs. Wet, wet – I know I'm wet even before I hear the liquid whisper of my lower lips parting. Now he's got all the proof he needs that my resistance isn't a matter of low libido.

'Wrestle with what, Kelda? Tell me.'

'Fallen angels. Lost souls. Misguided beings that fall out of the sky.'

'I've always known you were different. And I know I'll probably never understand you, but god, I've wanted you anyway. The booze made me brave enough to tell you.'

I'm pinned against the counter now, Sander's weight holding me firm against the tile. The muscles in his arms twitch as they brace my ribs, nerves sending me messages of their own. The stink of alcohol is gone, and I know now that it was a phantom stench, that in these past hallucinatory hours, he never drank a drop. The Fallen Ones can do that – intoxicate us with their wild, ephemeral substances, powerful as psychosis. In our struggle to figure out what's hijacked our brains, our senses step in with signals we can understand. The Fallen Ones wear our addictions like veils.

'It wasn't booze, Sander.'

'What are you talking about? I was plastered.'

I start to explain how the circuitry of a mortal brain can run haywire under the touch of a Fallen One, but he swallows my words with his mouth. Those lips, lips I always thought were a bit too thin, too hard in their refusal to express the inexplicable, are softer than I could have guessed when he kisses me. Molten tongue, gently insistent. Those healing hands clasping the back of my head, guiding my face in the rhythm of the kiss.

Something's in the room with us. Called up by my aborted ritual, and by the energy that Sander and I are making, it hovers in my kitchen. I smell the acrid, blood-bitter stench of its envy. I glance over Sander's shoulder as he turns my body and eases me against the counter, parting my robe with his hands. He hoists me up on the tiles and pushes my thighs apart.

I watch the Fallen One rise and spill her poison across the ceiling; she, it's definitely a she, all female in her sick hunger. As I unbuckle Sander's belt, I'm sizing up her power. As I unzip his fly, I'm watching her summon everything she has. She's a tough one. Been floating for centuries, chewing a massive grudge. She almost got Sander, but he's mine tonight.

Fuck off. I'll deal with you later.

I mouth the words at the ceiling while Sander's face is hidden in the hollow between my neck and shoulder. The Fallen One curls into itself, like a stingray recoiling for attack. She spews putrid smoke, filling the room with the stench of the charnel house, but it's going to take more than a foul odour to stop what's going on between me and Sander.

I've got his cock in both hands now, clasping it between my palms. The shaft springs up, nudging the heel of my hand, seeking something darker and deeper. Sander starts breathing in sharp, rough gusts when I open my thighs for him. I grab his taut ass and pull him into me. His groan is gut-deep, rusty, and I'm so wet that he slides in without a hitch. We've both been deprived and that bitch on the ceiling isn't getting any of what's mine.

'I can't believe this is finally happening,' Sander whispers.

'Me neither.'

I yank his shirt open and drag my nails down the hairless slope of his chest, watching him flinch as I scratch his nipples. His skin is humid, hot. His musky scent makes my pussy clench. Wearing his medical education like a superhero's shield, Sander thinks he's protected from my world. I'm about to take him to a place where those shields melt like cheap plastic toys.

He grabs my hips, tilting my pelvis so that he can ream me with deep, rhythmic thrusts. Each stroke hits me at my soft centre, unthawing a part of me that had been frozen for months. The changes in his face – slackening of the sceptical mouth, darkening of the tawny eyes – arouse me more than anything else. Still fucking me, he bends to cover my breasts with greedy kisses. His teeth grind the darkened tips till I shriek, then he comes back up to devour my mouth. His thumb furrows through the same wet place that his cock is filling, finds my swollen clit, and applies a gentle pressure while his shaft turns me inside-out.

I moan. He grins when he feels me soften. He thinks he's got me. I'm not willing to be gotten so easily.

So I show him. I unlatch the door that's been closed for so long, and let him see what's behind Door Number One. Here's your prize, Sander. A riot of ghosts and fallen angels, hovering in a milky netherland, waiting for their lucky break. Souls torn apart by what they want. Why do the things we want the most destroy us? Ask any one of these entities; they've been fighting with that question for eons.

Sander's pupils grow huge. He stares at me, and though he doesn't have Speak, I can see him wondering what on earth he's fucking. A naked chick on a kitchen counter, or Satan's slut?

'Who *are* you?' he says, his voice hoarse with awe and lust and something close to terror.

I'm not going to answer that question. I wrap my thighs around his waist and clutch his cock with my inner muscles before fear can soften him. I keep him rocking, keep his flesh from sleeping. Just before I come, pleasure fogs my mind again. The waves of my orgasm both bless me and rip me open. Sander rages after me. A groan stirs in the pit of his belly, rises through his throat, crescendos in a howl. At the climax, he pounds me hard, shakes all over, goes still.

He stays inside me for a long time before we slide apart. He sinks to the kitchen floor, pulling me down with him, and we pant and shiver together, clinging to each other. The toxic cloud on the ceiling has vanished, taking her slaughterhouse stench with her. She came, she watched, she fed on our desire. She's gone, but not before infecting Sander and me with her greed.

'Wild night,' Sander gasps.

'No kidding.'

I feel around the floor for my robe. It's lying in a white pool on the tile. I wrap myself up in it and double-knot the sash.

'I still have no clue what happened.'

'Let me put it this way, Sander. Nothing that you

think happened really happened. Except what just happened.'

Sander's laughter doesn't have that harsh flatness anymore. It's a boy's laughter, bright and innocent. No wonder the Fallen One dragged him out of bed and out to the Ninth Circle to flash her stolen goodies in front of his face – he's a lost soul's wet dream.

'You're unbelievable, Kel,' he says, running his finger-tips down the swan-swoop of my throat. 'Tonight was unbelievable.'

'Hold that thought. You'll only make things worse for yourself if you push that whole belief issue.'

Accepting the unbelievable, in my world, is never a bad thing. Forcing things to make sense can get you killed; I've seen stronger men than Sander torn in half when they refused to accept what their rational brains couldn't process.

He's lying on his back like a giant cat, his head in my lap, eyelids drifting down over his golden eyes.

'I wish I knew what you were talking about,' he says.

'You will,' I promise.

I stroke Sander's damp hair. He purrs, a half-dreaming lion. Tonight shouldn't have happened. It probably wouldn't have happened, if the Fallen One hadn't brought him to me. Every Fallen One has a shtick – maybe that's hers. Uniting mortal lovers. Playing the voyeur to their passion, for centuries on end.

No wonder she wants revenge.

3

I'm half expecting Lia's ballet school to look like the spooky, fairytale academy in Dario Argento's *Suspiria*, but aside from a tall, wrought-iron fence, the place has all the gothic charm of a juvenile detention centre. A row of posters on the school's windows catch my eye: dancers caught in mid-air, athletic bodies suspended, muscles taut, arms outstretched in mid-flight.

Lia must have danced like that. I picture a material angel, floating in a cape of red hair. What spirit stuck in the immaterial realm wouldn't long to occupy one of those gorgeous, soaring fleshforms? Energy exploding in space. Lust, envy, greed – and everything you need to feed them.

No wonder they want us so much, the Fallen Ones.

I walk around the building to the courtyard, where exquisite waifs wearing leotards and sweat pants perch around a circular table. One of them spoons yogurt from a carton. Another picks at a sushi roll with a pair of chopsticks. One lucky girl, who must have the metabolism of a hummingbird, is wolfing down a hoagie.

Four sleek heads on gazelle necks turn to me as I loom over them. My bod falls somewhere in the slim-to-skinny range, but next to the ballerinas I feel like a hippo in my snug jeans.

'Hey there. I'm looking for somebody. Her name's Lia.'

The two syllables turn the girls into mutes. They stare at me.

'Lia's, um, not here anymore,' pipes up the hoagie girl after a few speechless moments.

'Really? Did she quit the ballet?'

'She hasn't been part of the company for a few weeks. She's on leave, sort of.'

'Where'd she go? Rehab?'

I toss out the question as if it were a joke. No one laughs. The girl with the yogurt stabs her spoon into the carton, frowning as she stirs.

'She did have some issues,' says a lithe brunette who's eating nothing. 'But she didn't need rehab.'

'She needed a sex life,' mutters the hoagie girl. Judging by the size of her sandwich, she's more sensually engaged than her friends.

'I thought she had a boyfriend,' I say. 'Some musician guy.'

'Yeah, Brendan. He's hot. I don't know what her problem was; she was just dysfunctional or something. She was always having problems with him.'

'The ballet is very demanding,' says the brunette chick – arch little bitch. 'It takes a lot out of you, physically. Lia was just super-dedicated. She didn't have time for an intimate relationship.'

'So why was she involved with somebody? Why didn't she cut the poor guy loose?'

The girls exchange a four-way glance that means something I can't interpret. I'm getting bored with the coy allusions, the darting peeks. I'm not a detective, and I'm sure as hell not a therapist; I don't have the patience to read body language when all it's doing is reminding me, once again, of my perpetual outsider status. It's a miracle that the girls haven't asked me yet what I'm doing here – I can only assume that someone in the group wants to spill something. I glare at the Hoagie Girl, who's the only one of these creatures I can remotely relate to, until her cheeks go pink and her pretty mouth opens.

'Lia didn't like to be alone,' she says. 'Especially after she started having her out-of-body experiences.'

My pulse picks up. 'What do you mean, out of body? What was she doing, astral projection?'

'No, Lia wasn't going anywhere when this stuff happened. It was more like she was standing outside of herself, watching it all. She'd be lying in bed with Brendan, or practising in the studio, or even just taking off her clothes to get in the shower, when she'd feel something step inside her and shove her out of the way. That's how she described it – shove her out of the way. Then she'd have to stand to one side and watch whatever this thing did with her body. She'd watch herself do all kinds of stuff that she'd never have thought of in a million years. Weird, kinky things. Can you imagine how awful that must have been?'

It's only too easy for me to imagine. I know exactly where Lia went while the Fallen One was making her first, seductive moves on her fleshform. While the Fallen One glamoured her with promises of pleasure, Lia's spirit stood in the cold outer circle where we all end up, at one time or another, after we've been supplanted by something stronger.

The brunette looks like she's trying to swallow a mouthful of cow dung. 'Where the fuck are you coming up with this, Carrie? And what gives you the right to tell Lia's secrets to a complete ... stranger?' She turns to me, her small head recoiling. 'Who *are* you to Lia, anyway?'

Now all of the girls except Carrie are staring at me like *I'm* the cow dung, but I don't mind. Carrie's got a big heart, and an even bigger mouth. If I can get her away from her shallow friends, she'll tell me everything I need to know. Ten to one, when her spirit isn't muted by the white noise of the general public, Carrie has halfway decent Speak.

'I'm a friend,' I inform them. 'A friend who cares about what happens to her.'

Looking miserable, Carrie stares at the remains of her

sandwich. As usual, the one who least deserves the shame is wearing it like a crown of thorns. I silence the buzz of her friends' brains as best I can, and tell Carrie to Speak to me.

Lia couldn't take it anymore.

Take what?

Watching herself turning into someone else. She jumped off a building. But she's not dead. I know she isn't dead.

Thank you.

I smile at Carrie. Her mouth wobbles back. Her chin is streaked with mustard and her wispy hair straggles out of her ballerina knot. She's the least alluring of the ballerinas, but to me, by far the most beautiful.

As soon as I'm out of sight of the ballet academy, I pull my cell phone out of my pocket and punch in Brendan's number.

'Yeah.' A gasp. I can tell that his shortness of breath doesn't come from running. It comes from waiting.

'Why didn't you tell me that you and Lia had no sex life? You could have saved us both some precious time.'

He's silent.

'Brendan? You have to be honest with me. Tell me all the details, even the ugly, dirty, sordid shit that you'd rather keep stuffed in your closet.'

'I couldn't tell you. Maybe it's a guy thing. I couldn't accept that she didn't want me. Too much shame involved.'

'Shame. Are you kidding?' I snort with disbelief. 'Fallen angels don't have any, I can guarantee you that. You should have told me, Brendan. I need to know what kind of spirit I'm dealing with, how strong it is, and how much of a chance I have of getting Lia back. If there's no chance, I'm not risking my neck on this.'

'What are you saying? I don't know what you're talking about. What fallen spirits? I just want my girl-friend back.'

'I'll give you the ten-minute tutorial on fallen souls later. Right now I need to gather as much information as I can. Human spirits don't last all that long in the place where Lia is right now.'

'You mean she's still alive?' The hope in his voice would shatter my heart, if I had enough cohesive fragments of it left to break.

'Sort of. Maybe. Lia's in a waiting place right now. It's not a good place to be. Not at all. From what I've learnt about her, she wasn't all that strong to begin with; she's not going to last where she is. Is there anything else I should know about her? Besides the fact that you two hadn't seen any action for awhile?'

Brendan gives a deep sigh. Behind the sigh, I hear glasses clinking, a few random piano chords. 'I'm at the club right now, getting set up for tonight. I can be out of here and meet you at Lia's apartment in half an hour.'

The building where Lia lived is only two blocks from where I'm standing as I disconnect the call and fold up my phone. I can see it from here, a 1950s skyrise, sad traces of a generation that was too egocentrically optimistic for its own good. High enough to look down on the entire city, with its impassive circle of mountains, that building was also more than high enough for a suicidal leap.

With no intention of hanging around till Brendan gets here, I hurry towards the last place that Lia was seen alive.

Amara almost had him. She *would* have had him, if his soul hadn't been so rigidly restrained by a fence of scepticism. He was a self-deluded fool of a healer, but the combination of virtue and tan skin made her hungry; she had wanted the young doctor since he touched her breasts at the ER. At the club, when she opened her pussy for him onstage, she'd almost engulfed him, but he pulled back just before falling into her fragrant snare.

Pacing the alley, pantherlike, Amara lights a cigarette and presses the red tip into her right breast until she smells burning meat. Sheer, searing joy: the pain sings so sweetly along her nerves that she almost comes from the force of it. Mortals fall over themselves trying to avoid sensations like this – weak, ungrateful humans, stunted things. Earlier that night, Amara dug her finger-nails into another stripper's soft upper arm, just to see how she'd react. The blonde's face had melted into a snarl of red-lipped rage, then collapsed into something far worse than anger when she saw the black voids of Amara's eyes.

What had the blonde seen there, Amara wondered? Something that turned her into a little girl again, piss going cold on her thighs as she waited for the most terrible thing that had ever happened to her.

And that was only from a touch. Something inside Amara is flexing itself, waking with a low howl, reaching, craving. This pull is different from the flat, barren yearning she remembers so well. Then, she couldn't reach through space to touch matter; what would she have touched it with? Now she has everything she needs, and so much more.

Not only to watch, but to touch.

Not only to touch, but to tempt.

Not only to tempt, but to seize.

'Hey, sweetheart. I'm lonely tonight. How about a date?'

A man peers up from the inside of a car. His face, half-hidden by a tinted window, is a pallid mask with twin holes for eyes. The window lowers. Amara sees sunken shadows under high cheekbones, a serious mouth. Hand-some enough, but like so many of the mortals she's seen, he's already a vacant shell.

Amara, standing on the sidewalk, plants her hands on her hips and thrusts her pelvis forward in an age-old invitation. She tosses back her hair, lifts her shoulders, watches sparks of greed ignite in the pigeonholes of the man's eyes. Still young, but he's already drained life of whatever it has to offer.

'Lonely? You don't know what lonely is,' she says. Her voice still sounds like a rusty gate opening, the vowels stunted, unnatural.

'You've got a sexy accent. Where are you from? No, let me guess. Eastern Europe.'

Amara flicks her tongue across her lower lip. She shakes her head.

'France?'

'Nowhere you've heard of. Or would want to hear of.'

He's leaning out of the window now, one elbow over the edge. All hunger, but he's holding it in. His need triggers Amara's. The throbbing starts at the root of her spine, rises like a drumbeat through her belly.

'Tell me. Where is it? I'm curious now,' he insists.

'Somewhere close to Hell.'

He smiles, showing teeth. 'I love a gorgeous woman with a sense of humour.'

'That wasn't a joke.'

He laughs anyway. 'Want to take a ride someplace?'

'No. You come out.'

His face slackens, mouth quivering. The mask slips. The hunger shrinks into something small and cold. As he's turning back to the steering wheel, Amara steps forwards and rests her hand on the roof of the car. His nostrils quiver at the scent of her skin – musk and flowers, temple smoke, and something older than anything human.

'What's that perfume you're wearing?' he asks.

'It's called Fallen Soul.' She softens her voice for him. 'Like it?'

'Yeah. I think I do.'

'Why don't you come out, then? Get closer.'

'I thought we could go someplace more private.'

Amara glances to the left, then to the right. The street

stretches out in both directions, empty as a cold throat. 'I don't see anyone else here. We've got the whole night to ourselves. Don't you like to fuck outside?'

He stares up at her, half-pleading now. 'This isn't what I'm used to.'

'If you were looking for ordinary sex, you wouldn't be here, would you?'

He gets out of the car, his limbs moving like a puppet's. Stiff, unwilling, but some buried part of him is *all* will. That part wants Amara more than he's ever wanted anything. He approaches, arms raised to hold her, but she turns her arse to him and flattens her palms on the roof of his car. She hikes her miniskirt and spreads her legs wide, aware of the impact of the long white V they make, pointing up to the hidden tunnel between.

'Like this. Like animals,' she says. 'Hurry!'

She raises her round bottom. He groans, and the sound seems dragged from the pit of his gut. No fool, this stranger – he doesn't know what he's getting into, but he's smart enough to realise that he might not get out of it with his soul intact.

Amara hears him unzipping his pants. Even before he grasps her body to take her, she feels the electric tremor of nerves gone haywire, blood pumping out of control, muscles twitching helplessly. That energy – the amazing life force of living matter – that's what she's been craving for so long. He enters her exactly the way she wants him to, in a single hungry thrust. She arches, throws her head back, gasps. Human beings, fucking in their safe beds, don't know what true union really means. They never truly feel the clash of material, skin and meat, the collision of bones. As his shaft breaks her pussy's slick resistance, Amara relives the moment that she slid into the dancer's falling body and claimed it as her own. First there was the moment of alien ownership, then the merging of herself with the ballerina, and finally the disappearance of the other girl altogether.

Yes, possession was better than fucking. But this is still good, so good it's unholy. Amara grinds her teeth, growling in time to the rhythm of her lover's hips. He's clutching her from behind like a dog mounting a bitch – and bitch she is, gnashing and whining, wordless and wild.

The rough skin of his palms chafes her breasts, tearing her cheap blouse to get at the small mounds with their tight pointed nipples. Tiny dancer's titties, toys tipped with bells, they dangle in his greedy hands.

'God, you're beautiful. You feel so fucking beautiful.'

He grabs her breasts, twists the long nipples. Amara grunts. She shoves her arse back to meet his cock; his paws leave her tits and land on the hood of the car, on either side of Amara's shoulders. She rubs her clit with nimble fingers, heightening the rough pleasure of the animal mating with the delicate hum that the tiny bud produces. Amara's inner muscles tighten around her lover's prick, and the tightening pushes her closer to climax. She bites her lips; pain will help her draw this out. She wants this first coupling to last as long as it can.

But when he stiffens, moans, then shudders, and pounds her hard to orgasm, Amara can't ride the edge of the cliff anymore. She falls headfirst into release, the spasms long and slow, holding all the hunger of her centuries of exclusion. She's still swaying against the car, riding it out, when her lover backs away. She doesn't hear him fall to the street, spent. She's still coming.

Coming to life. It feels, as the man on the ground said, fucking beautiful.

Counting my steps, more from obsessive-compulsive mania than superstition, I walk along the sidewalk outside Lia's building. I look up at the sky, but I see only the brutalist angles of a concrete tower. It's not as if there were any stains, or a big red X to mark the spot where she fell, but when I reach one particular segment of the walkway, I feel a stirring from the spirit who took her, the fallout of the splendid world. I sit down, tailor-fashion, right in the middle of the sidewalk, pressing my palms against the concrete. I try to make my mind blank; it's all too easy to spin my own stories about the Fallen Ones, tales from a lonely, hyperactive imagination.

'What are you looking for? Trying to figure out where she landed?'

Brendan is standing over me. I feel a shiver resonating from his presence before I look up into his face. Our eyes lock. Something tingles in the space between our bodies. I remember the night I felt him dreaming about me.

He's so different from Sander, with his radiantly uncluttered mind. As soon as Brendan and I make eye contact, I'm flooded with a jagged stream of messages. Pain, memory, loss, desire, hope – a code coming so hard and fast that it makes my mind whirl, and I lose the staring contest with those pitch-black eyes.

'Lia didn't land,' I tell Brendan. 'She never made it to the ground. By the time she hit the sidewalk, she'd been taken.'

'I wish I knew what you were talking about.'

No, you don't.

Brendan sits down on the sidewalk beside me. His long fingers reach for the same patch of cement that I'm touching.

'What exactly are you trying to figure out?' he asks. 'What are we supposed to learn here, sitting around feeling the sidewalk?'

I give him a sharp sideways glare. 'Hey, sarcasm is *my* prerogative. You can't afford to be anything but dead serious about this.'

He's silent for a moment. 'I'm sorry. Tell me what you're looking for. Please.'

His plea melts something inside me. Brendan's broad shoulder is so close to mine that I could touch him. I could touch his unshaven cheek. I could take his head in my hands and kiss his mouth.

'I'm trying to figure out what took Lia. I need to know what kind of spirit it is, how powerful it is, and whether I have a chance of releasing it from your girlfriend's body.'

Brendan's staring at the ground, but his hands are folded safely in his lap now. At some level of his being, not all that deeply submerged, he's willing to hear. Maybe even to believe.

'What do you know so far?'

'It's an androgynous spirit, like most of them,' I tell him. 'But it mostly identifies with the feminine. It's been hanging around for a long time, watching and wanting. It's wanted more than anything to be a woman.'

'So why does it take so long? How long are we talking about, anyway?'

'Hundreds of years, maybe thousands. Waiting gives these entities power; the longer they hang around, feeding their grudges, the stronger they get. They might make a few attempts to possess a material body before they actually hit the jackpot. It's a matter of being in the right place at the right time, with a desirable mortal who happens to be very weak. A girl like Lia – weak sense of self, confused – would have been a prime target. She'd probably been stalked for months. Do you remember when she started to change?'

He mulls this over for a few seconds. 'Last time we made love, if you can call it that, was back in January. I got stuck at her place for a couple of days during the blizzard. The heat in her apartment wasn't working; her pipes froze. Everything was cold; we could see our breath in the air while we were lying in her bed. Her skin felt like ice. She kept trembling. I spent most of those two days holding her. I felt like I was trying to keep her alive.' He goes quiet, his gaze focusing on a point far away from me.

'So the sex must have been pretty cold, too,' I prompt.

He shakes his head. 'No. Not at all. That's what was strange about it. She woke me up in the middle of the night, and she was on fire. All over me – mouth, hands, thighs – she was starving. And she was so hot inside. Like lava. At first I thought some other chick had broken in and taken her place; we'd never fucked with that kind of intensity. Not even when we first met.'

A purse-lipped woman in stretch pants, walking her Pomeranian, catches the word 'fuck' and gives us a dirty look.

'We're blocking the lady's way,' Brendan says. He unfolds his long legs and gets to his feet. I do the same. Reaching into his pocket, Brendan pulls out a ring of keys. 'I've still got her key here, somewhere. Should be exactly the way she left it. I told her landlord she was still in the hospital.'

I smile at him. 'You're keeping the faith, aren't you?'

He shrugs. Under the shadow of a twenty-four-hour beard, his cheeks flush. 'My senses tell me she's gone, but I still feel her – here.'

Brendan's hand goes to his solar plexus. His fingers have a ghost of a tremor.

'That's a good sign,' I tell him. I want to offer him some small form of comfort, but the more I learn about Lia, the more I think she doesn't have a chance of reclaiming her body. I feel a ghost of a girl, already slipping out of herself before the Fallen One found her. Brendan may need to hold that flashlight of faith for both of us.

'Did you love her?' I ask Brendan, as we're riding the elevator up to the eleventh floor, where Lia lived.

'I don't know.' He looks startled, not so much by my question, but by his own response.

'You don't sound as certain about her as you did the other day. Having second thoughts?'

His laugh rings hollow. 'Hell, I'm having all kinds of

thoughts. Like maybe I really just wanted to save her. Lia was that kind of girl. Her beauty was all about her fragility.'

I bite back a bitchy retort, digging my nails into my palms. The guy's confused. He's almost, but not quite, grieving his lost girlfriend. That's what inspires him to say something inane like that: *her beauty was all about her fragility.* What is it about men and weak women? Why do they get hard over females without spine or substance?

I could show Brendan what it's like to fuck a strong woman, with appetites as huge as his own. Maybe it's just good old female sexual jealousy, but for a moment I wish I could knock Lia out of the way and jump her lover in the elevator. She's a Lost One now, and from everything I've gathered, she wasn't much more than that when her body still belonged to her. A wraith too pretty for her own good, she would have been alternately pampered and ignored by the people who supposedly loved her. A little less beauty would have done her good; she would have had no choice but to learn a few survival skills.

'Here we go.' Brendan's voice has a note of relief as the elevator doors open. I wouldn't be at all surprised if he had caught a few of my thoughts.

'Great. You lead the way.'

The hallway of Lia's floor smells of cooking oil, cat piss and cigarette smoke. Following him, I check out the feline angle of his shoulders, the way they shift rhythmically in synchronisation with his hips. I try not to think about the way that innate rhythm would accelerate with him lying on top of me, driving that lean body against mine. I try not to imagine the way my thighs would look wrapped around his neck, my knees snow-white against his coal-black hair, or the way that hair would feel as his head glided down, down to the notch between my legs.

'This is it.'

Brendan stops in front of a door marked with the number 1111. I don't like that number, and I don't like the way the air sizzles outside Lia's door. Neither does Brendan. He stands there tossing the keys in his hand.

'Go ahead. It's OK.'

He turns to me. Haunted. 'I'm thinking maybe we should let her go.'

They always do this, the lovers and sisters, mothers and best friends, when they're right on the verge of finding a Lost One. There's always that frozen second of doubt, when they're like kids at a carnival spook house, too frightened to step forwards or back. I don't blame them. Not at all. If I hadn't been cursed the way I am, I'd never step into the world beyond McDonald's, reality TV and my local bar.

'It's OK,' I tell him again, and this time I let myself touch Brendan, and I let him see everything I've been thinking. Only for a second, but in that second, I feel his muscles go electric and he's all thrumming sinew. I take my hand off his arm. The currents still crackle, like feedback from an amplifier, but he can move again.

He unlocks the door. I follow him inside. The blinds are closed and the objects in the room are suspended in the silent aftermath of something gone wrong. The lingering air of confusion, the feeling of being forsaken, is almost more potent than I can bear.

'This girl definitely had issues,' I say.

He cracks a smile. 'Told you.'

'She didn't do much with the decor in here.' I look around at the beige sofa, the glass coffee table, the standing lamp. 'This might as well be a hotel room. I thought she'd be more creative with her living space.'

'Lia really lived at the studio. This was just a place for her to sleep and change clothes. She was always experimenting with new costumes. And she'd change her outfit ten, fifteen times a day, like she could never figure out who exactly she wanted to be.'

'Let's go check out her closet, then.'

On the way to Lia's bedroom, I glance at the window she must have jumped from. Someone had closed it, and covered the glass with an X of black electrical tape.

'Who taped the window?' I ask Brendan.

'I have no idea.' His lip curls. 'The cops, probably. Just to prove they actually showed up. They haven't done shit to help me.'

'Why should they? As far as they're concerned, Lia's alive. She ended up in the ER and she's out on the streets now. From their point of view, she did a personality makeover. Nothing illegal about that.'

It never ceases to amaze me how much trust people put in the legal system, as if the police were kindly parents, waiting to catch falling girlfriends and wayward lovers on their way to the ground. We put so much faith in our ability to save each other from the forces of circumstance, nature, bad juju, whatever, when really there's nothing between us and the sidewalk but a thin film of coincidence.

Brendan opens the door to Lia's bedroom. Suddenly, everything shifts. The room is an explosion of fabric, feathers, dirty panties, takeout containers, fashion magazines. Hairbrushes. Lipsticks. A dressmaker's dummy, wrapped haphazardly in black nylon, lies at half-mast across the bed, a headless guardian.

'She was hiding out in here. This was her warren.'

'Yeah. That's exactly it. When she wasn't dancing, she used to hole up here like a scared animal,' Brendan agrees. 'She was either at the academy, or at her shrink's office, or here. Her life was a closed circuit, at the end. She wasn't always like that. I can remember when she had passion.'

He stares down at the chaotic bed as if he were trying

to conjure a memory of that passionate dancer. Back in the hallway, I'd had this brief, crazy-evil thought that Brendan and I would make love on Lia's bed. A cocktail of jealousy and lust can turn anyone bad. Now I know it could never happen. Not just because the mattress is buried under a mountain of junk, but because I'm feeling Lia too strongly. I couldn't screw her boyfriend in the afterburn of her madness.

And she was mad, at the end. Stark raving.

'I had no idea it had gotten this bad,' Brendan says. 'I knew she had problems, but this is insane.' His fingers light on the fringe of a seafoam scarf. He draws the filmy skein of fabric out from under a pile of garbage. 'I gave her this last Christmas.'

'What about this? Somehow this doesn't look like your taste.' I'm holding up a G-string with a split gusset, red satin rimmed with metallic sequins. A pussy would be a flash of glistening pink meat, snared in gold.

'It's not. Not Lia's, either. She wouldn't be caught dead in that.'

Not dead, maybe. But not living, either. Somewhere in between. I flip the G-string back into the rubble, then rub my hands on my jeans. I wish I could wash my whole body with scalding water, but I don't know that it would help; nothing in this place feels clean.

Brendan's gaze is still fixed hungrily on the red-gold scrap. I can feel him dying to touch it. He wants to finger the open diamond that would have surrounded Lia's lips. He wants to rub the cloth against his cheek, his lips. His Speak tells me that he's starting to see what Lia was becoming before she fell; still, he wants to taste whatever is left of her.

She's gone, isn't she? he Speaks.

Not quite. Not yet.

I walk over to the vanity table, a dainty antique that looks like it once graced a prom queen's bedroom. The vanity table has a three-way mirror, perfect for a perfectly pretty girl, but all three panels are draped with a white sheet. One hem of the sheet is singed and streaked with brown, I'm guessing by a burning cigarette. Using my fingertips like a pair of tweezers, I pull back a corner of the sheet. I'm not surprised to find the glass panels coated with black spray paint. On this point, I sympathise with Lia. Bad shit lives in mirrors, and I'm not just talking about the hagged-out reflection of a hungover face.

'Did she always cover up her mirrors like this?'

'No. That's new,' Brendan says. 'So's the mess on the table. She was almost religious about her make-up; that tabletop used to look like a shrine.'

The surface of the table is yet another reflection of Lia's inner war zone: a litter of cosmetics and overflowing ashtrays. Back issues of *Vogue* and *Cosmo* lie open under the litter, their glossy pages shredded, as if someone had taken a razor to the models' faces in a fit of manic envy.

On a corner of the table sit two amber plastic bottles. The bottles are almost full, and the prescriptions are dated only two weeks ago. I bend down to glance at the labels. One bottle contains Ativan, the other, Seroquel.

I turn to Brendan, who's standing with his hands stuffed in his pockets, hulking in the doorway.

'Did you know what kind of medication Lia was taking?' I ask him. 'Or more likely, *not* taking?'

His eyes are hooded. 'Antidepressants. That's what she told me.'

'Hah.' I straighten up. 'One of these is a sedative. The other is an antipsychotic.'

'My girlfriend was not psychotic. She had a few problems.'

'Yeah,' I snort. 'Like hallucinations? Delusions? The urge to fly out of her window?'

Brendan pulls his hands out of his pockets. His fingers pump against his thighs, a pantomime of frustration. 'I should have taken better care of her. Looked out for her. I had no idea it had gone this far.'

I shrug. 'You were her boyfriend. Not her parent. Some "problems" are way too big for one person to deal with.'

'Maybe. But I should have known she was mentally ill. She was my lover, for god's sake.'

'Who says she was mentally ill?'

Brendan looks puzzled. 'What else would she be?'

Something silver winks at me from the ravaged pages of a magazine. It's a disk the size of a half-dollar, attached to a red velvet ribbon. A pendant with two intermeshed knots. Celtic, probably. It's the kind of piece you could buy at any New Age shop or art fair, but this thing makes my tiny neck hairs wriggle.

'Did you give this to Lia?'

I don't want to pick up the pendant, but I don't feel I have a choice. I hold it out like a hypnotist, letting it swing in front of Brendan.

'No.' He shakes his head. 'The only jewellery Lia ever wore was a pair of diamond earrings that her father gave her for her high-school graduation. She only used jewellery with her costumes. What *is* it?'

Brendan reaches for the pendant, but his hand stops shy of touching it. His twisted lip tells me he's having the same reaction as I am, only he has no clue why. In the glamouring phase of possession, Fallen Ones are a lot like infatuated humans – they shower their would-be hostages with gifts.

'I've seen enough. Let's get out of here.'

'Where do you want to go?'

I grab his hand and drag Brendan out of the bedroom. 'Ever been to the Ninth Circle?'

'Of hell, you mean?'

'Why, yes, Brendan. That's exactly what I mean.'

He shakes his head.

'Then this is going to be a real thrill-ride. But hell doesn't open its gates until seven pm, so we're going to make a pit stop at the library. There's someone I want you to meet.'

Totally befuddled now, Brendan lets me lead him out of the insanity of Lia's apartment, down the elevator, and back into the mundane madness of a downtown rush-hour.

4

Sitting cross-legged in a service entrance behind the alley, in a doorway that stinks of urine, Amara pets the satin skin along her inner thighs. Her snowy hide isn't as flawless as it used to be; after the past two days and nights, her legs and arms and breasts are spotted with fingerprints and streaked with a crazed scarlet alphabet of scratches. She frowns.

Damage.

Her sex feels raw. The pearly pink folds, so tightly sealed, are red and angry, the labia gaping. She strokes her lower lips, waiting for that sly hum to begin, so she can coax another dazzling nerve-shower from her flesh.

All she feels is a keen, stinging pain. And once the flash of pain dies, her nerves give her nothing but a dead resistance. She groans out a feral curse, in a long-lost tongue, and bangs the back of her head against the concrete wall behind her. Anything to feel *something*, that numbness is unbearable.

If she hadn't fallen, she'd have lived in that splendid suspension forever. Hovering in a soft, neverending explosion of joy. The orgasms that she has in this body are just flickers of that glory. She had that once, before she fell, while she was still a fruit hanging on the tree. Some of the fruits turned into ruby stars and rose to the heavens. Others dropped like beads of blood to the ground, joining, but never quite joining, the world of loss and discontent and decay below. Who made the choice? It wasn't Amara. She never would have chosen the fall, no matter what the Snake promised.

Flesh brings knowledge. But it also brings craving.

Before she had a fleshform, Amara never knew what it was to feel this gnawing inner emptiness.

What do mortals do with this?

Anything. Anything to fill the void.

'Eros and chaos. They're inextricably bound – the force of life and fertility, the energy of destruction and damage. When Eros is suppressed, it turns into rage. Imagine that volcanic energy, pushed underground for centuries. Think of that stifled longing, the force it exerts when it finally explodes to the surface!' Max says.

'The story of my sex life,' I break in.

I couldn't resist that barb. As much as I adore Max, there's something evil in me that always wants to prick his bubble when he goes into his professorial mode. Max lifts an elegant eyebrow, then snubs me, turning to Brendan.

'It doesn't surprise me that your Fallen One chose a woman who suffered from a deadened libido and a troubled mind. Your lover would have been the perfect vehicle for a Fallen One: young, supple, lovely and open to invasion.'

Max offers us chairs at the theological library's study table. Max and Brendan and I are the only ones in the library this afternoon. An evening summer storm is brewing outside, blocking any sunlight that would have leaked through the library's single window. Max switches on a couple of reading lamps. The shadows that they throw on Brendan's face make him look haunted. Haunted and hunted, and somehow even more attractive. I don't know what it is about me; I just get hot for a man with a mystery.

'What's a Fallen One?' Brendan asks. He leans forwards hungrily.

Max's long mouth curves into a sickle. Max is an ex-priest who now intercedes for lost souls from the privacy of his cramped cell of an office. He's been my guide, my mentor, since the day he found me hanging out in front of the liquor store across the street from the seminary, a seventeen-year-old runaway trying to get skeevy guys to buy her packs of Camels and pints of Jack Daniels. Max is the one who discovered my Speak, helped me turn it into a full-blown power. And he's the one who helped me find my deeper gift, or my curse, whatever you call it.

A few years ago, Max also became my lover. No one could have been more shocked than me to find out that he's a genius at cunnilingus; no man has ever paid such thorough, tantalising court to my pussy, or bothered to learn its topography so lovingly with his tongue. He's the one who convinced me to have the hood of my clit pierced with a tiny sterling barbell, so he could tug delicious, orgasmic cascades out of my vulva. Max can give me more gut-wrenching joy than I've ever thought I deserved; so much that he's had to bind my wrists with a leather belt to keep me from pushing him away while he's down between my thighs.

'My captive orphan. My beautiful, motherless girl,' he croons, whenever he takes a break from licking to fuck my pussy slowly with two fingers. I squirm until the leather around my wrists chafes the skin, but I really don't want to break free. The twisted skeins of our shared pleasure, the wounds we open in each other, bring me to climaxes that are close to seizures.

Max once confessed to me that my pussy is his one remaining addiction; he's learnt how to conquer his other cravings. Every now and then, on a quiet afternoon like this one, I'll lie back on this table and let him have his way with me. He never asks for anything in return; I've always assumed he finds his pleasure later, alone.

'Have you ever heard of Lilith?'

Brendan glances at me. 'Like the music festival for women?'

'Well, sort of. Lilith was Adam's *first* wife. The one he couldn't introduce to his family,' I pipe in. 'You can read about Adam and Eve in the Old Testament, but you won't hear about Lilith. You have to go to rabbinical myth to get the dirt on her. The way one of the legends goes, she got pissed off when Adam wanted to screw her in the male-superior position, and she ran away to the Red Sea. She hooked up with some demon, and she was so incredibly fertile that she had a hundred babies a day. Must have been hell on her body, especially if she was breast-feeding.'

Brendan and Max gawk at me.

'The rabbinical scholars had nothing on you, darling,' Max finally says.

I shrug. 'I just tell it like it is. You can tell the rest. About the Fall, and all that.'

'Why? I couldn't hold a candle to your contemporary vernacular.'

'OK,' I continue. 'Lilith had hundreds of offspring, all of them spawned by a demon. But because she gave birth to them before the fall of mankind – you know about the doctrine of original sin, right? – they were also divine. They weren't quite demons, but they weren't angels, either. Lilith was a goddess. When you're the child of a goddess and a demon, you can imagine how that messes with your identity.'

Brendan nods. His full mouth is slack. He's not quite following me, but he hasn't dropped away, either.

'Sometimes I wonder if you're a daughter of Lilith, yourself, Kelda,' Max muses. 'Half divine, half demonic. No record of your birthplace, or your biological parents. A childhood spent in foster care. Who knows where you really came from?' Max's voice is soft, the way it gets before we do our secret table dance.

'Nobody. Me included,' I say sharply.

'So do you think you're more divine or demonic?'

My left thigh starts pumping up and down, the way

it does when I'm nervous, or pissed off, or both. I glare at Max. He smiles back, thin lips parting his Van Dyke beard.

What's with the fucking third degree? I use Speak, hoping Brendan's gifts are too unformed for him to pick up on it. *You know I don't have a history.*

Oh, yes you do, Max Speaks back. *You just don't want to know it.*

Something firm, like a warm ledge, is pressing against my shaking leg. It's Brendan's thigh. I take a deep breath, and my leg stops jiggling. I give him a look that says 'thank you'. He returns the look, along with a small smile. I wish I had the whole weight of his body on top of me, something solid to pin me down.

I look at Max's tight face, waxy from so many days spent in this catacomb of a library. His pale blue eyes dart back and forth between me and Brendan. Along with being my now-and-then lover, and my guide to the realms of printed and invisible knowledge that help me do my work, Max is the closest thing I have to a father. He's never seen me with another man – a young one, with a powerful body and energy to burn. I shut down my mind, not wanting to see the storm that must be roiling in Max's skull right now.

'Tell us the rest of the legend, Max,' I say gently. 'Help us figure out who this Fallen One is.'

We've told Max everything we know about Lia: the troubled days before her fall, her dive from the eleventh-storey window, the appearance of an oversexed redhead at the ER. Her friend's second-hand account of Lia's erotic possession.

At first I don't think Max will talk. Then he sighs, tents his tapered hands, and picks up where I left off.

'Picture a tree,' Max says, 'a tree hung with fruit. Those fruits were Lilith's children, equally weighted with the promise of divine life or death. Some of the fruits flourished and were harvested. Others fell to the ground and rotted. Their beauty and promise reached an early end. Those are what we call the Fallen Ones. They're suspended in a state between life and death. More powerful than mortals, less so than angels, they hang between the material and the immaterial. It's a state of perpetual longing. A kind of hell.'

'Why did some of them fall?' Brendan asks. 'Were they just born bad?'

'I've spent my life trying to figure that one out,' Max says. His smile includes Brendan now, as well as me. 'I can only speak for myself, and for several other religious traditions, when I say that I don't believe their fall is predestined. After all this time, I've come full circle, back to the roots of my childhood faith, and the story of Lucifer. I believe it's the result of a shift that happens when the spirit becomes self-aware. There comes a moment of choice, when the spirit chooses union with the divine, or the pursuit of its nascent will. That's when the fruit drops, and the fall begins.'

'So it *is* predestined. The Fallen Ones are doomed.'

'No. They still have free will, the power to make a choice. And they have the potential for redemption, by fulfilling a task that retrieves their divine character.'

'It's kind of like a work release programme,' I add, noting the blank look on Brendan's face. 'Basically, each Fallen One has the chance to prove that they're willing to reverse the fall by giving something of themselves. They have a job to do. Once they've proven they can do it, they're allowed to come back to the fold with the angels. But a lot of them get bored. Who wouldn't, hanging around working for thousands of years? They spend so much time dealing with mortals that they start to envy us. After all, our lives are great, right? We go to work, we pay our bills, every now and then we delude ourselves into falling in love, and we fuck. Who *wouldn't* want to be human?'

'Your demonic side is showing, Kelda,' Max chides

me. 'Sarcasm won't help us here. Remember, the Fallen Ones are in a state of limbo. Neither flesh nor spirit. At times they're powerfully drawn to the immaterial world; at others, they crave the joys of the flesh. When those cravings become unbearable, a Fallen One will take possession of a human body. Give it a test drive, so to speak.'

'What happens if they like the vehicle? Do they get to keep it?'

Awareness dawns in Brendan's eyes as he starts to put the pieces together.

'That depends,' Max says.

'On what?'

'On how strong the Fallen One is. On how strong the soul of the lost mortal is. And sometimes, if the victim of the possession is lucky, another mortal – like our gifted Kelda here – will intercede and release the Fallen One from the human body.'

Max and Brendan turn to me. Max looks expectant. Brendan just looks desperate. I squirm in my chair. I keep hoping that one day I'll wake up and find out that I've always had a secret, undiscovered vocation – maybe playing bass guitar, or styling hair, or driving a dump truck. Anything but being an exorcist. The work is hard, it doesn't pay shit and it's a threat to your body *and* soul.

'If you could bring Lia back, would I even know her?' Brendan asks me.

Under the table, where Max can't see, I cover Brendan's hand with mine. There's that charge again – *zap*, like a tiny lightning bolt connecting us.

'Did you know her when she was alive?' I ask him.

He shakes his head.

We think we know our lovers better than anyone who shares our genes – we tell ourselves that because we're so familiar with our lover's flesh, our souls are interchangeable. We trust feverishly in the make-believe of desire; when we touch a raw sore in the beloved, we slap a fantasy over the wound and call our delusions tenderness. We take our lovers into our mouths, bodies, hearts. Our edges merge. We can't – or won't – imagine a time when our soulmate will turn into a hostile stranger. Once the beloved goes alien on us, we become alien to ourselves.

I don't have to say any of this aloud. Brendan already knows it. I pull the silver pendant out of the pocket of my jeans and place it on the table in front of Max.

'OK, Max. Here's the last of the clues we found. Tell us who we're dealing with.' I'm addressing Max, but I haven't taken my eyes off Brendan's. I can't look away; there's too much I'm dying to see.

Max's deep sigh tells me he knows what's going on under the table. *So you're going to start bringing your dates to the library, Kelda?* His Speak is as dry as an old sherry. Making my mind a blank wall, I bounce the barb right back at him. He picks up the pendant. The disk swings once, twice, then settles into a slow spin. In the light cast by the green reading lamp, the two knots writhe, intermesh. Their cords tighten to a point that's no longer union; it's mutual strangulation.

'We found that in Lia's room,' Brendan offers. 'I don't know where Lia got it.'

'You mean you never knew that your girlfriend had a secret admirer?' Max's voice is lightly taunting.

'What do you see in it?'

'Desire,' Max says. 'Obsession. Coveting. An intent to bond, not out of love, but out of bottomless need. If there's any authentic love in this Fallen One, it's been smothered by her envy.'

'Who is she?' Brendan asks.

'I can't identify her with any certainty, but I can make a reasonable guess. There's a Celtic legend about a fallen spirit who goes by the name Er Shaghryn,' Max says. 'It means "the lost", "the stray", "the misguided one", and

235

she's all of the above. She's described as being very beautiful, but only half-visible. Most often, she's identified as a streak of flaming red hair. As a lost soul, she's been promised a reunion with the divine if she spends an indeterminate amount of time reuniting lost lovers. But her work makes her hungry to experience love – especially in its erotic form – herself. She longs to possess a human woman's body, so she can taste all the pleasures of human sensuality. Until she stops coveting the flesh, she'll never be completely immortal.'

'Or she'll find herself a fleshform to inhabit,' I break in. 'Often it's a form that looks something like the Fallen One, herself.'

'Like Lia,' Brendan says, bringing the story to its ugly conclusion.

'You say your lover jumped out a window,' Max goes on. 'When a human body, an open human body, is in mid-air, they're exceptionally vulnerable to being stolen. The Fallen One will often have stalked them, glamoured them for weeks, waiting for the right time to take possession. There are certain states, like falling, or severe intoxication, or madness, or seizure, when possessing a mortal's body is as easy as snatching a sleeping man's wallet. Er Shaghryn is a very old spirit. Her envy, her lust and rage, make her strong.'

'In other words, Brendan, we're dealing with a supernatural bitch. Finding her will be a lot easier than making her give up Lia.'

'I have faith in you,' Max says to me, 'you're a strong girl. And you obviously know what you're looking for.' Then he throws me a line of poetry, delicately twisted, like all his weapons: 'The Eye sees more than the Heart knows.'

I'm no scholar, but I recognise the line from William Blake. Max used to read me Blake's visionary poetry, when I was first learning with him, before sex warped our mentor/pupil relationship into something kinky.

Max pushes in the battered oak library chair, walks to his office, and closes himself inside with such passive-aggressive tenderness that the meeting of door and frame makes no sound at all.

Brendan's hand is gripping mine now; his tendons twitch, his skin is ice cold. I'll have to deal with Max later. For now, I have to take care of the shaken mortal sitting beside me.

'I need a drink,' he says. 'I need a lot of drinks.'

'Come on,' I say in a brisk, take-charge voice that makes me sound about ten times more confident than I feel. 'I'll buy you a cocktail in hell.'

It's all way too familiar: the mesh of hungering humans, the concussive percussion of industrial rock, the red strobes bleeding over female flesh writhing on platforms and in chainlink cages. Only the thin boundary of skin separates my soul from the infernal grind of the Ninth Circle.

My body orients itself instinctively to the cage where I used to dance. The first time I danced there, I was barely over the safe side of eighteen, but that was OK. That was better than OK. I had pierced nipples and a shaved pussy with the words *memento mori* tattooed right above the slit, and I was hotter than a .38 special on a Saturday night. Whipping back and forth like a rattlesnake, I flashed the geography of tattoos that crossed my arms and tits. I got down on all fours and pumped my hips, while men pelted my hard little heated-up arse with wadded money.

I can't believe I did that. I can't believe I gathered up those grimy bills, straightened them as if they were inscribed with precious messages and used them to feed myself.

It's early yet. The night is just beginning its down-slide to madness. The beat of industrial grunge is still slow; the dancers sway in a desultory, hungover trance.

Only one of them moves with any passion, a dancer on a stage beside the bar. Her limbs slash across her torso, her hips rotating faster than the music's rhythm as she spasms to a beat all her own. She's already got her own fan club, a clutch of horny fools standing around her platform like zombies. Curtains of red hair toss across her face, but Brendan recognises her, from all the way across the vast warehouse floor. Without touching him, I can tell every nerve is as tight as piano wire.

I brought Brendan here to make a positive ID, to identify stolen property. If there was any lurking doubt that the body undulating on the platform belonged to Brendan's girlfriend, it's been blasted into oblivion.

I thought she'd be harder to find. I thought she'd be hiding from me.

No, Brendan. She wanted you to find her. Now you have.

Aside from being a powerful channel of soul-level communication, Speak is also a great advantage when you're trying to hold a conversation in a noisy club. Brendan's hand fumbles for mine. I bury my fingertips in the clammy meat of his palm and keep the pressure steady as I guide him across the room. The crowd is still thin, for the Ninth Circle, but there are enough bodies to shield us until we can move close enough for Brendan to see the Fallen One in her full, sensual monstrosity, before she can morph herself into something he'd find more seductive.

What does she want from me?

Everything. Everything she couldn't take when she was Lia.

The dancer shakes her hair off her face, and her eyes meet Brendan's. All black pupil, they're twin circles cut from an abyss. She freezes, a mechanical doll from hell, broken in mid-contortion. Brendan's large body turns to dead weight. I try to drag him forwards, but I might as well try to pull a concrete pillar off its moorings.

'Come on!' I shout over the techno-drone. 'We have to get closer.'

'Why?' The question is a raw howl. 'So she can rip my fucking soul out?'

I haven't told Brendan the second reason that I needed him to come here tonight, but as he towers over me, staring down, his stricken face tells me that he's clued in.

'No. I'm not going to be bait for that thing.'

It takes every molecule of strength in my small frame to keep him from bolting, but I hold him still. A herd of horny college kids come to my aid, blocking the way back to the door.

'Listen. We have to get her to follow us. We can't release Lia unless we can get her to come to a neutral space. She has too much energy here. We have to lead her someplace where she'll be weak.'

'I don't care anymore. Lia's gone.'

I reach up and clasp Brendan's head between my hands. 'Not yet. Please.'

'This is bullshit. My girlfriend's dead. Why the fuck do you care, anyway?'

Good question. Why do I care? Must be my saviour complex kicking in. With all my orphan spirit, the spirit of a child weaned on the fundamentalist rants of a foster mother and solitary afternoons watching Walt Disney videos, I want to believe that inside every corrupted angel, there's a pure soul dying to be saved.

I should have become a freaking social worker.

With one mighty heave, Brendan shakes himself free from me, shoving me into a cocktail waitress carrying a tray of drinks over her head. In the hubbub of shrieks and shattering glass, he disappears, leaving me in the midst of a lost life.

When I've made my apologies, reoriented myself, I look up to find Brendan gone. On the platform, Lia's body is still going through its sensual contortions. Her eyes shoot me a triumphant taunt. I telegraph four words to her from across the room:

Catch you later, bitch.

Lia never knew what caught her. First she was climbing up onto her windowsill, crouching like a gargoyle, then shooting towards the street. Then she was landing on concrete. Dead. She could only be dead; the head-on crash with the sidewalk felt like the end of the world. Pain, massive and jarring, set off an explosion of stars and twitters in her head – just like in the cartoons, she thought, before her brain went blank. The agony shook muscle and bone and lung tissue, bringing her heart to a standstill before something got the organ beating again.

In the days before her fall, everything had seemed unreal. Her apartment wasn't anywhere she'd ever lived. The strange man who rolled over, snoring, on her living room couch didn't look like anyone she'd ever have wanted to touch. Nothing was familiar, not even her own hand picking up the prescription bottles and lifting the pills to her mouth. She had painted her mirrors, because she didn't know the face that gazed back at her, and she had marked her windows with black tape, because she kept forgetting that the windows were there. Her apartment seemed to open up straight into a sky that was constantly, constantly inviting her to jump. She didn't want to jump, but she couldn't resist forever.

As soon as she hit the ground, the pieces that made up reality became as lucid as freshly washed glass. But that clarity hurt, because she was no longer part of it.

Instead, she was standing outside of the world, and outside of her body, watching from behind a sort of two-way mirror. On the other side of the mirror, she saw herself being surrounded by people, then whirling lights, which all merged into a drama of rescue. When she turned to face her own side of the looking glass, she saw an endless grey tunnel, like the hallway of an institution, where humanoid shapes wandered without purpose, colliding with walls, and sometimes melting into them and vanishing.

Meanwhile, Lia's body went on. She watched herself being lifted into an ambulance, and then the scene changed to a maze of rooms, where her limbs were palpated, and a tubular metal coffin, where images were taken of the scrambled contents of her skull. Then came the miracle – she watched herself become reborn into something else. This creature was as vicious as she was gorgeous; she was all fire and lust, where Lia had been fear and clutching need. It was like a movie of her own life, played by an actress far more seductive. Lia couldn't stop watching, especially when she saw the way she danced in front of men, absolutely free from shame.

Lia had been dancing that way, at the Ninth Circle, in the days before the honeyed voice in her head had convinced her that she'd be better off as a heap of shattered bones – at least the flight would give her a brief shot at ecstasy. Lia had never been able to shed the queasy feeling that she wasn't really herself when she danced at the club. When she watched her fingers hooked like claws through the chain links; when she climbed to the top of the cage and clung there, baying like a she-wolf; when she found strangers in the streets and took them home to fuck the animal she was suddenly becoming, Lia knew she was lost.

She has no idea where she is now. The place feels like purgatory, and looks like the Department of Motor Vehicles. Wherever she is, it's safer than where she was. The pleasures of having a body that breathes and leaps and fucks are lost to her, but at least her heart doesn't beat like a scared rabbit's anymore. She doesn't collapse into crying jags, or bang her head against the wall to drive the voices out of her skull.

Not a bad place, really, compared to where she came from. Why would she ever want to go back?

5

The night offers a thousand hiding places, but I have no idea which one Brendan chose after he fled the club. By the time I beat a path out of the Ninth Circle, he's gone. I stand in the middle of the street, listening for the trailing stream of his Speak. All I hear is the tidal rush of traffic on the freeway overpass, and the strangled moans of someone being brought to orgasm in the back seat of a car.

At least I hope it's an orgasm. In this neighborhood, a human howl could mean just about anything.

I scan the streets for one of the rare taxis that venture down the lightless corridors of the Warehouse District at night. Cabs don't come down this way unless they're bringing someone who knows exactly where they want to be. Once you find the Ninth Circle's narrow, unmarked door, you need a guide to find your way into the warehouse and a trail of bread crumbs to find your way out. There's a labyrinth of hallways to negotiate before you even reach the bouncer. The space on the street where Brendan parked his black Lincoln is empty, and I don't have any other means of escape.

I realise now that I could fit everything I know about Brendan on the back of a business card. He's a musician. He has the beginnings of Speak. He has/had a lover who's been taken by a Fallen One. But I don't know where he works, or lives. I don't even know his last name. After getting an eyeful of what his angelic girlfriend has turned into, I doubt he wants her back, not if he has to be the bait that lures her to me.

Without that bait, I'm screwed. Fallen Ones don't line

up on my doorstep to offer me their hostages. Those mortal bodies are their prizes, their juicy rewards for centuries of hanging in limbo. The only way I can get close to Lilith's offspring is to lure them into a clear, open space with something that they desperately want. The space doesn't have to be sacred, but it can't be charged with vice or rage or passion, or anything that fires up a fallen angel.

Judging by the infernal libido of the Fallen One who's taken Lia, I could probably use any mortal with a pulse to draw her out of the club tonight. But once I get her where I want her, I want the Fallen One's predatory soul to be glued to the floor by longing, by jealousy and maybe even a trace memory of Lia's love for Brendan.

The yellow bar of a taxi's light floats down the street. My heart jumps. I wave my arms, screaming like a mugging victim. The cab slows in front of me. Before the vehicle comes to a full stop, I'm already pulling the driver's side door open. In my Brendan-focused tunnel vision, I barely see the cab's passenger. Even if I'd noticed him right away, I wouldn't have recognised the hollow-eyed man as Sander. Spiky stubble furs his thin cheeks, and his unwashed hair hangs below his ears.

'Kelda!' The shadows can't hide the sudden illumination of his face. 'What are you doing here?'

'I should be asking *you* that, Sander. Didn't you get enough hell the first time?'

Sander doesn't answer. His stricken face makes me go cold all over. Last thing I remember, the ER doctor was lying in my lap like a golden lion – worn out from impromptu kitchen sex and a delusional encounter with a Fallen One. Now he looks like a drunk on the tail end of a three-week bender. I can always recognise the raw, stunned stare of an addict who's almost, but not quite, had enough. You never get enough till you're dead. That's the kicker.

'This isn't the first time you've been back, is it?'

He shakes his head.

I cross my arms over my chest. 'How many times has she had you, Sander?'

He sighs and lowers his head between his shoulders, one arm draped over the back seat. 'I can't remember. Twice, I think. I know I've been with her twice here at the club, and she comes to me in my bed at night. She *feeds* on me, Kelda. She takes so much out of me, it almost kills me, but I can't stop it from happening. I haven't slept since you and I...'

His voice drags off into something between a groan and a sob. He looks up at me with a flicker of that desire that I remember from the bar, on those mornings he'd come in after a killer night shift. I wonder how long it's been since he reported to the hospital. I wonder if he has a career left.

'Hey! You gonna pay the fare or what?' the cabbie barks. 'I ain't hangin' out in this hellhole all night.'

I shove a twenty into the cabbie's outstretched palm. His hand shakes. I don't blame him. Some scary shit is about to go down; maybe the driver feels the evil vibe even more keenly than I do. Seconds after Sander gets out of the taxi, even before he's slammed the door shut, the cab tears away. Sander leans into me. I can tell he's resisting the urge to collapse against me; I'm strong, but I'm still no match for his size. It's all I can do to keep him upright.

'We should have taken that cab home,' he says. 'Back to your place. You're the one I want, Kel. Why won't you be mine?'

'We can talk about the Valentine stuff later, Sander. Right now, this is where we need to be.'

'*Alek-ssssander.*'

A drawn-out whisper, accented with the alien trill of a dead language, fills the silent street. The hissed second syllable dies out into an echo. Sander bolts upright, no sandbag anymore. He's all high-voltage lust, triggered by the call of a succubus.

I look up and down the street. Empty. Nothing crouches behind the cars. Leaving Sander, I dart into the alley beside the club. Empty. I scan the tops of the buildings, but nothing's perched up there, waiting to fall.

Then I feel her. I don't see her, but I feel her, and I smell her, that slaughterhouse perfume, the tang of decay underlying the musky fragrance of aroused flesh. I hear someone whimpering. It's the plea of doomed longing, not coming from Sander's mouth, but from his soul.

'Sander! Go over there, sit on the ground and *do not move.*'

I point to the doorway of the warehouse. Not much space there, but it's enough to give him temporary shelter. Fallen Ones get squeamish around doorways. They hate horizontal points of transition. The only time you'll see one of them using a door is when they're trying to pass as mortal. Otherwise, they'd rather drop through the roof; all that stuff that makes up the ceiling doesn't get in their way at all. Falling is their natural state, as Max once told me. Walking through a door feels like a form of death to Fallen Ones – how do they know what's on the other side?

Sander doesn't budge. I sense him wanting to hide behind me, hide inside me, but the only motion in his body is a useless, head-to-toe trembling. I grab him by the elbow and pull with all my might, dragging him to the door. Somehow I shove his quaking limbs into a crouching position on the ground. I hope it doesn't open up and disgorge a stampede of clubbers while he's crouching there. It would suck if Sander got trampled to death; on the other hand, if he hangs out in the open, he'll go into a seizure.

And once he's in a seizure state, she'll take him again.

I walk out into the middle of the street, stripping off

my jacket. Slow and seductive, I shrug off the leather skin, then I unbuckle my belt, unbutton my jeans, and loosen my top. She's watching me. Can't take her eyes off my hips as I roll the T-shirt up above my waist with one hand, while unbuttoning the fly of my jeans with the other. As I sway back and forth, dancing to the memory of music from that chainlink cage, the Fallen One's desire snakes around my body. The throb of percussion from the Ninth Circle guides my torso as I slither out of my bra and let it fall to the asphalt. Anyone who steps out here is going to get one hell of a free show, but I don't care.

I'm not going to let that bitch have Sander. Or Brendan. Lia might already be lost, but this Fallen One isn't going to have either of my men.

She's standing behind me now, inches away. Her breath moistens the skin on the back of my neck; her lips leave velvet prints across my shoulders before she's even kissed me. I tug at my nipples, rub my swelling clit. My fingertips sink deep into the juicy folds. I have to confess – exorcism makes me wet.

With the stealth of a tiger she grabs me, restraining me just enough that I can keep moving my hips as she grinds her mound against my rotating bottom. She wraps an arm around my waist and grazes my skin from breasts to belly with the dagger-points of her fingernails. Her tongue dabbles in the pearls of sweat on my neck, then trails along my shoulder blade; she tastes me with the leisurely curiosity of a predator who's confident of enjoying a full meal.

Er Shaghryn. I feel her wither as I Speak her real name. *You're the Lost One, aren't you? An orphan, like me.*

Not like you. Nothing like you, she Speaks back, in a hiss.

I've pissed her off, sapped a bit of her power, but not much. All sex-driven, she makes a quick comeback and thrusts her pelvis against my arse, biting my throat. She lets her long hair caress the bare length of my back. Her hand dips down under the hem of my panties to join mine in bringing me to my first orgasm of the evening.

I didn't know I was so wound-up, and the climax comes so fast that I cry out in surprise. Feeding off my energy, she tightens her grip, stronger now than ever. I squeeze my eyes shut, trying not to come again, but she's rippling all around me with her skin and hair and claws, and I can't hold back. A second orgasm jolts me, fierce in its supernatural intensity. It's a damn shame, but no mortal lover can make me come like a Fallen One.

She cackles into my ear, a laugh like a steel hyena. With one cruel motion, she yanks my pants to my knees, her nails shredding my skin as they rake my thighs. Still panting, still throbbing, I close my eyes as tight as I can, like a child who thinks she's hidden, as long as she can't see the monsters around her. I'm not ready to look Er Shaghryn in the eye, but she's manipulating my body as she pushes me to the street, and I know I'll have to confront the abyss behind her flesh-mask if Lia is ever going to be released.

I open my eyes. Red hair falls across her face, backlit by the glare of a security light overhead. She's got me pinned to the ground, my shoulders against the asphalt. Her gorgeous body hovers over me, spiked nipples scratching mine. With one of her muscular dancer's legs, she shoves my thighs apart. I twist, clench, pump my knees against her belly, but she's too strong, and she enters me before I'm ready. I've never fought a Fallen One like this. Her doomed spirit explodes inside me. Don't be fooled – this feels like no human fuck. It's a soul-screwing, a theft of one spirit by another, and she's pouring a thousand years of rage and desire and envy into me.

This is the part of the game where I usually have my things around. I reach for a prop – a crucifix, a candle, a vial of holy water – and I make the drama my own. The

Fallen One does a double-take as she surges into me, and in that flicker of surprise, I seize the advantage. But this bitch, Er Shaghryn, has me paralysed. I watch the whole ugly scene going down, but I can't even twitch. All I can do is accept what she's giving me.

And come. And come again. The only thing more intense than my terror, at this moment, is the pleasure wracking my body. I hate the moans that pour from my mouth, but I'm as powerless to stop them as anything else. While she takes me, Er Shaghryn stares into my eyes, and I swear it's like descending into hell.

Hell, for Er Shaghryn, isn't hot. Hell is bone cold, and absolutely silent. Plunging into the world that she comes from, I'm suddenly gripped by a keen knowledge of this Fallen One's pain. It's the pain of an outcast, the utter loneliness of a solitary prison, from which you can watch, but never touch, the beauty that lies inches past your fingertips.

My heart opens. My soul opens.

By the grace of some warped miracle, she lets go.

I hold my breath, waiting a few beats for the Release, but something in this scene isn't spinning the right way. Like a woman in the spasms of a labour going wrong, I don't know what's happening, but I know this doesn't feel right. The Fallen One should be flowing out of me, a gust of supernatural substance returning to its source. That's what I do for these beings. It's not happening here. I don't see or feel or hear the Fallen One anywhere.

Meanwhile, Lia's discarded body rolls off mine. She lies in a shattered heap on the street beside me. If we were lying together in a bed, you'd think we were recovering from a heaving bout of passionate love-making, instead of picking up what's left of our souls, scraping the gravel out of our wounds.

The fleshform heaves. The slender rib cage rises. A faint rattle leaks from the slack mouth, then the body goes limp. The being that was Lia is a vacant skin. I'm struggling to pull myself onto my elbows, whimpering as an arrow of pain shoots down my side, when someone squats beside me and holds me still.

'Don't move, Kelda. Let me check you out.'

It's Sander, back from the netherworld where the Fallen One was holding him. With Er Shaghryn gone, he's been released, too. His mind feels clear again, and his hands are competent and clinical as they rove across my limbs. The fact that I'm naked, with my jeans around my ankles, doesn't faze him. He's all business as he reads my bones with his fingers. Nothing makes me flinch, until his thumb brushes one of my ribs. I bite back another whimper. Not much you can do about a cracked rib, so there's no point in playing up the agony.

'I'm fine, Sander. You should be examining *her*.'

I nod at the shell lying next to me.

'You're the one I care about,' he says. 'Fuck that bitch.'

I grin, giving myself another shot of pain as my scraped cheek rises. 'Never thought I'd hear you violate the Hippocratic oath.'

'That only applies to humans. She – *it* – was anything but human.'

That statement, coming from Sander, couldn't have shocked me more than if he'd pulled a crystal out of his pocket and waved it around in front of my forehead. Whatever happened to him over the past couple of days must have shaken his rational belief system to the core. Before I can reply, the street fills with the echo of footsteps, bouncing back and forth against the warehouses.

'Lia! *Lia*!'

Brendan's cry, coarse and desperate, rings through the darkness. His tall form, in silhouette, suddenly looms over us, then crouches next to the lifeless dancer. The night rages with the scream of sirens

Then, unbelievably, Lia moves, like a fairytale beauty waking from a coma.

'Don't touch her!' Sander barks.

This time Sander isn't trying to protect a broken body; he's trying to protect a lovestruck mortal. But Brendan has already scooped Lia into his arms. Her limbs are limp, but her rib cage is rising and falling again. Brendan's face is buried in her hair, so I can't see his response. I can't hear Brendan Speaking to me, either; his mind is absorbed in the bundle of flesh and bone he's cradling. We put so much faith in our lovers' bodies, their gorgeous shells – Brendan is a bit more sensitive than most men, but at heart, he's no different from any other mortal flesh-junkie.

The ambulance crew crowds around the reunited lovers, and I almost choke on my envy as I hear the joy and relief in Brendan's gasps. In my fantasies of this Release, Sander was never my saviour, or my prince. A couple of the medics try to tend to me, but Sander waves them away; his arms are a circle of strength around me. As the medics drape Lia's nude back with a blanket, she turns her head. She looks at me over her shoulder as one pale hand reaches for my arm. In profile, I can only see one of her eyes, but that's enough.

Who are you? I Speak to her.

A smile lifts her lips. That smile turns my blood to ice. Brendan doesn't see the smile, or the dead onyx of his lover's enormous pupils. One flash, and in the spinning lights of the ambulance, that flatness is illuminated by a peaceful radiance. Lia's eyes, the blue of heaven, are her own again.

The blackout curtain blocks all forms of light from my bedroom. My ears are firmly plugged with the earphones of my iPod, and the holy drone of a Gregorian chant fills my skull. I've got a pillow planted over my face, and I've just taken two extra-strength aspirin and a Benedryl to coax my brain to sleep. But no amount of sensory deprivation can drive that image of Lia out of my mind. I keep seeing her rising to her feet, arms held out in front of her like a sleepwalker coming to life. Her face is radiantly beautiful, but her eyes, two scorched pits in the mask of a Botticelli angel, give her away.

I see her dove-white hand reaching for me, trying to convince me that she's human again, but when she touches me, my skin sizzles from the heat of her need. Where is she now? I don't even know what new hungers drive her, and at the moment, I'd be scared to guess.

I've never had a Release go down like that before. I've won a lot of mortals back from the Fallen Ones who stole their fleshforms, and I've lost more than I'd care to admit. But I've never left a mortal half-possessed. I didn't even know it was possible. What would a Half-Fallen One be? What space would she claim, between the seen and the unseen?

At times like this, I wish I still drank. I'd be under the bar at the Ofice by now, or maybe under a freeway overpass, blissfully passed out. Somehow I fall into a dense, medicated sleep. The only reason I know I've dropped off is that I find myself waking up to the pressure of another body against mine. Long, cool and naked, it surrounds me and rocks me like a hammock made of muscle and bone. Lips leave trails through the forest of hair-sensors on the back of my neck, and a hand finds its way to my breast, cupping the swell of flesh.

I open my drugged eyes. The hand is masculine, furred with black hair.

'Brendan? How did you get in here?'

'You left your door unlocked,' he murmurs. Lust thickens his voice, and a corresponding hardness between my cheeks gives more evidence that he wants me.

'I never leave my door unlocked.'

But last night, anything was possible. Last night, the world as I knew it veered in a strange direction; the natural and the supernatural both proved me a fool. When Sander dropped me off at my building, he wanted to spend the night. He'd sleep in my bed, on my floor, on my couch, he said – anywhere I wanted, as long as I'd let him watch over me.

I sent him home to his own bed. I didn't want a guardian, and I didn't want to have to wake up to the aftermath of the soul-rape Sander had experienced. I wanted to be alone, cocooned in my safe apartment.

So in my self-protective paranoia, how did I forget to lock up for the night?

Walking through a door feels like a form of death to Fallen Ones. Max's words echo in my head.

'Where's Lia?'

'They took her to the hospital,' he says.

'Why aren't you with her?'

'Because I wanted to be with you.'

I swallow. The Benedryl has left my mouth cottony. 'Do you still love her?'

'I don't know. She's not what she used to be.' His palm paints circles on my belly. Lower, lower, his hand goes, till it's petting the fur between my thighs.

'No one ever is, when you love them long enough. People change.'

He gives a bitter little laugh. 'No, they don't. Not like that. Lia's different now. You, on the other hand, are the same sexy bitch that you were when I met you.'

Is it just lust that makes Brendan's voice so husky? Desire, or maybe something else, turns his accent vaguely alien. I stiffen. I try to twist around to check Brendan's eyes, but he's already rolled me over onto my belly. He's climbing on top of me, bracketing my hips between his thighs as he mounts me, and the pulsing, breathing mass of him feels so good that I can't stand to face anything but the reality of his weight.

Before he enters me, he reaches under my hips to find my pussy, and rubs the outer lips between my fingers. I lift my arse, lower my chest to the bed, part my thighs – all open for him, all animal. He finds the bar on the hood of my clit and tugs at it, pulling the tender sheath until my yelp lets him know he's gone too far. He plays with me till we can both hear and smell my wetness, then he spreads my cheeks and slides into my pussy, up to the hilt with one long glide. His pelvis hits my arse hard, knocking a soft grunt out of me. No apologies, no sweet-talk; he's just taking me at a hungry tempo. I deepen the arch of my spine, and his cock sinks in so deep that his thrusts spear my core.

His cock. I've wanted Brendan something fierce, and he's finally doing me, and I haven't even seen the cock that's plunging in and out of my hungry hole. I haven't seen his face, or his body. His fingers dig into my shoulders; my teeth bite down on my pillow. The growl rising from his chest doesn't sound human, but how many men sound human on the brink of a skull-splitting orgasm? He clutches a handful of my hair at the roots and uses it to reinforce his hold as he rides me even harder.

I'm gasping for air. My eyes stare blindly into the depths of my pillow. His shaft strikes me at an angle that tweaks a nest of nerves, and the friction against that tender spot lights me up from head to toe. I'm growling, too, arse in the air like a little beast, and it's so good to be back in this sweating, grunting, animal world that I come partly from the sheer joy of having a body. Then Brendan's climax tears a howl out of him and our spasms ricochet off each other. Him into me, me into him; this energy exchange is as intense as any Release. Sex with humans is never like this.

Who are you? I seem to be Speaking that question a lot lately. Simple question, but no one wants to give me a straight answer.

Brendan doesn't Speak back. I can feel him listening, but all I hear is the static of fading pleasure, and the harsh panting as he catches his breath. I take advantage of his post-come weakness, and my sweaty slipperiness, to squirm around so that I'm lying underneath him, staring up into his face. Shaggy black hair falls over dark eyes. Brendan's eyes are always dark, even darker now with his dilated pupils edging out the coffee-brown irises.

'I knew it would be amazing,' he says. Brendan's voice, soft with wonder, is utterly his own again. 'From the first time I saw you, I knew you weren't like any woman I'd ever known.'

The joy in his face – the glee of a kid under a Christmas tree – is sheer mortal. I've never seen a pussy-eating grin like that on a Fallen One's face. No chance he's been possessed; a fleshform just can't hold a human spirit and a lost soul at the same time. I've never seen a Half-Fallen soul. Then again, I've never been fucked with such raging intensity by an entity with an expiration date.

Somewhere between the man who just took me like an animal, and the man who's now gliding into me again, tenderly this time, as if he's scared of breaking me, is a being I don't know. I could ask him, one more time, to identify himself, but what good would that do? We can ask our lovers who they are until we run out of breath. Maybe the only honest answer is no answer at all.

Visit the Black Lace website at
www.black-lace-books.com

FIND OUT THE LATEST INFORMATION AND TAKE
ADVANTAGE OF OUR FANTASTIC FREE BOOK OFFER!
ALSO VISIT THE SITE FOR . . .

- All Black Lace titles currently available
  and how to order online
- Great new offers
- Writers' guidelines
- Author interviews
- An erotica newsletter
- Features
- Cool links

BLACK LACE – THE LEADING IMPRINT
OF WOMEN'S SEXY FICTION

TAKING YOUR EROTIC READING
PLEASURE TO NEW HORIZONS

LOOK OUT FOR THE ALL-NEW BLACK LACE BOOKS – AVAILABLE NOW!

All books priced £7.99 in the UK. Please note publication dates apply to the UK only. For other territories, please contact your retailer.

A GENTLEMAN'S WAGER
Madelynne Ellis
ISBN 978 0 352 33800 6

When eighteenth-century young lady Bella Rushdale finds herself fiercely attracted to handsome landowner Lucerne Marlinscar, she does not expect the rival for her affections to be another man. However, the handsome and decadent Marquis Pennerley has desired Lucerne for years and, when they are brought together at the remote Lauwine Hall for a country party on the Yorkshire Moors, he intends to claim him. This leads to a passionate struggle for dominance – at the risk of scandal – between the highly sexed Bella and the debauched aristocrat. Ultimately it will be Lucerne who will choose the outcome – and his decision is bound to upset somebody's plans.

THE SILVER CAGE
Mathilde Madden
ISBN 978 0 352 34165 5

Iris and Alfie have been driven apart by the strongest forces in the werewolf world – the powerful thrall of the Divine Wolf – the mother of them all. Now Iris needs to win Alfie back, not just for herself, but because the fate of the world could rest upon it.

But the only way to free Alfie from the power of the Divine Wolf is to kill her. Something that could end the lives of all werewolves. Including Alfie himself – Iris's true love.

To be published in March 2008

CASSANDRA'S CONFLICT
Fredica Alleyn
ISBN 978 0 352 34186 0

A house in Hampstead. Present-day. Behind a façade of cultured
respectability lies a world of decadent indulgence and dark eroticism.
Cassandra's sheltered life is transformed when she gets employed as
governess to the Baron's children. He draws her into games where lust
can feed on the erotic charge of submission. Games where only he
knows the rules and where unusual pleasures can flourish.

Next collection of novellas coming in February 2008

PHANTASMAGORIA
Madelynne Ellis
ISBN 978 0 352 34168 6

1800 – Three years after escaping to London with her bisexual lovers, Bella Rushdale wakes one morning to find their delicate ménage-a-trois on the verge of shattering. Vaughan, Marquis of Pennerley has left abruptly and without any explanation. Determined to reclaim him and preserve their relationship, Bella pursues the errant Marquis to his family seat on the Welsh Borders where she finds herself embroiled in his preparations for a diabolical gothic celebration on All Hallows Eve – a phantasmagoria! Among the shadows and phantoms Bella and her lovers will peel away the deceits and desires of the past and future.

To be published in April 2008

GOTHIC HEAT
Portia Da Costa
ISBN 978 0 352 34170 9

Paula Beckett has a problem. The spirit of the wicked and voluptuous sorceress Isidora Katori is trying to possess her body and Paula finds herself driven by dark desires and a delicious wanton recklessness. Rafe Hathaway is irresistibly drawn to both women. But who will he finally choose – feisty and sexy Paula, who is fighting impossible odds to hang on to her very existence, or sultry and ruthless Isidora, who offers him the key to immortality?

GEMINI HEAT
Portia Da Costa
ISBN 978 0 352 34187 7

As the metropolis sizzles in the freak early summer temperatures, identical twin sisters Deana and Delia Ferraro are cooking up a heat wave of their own. Surrounded by an atmosphere of relentless humidity, Deanna and Delia find themselves rivals for the attentions of Jackson de Guile, an exotic, wealthy entrepreneur and master of power dynamics who draws them both into a web of luxurious debauchery. The erotic encounters become increasingly bizarre as the twins vie for the rewards that pleasuring him brings them – tainted rewards which only serve to confuse their perceptions of the limits of sexual experience.

THE NEW BLACK LACE BOOK OF WOMEN'S SEXUAL FANTASIES
Edited and compiled by Mitzi Szereto
ISBN 978 0 352 34172 3

The second anthology of detailed sexual fantasies contributed by women from all over the world. The book is a result of a year's research by an expert on erotic writing and gives a fascinating insight into the rich diversity of the female sexual imagination.

Black Lace Booklist

Information is correct at time of printing. To avoid disappointment,
check availability before ordering. Go to www.black-lace-books.com.
All books are priced £7.99 unless another price is given.

BLACK LACE BOOKS WITH A CONTEMPORARY SETTING

☐ THE ANGELS' SHARE Maya Hess	ISBN 978 0 352 34043 6
☐ ASKING FOR TROUBLE Kristina Lloyd	ISBN 978 0 352 33362 9
☐ THE BLUE GUIDE Carrie Williams	ISBN 978 0 352 34132 7
☐ THE BOSS Monica Belle	ISBN 978 0 352 34088 7
☐ BOUND IN BLUE Monica Belle	ISBN 978 0 352 34012 2
☐ CAMPAIGN HEAT Gabrielle Marcola	ISBN 978 0 352 33941 6
☐ CAT SCRATCH FEVER Sophie Mouette	ISBN 978 0 352 34021 4
☐ CIRCUS EXCITE Nikki Magennis	ISBN 978 0 352 34033 7
☐ CONFESSIONAL Judith Roycroft	ISBN 978 0 352 33421 3
☐ CONTINUUM Portia Da Costa	ISBN 978 0 352 33120 5
☐ DANGEROUS CONSEQUENCES Pamela Rochford	ISBN 978 0 352 33185 4
☐ DARK DESIGNS Madelynne Ellis	ISBN 978 0 352 34075 7
☐ THE DEVIL INSIDE Portia Da Costa	ISBN 978 0 352 32993 6
☐ EQUAL OPPORTUNITIES Mathilde Madden	ISBN 978 0 352 34070 2
☐ FIRE AND ICE Laura Hamilton	ISBN 978 0 352 33486 2
☐ GONE WILD Maria Eppie	ISBN 978 0 352 33670 5
☐ HOTBED Portia Da Costa	ISBN 978 0 352 33614 9
☐ IN PURSUIT OF ANNA Natasha Rostova	ISBN 978 0 352 34060 3
☐ IN THE FLESH Emma Holly	ISBN 978 0 352 34117 4
☐ LEARNING TO LOVE IT Alison Tyler	ISBN 978 0 352 33535 7
☐ MAD ABOUT THE BOY Mathilde Madden	ISBN 978 0 352 34001 6
☐ MAKE YOU A MAN Anna Clare	ISBN 978 0 352 34006 1
☐ MAN HUNT Cathleen Ross	ISBN 978 0 352 33583 8
☐ THE MASTER OF SHILDEN Lucinda Carrington	ISBN 978 0 352 33140 3
☐ MS BEHAVIOUR Mini Lee	ISBN 978 0 352 33962 1
☐ PAGAN HEAT Monica Belle	ISBN 978 0 352 33974 4

BLACK LACE BOOKS WITH AN HISTORICAL SETTING

BLACK LACE BOOKS WITH A PARANORMAL THEME

To find out the latest information about Black Lace titles, check out the website: www.black-lace-books.com or send for a booklist with complete synopses by writing to:

Black Lace Booklist, Virgin Books Ltd
Thames Wharf Studios
Rainville Road
London W6 9HA

Please include an SAE of decent size. Please note only British stamps are valid.

Our privacy policy
We will not disclose information you supply us to any other parties. We will not disclose any information which identifies you personally to any person without your express consent.

From time to time we may send out information about Black Lace books and special offers. Please tick here if you do <u>not</u> wish to receive Black Lace information. ❑

Please send me the books I have ticked above.

Name ....

Address ....

....

....

....

Post Code ....

Send to: Virgin Books Cash Sales, Thames Wharf Studios, Rainville Road, London W6 9HA.

US customers: for prices and details of how to order books for delivery by mail, call 888-330-8477.

Please enclose a cheque or postal order, made payable to Virgin Books Ltd, to the value of the books you have ordered plus postage and packing costs as follows:

UK and BFPO – £1.00 for the first book, 50p for each subsequent book.

Overseas (including Republic of Ireland) – £2.00 for the first book, £1.00 for each subsequent book.

If you would prefer to pay by VISA, ACCESS/MASTERCARD, DINERS CLUB, AMEX or SWITCH, please write your card number and expiry date here:

....

Signature ....

Please allow up to 28 days for delivery.